The City Of Beautiful Nonsense

By
E. Temple Thurston
Author Of
"The Apple Of Eden," "Mirage," Etc.
1911

BOOK I
THE ROAD TO THE CITY

BOOK I
THE ROAD TO THE CITY

The City of Beautiful Nonsense
CHAPTER I
A PRELUDE ON THE EVE OF ST. JOSEPH'S DAY

Of course, the eighteenth of March--but it is out of the question to say upon which day of the week it fell.

It was half-past seven in the evening. At half-past seven it is dark, the lamps are lighted, the houses huddle together in groups. They have secrets to tell as soon as it is dark. Ah! If you knew the secrets that houses are telling when the shadows draw them so close together! But you never will know. They close their eyes and they whisper.

Around the fields of Lincoln's Inn it was as still as the grave. The footsteps of a lawyer's clerk hurrying late away from chambers vibrated through the intense quiet. You heard each step to the very last. So long as you could see him, you heard them plainly; then he vanished behind the curtain of shadows, the sounds became muffled, and at last the silence crept back into the Fields--crept all round you, half eager, half reluctant, like sleepy children drawn from their beds to hear the end of a fairy story.

There was a fairy story to be told, too.

It began that night of the eighteenth of March--the Eve of St. Joseph's day.

I don't know what it is about St. Joseph, but of all those saints who crowd their hallowed names upon the calendar--and, good heavens! there are so many--he seems most worthy of canonisation. In the fervent fanaticism of faith, the virtue of a martyr's death is almost its own reward; but to live on in the belief of that miracle which offers to crush marital happiness, scattering family honour like dust before the four winds of heaven--that surely was the noblest martyrdom of all.

There is probably enough faith left in some to-day to give up their lives for their religion; but I know of no man who would allow his faith to intercede for the honour of his wife's good name when once the hand of circumstance had played so conjuring a trick upon him.

And so, amongst Roman Catholics, who, when it comes to matters of faith, are like children at a fair, even the spirit of condolence seems to have crept its way into their attitude towards this simple-minded man.

"Poor St. Joseph," they say--"I always get what I want from him. I've never known him to fail."

Or--"Poor St. Joseph--he's not a bit of good to me. I always pray to the Blessed Virgin for everything I want."

Could anything be more childlike, more ingenuous, more like a game in a nursery--the only place in the world where things are really believed.

Every saint possesses his own separate quality, efficacious in its own separate way. St. Rock holds the magic philtre of health; you pray to St. Anthony to recover all those things that were lost-- and how palpably stand out the times when, rising from your knees, your search was successful, how readily those times drop into oblivion when you failed. It is impossible to enumerate all the saints and their qualities crowding the pages of those many volumes of *Butler's Lives*. For safety at sea, for instance, St. Gerald is unsurpassed; but St. Joseph--poor St. Joseph!--from him flow all those good things which money can buy--the children's toys, the woman's pin money and the luxuries which are the necessities of the man.

Think, if you can--if you can conjure before your mind's eye-- of all the things that must happen on that eve of the feast day of St. Joseph. How many thousands of knees are bent, how many thousand jaded bodies and hungry souls whisper the name of poor St. Joseph? The prayers for that glitter of gold, that shine of silver and that jangling of copper are surely too numerous to count. What a busy day it must be where those prayers are heard! What hopes must be born that night and what responsibilities lightened! Try and count the candles that are lighted before the shrine of St. Joseph! It is impossible.

It all resolves itself into a simple mathematical calculation. Tell me how many poor there are--and I will tell you how many candles are burnt, how many prayers are prayed, and how many hopes are born on the eve of St. Joseph's day.

And how many poor are there in the world?

The bell was toning for eight o'clock Benediction at the Sardinia St. Chapel on that evening of the eighteenth of March-- Sardinia St. Chapel, which stands so tremulously in the shadows of Lincoln's Inn Fields--tremulously, because any day the decision of the council of a few men may rase it ruthlessly to the ground.

Amongst all the figures kneeling there in the dim candle-light, their shoulders hunched, their heads sinking deeply in their hands, there was not one but on whose lips the name of poor St. Joseph lingered in earnest or piteous appeal.

These were the poor of the earth, and who and what were they?

There was a stock-broker who paid a rent of some three hundred pounds a year for his offices in the City, a rent of one hundred and fifty for his chambers in Temple Gardens, and whose house in the country was kept in all the splendour of wealth.

Behind him--he sat in a pew by himself--was a lady wearing a heavy fur coat. She was young. Twenty-three at the utmost. There was nothing to tell from her, but her bent head, that the need of money could ever enter into her consideration. She also was in a pew alone. Behind her sat three servant girls. On the other side of the aisle, parallel with the lady in the fur coat, there was a young man--a writer--a journalist--a driver of the pen, whose greatest source of poverty was his ambition.

Kneeling behind him at various distances, there were a clerk, a bank manager, a charwoman; and behind all these, at the end of the chapel, devout, intent, and as earnest as the rest, were four Italian organ-grinders.

These are the poor of the earth. They are not a class. They are every class. Poverty is not a condition of some; it is a condition of all. Those things we desire are so far removed from those which we obtain, that all of us are paupers. And so, that simple arithmetical problem must remain unsolved; for it is impossible to tell the poor of this world and, therefore, just so impossible it is to count the candles that are burnt, the prayers that are prayed or the hopes that are born on the eve of St. Joseph's day.

CHAPTER II
THE LAST CANDLE

When the Benediction was over and the priest had passed in procession with the acolytes into the mysterious shadows behind the altar, the little congregation rose slowly to its feet.

One by one they approached the altar of St. Joseph. One by one their pennies rattled into the brown wooden box as they took out their candles, and soon the sconce before the painted image of that simple-minded saint was ablaze with little points of light.

There is nature in everything; as much in lighting candles for poor St. Joseph as you will find in the most momentous decision of a life-time.

The wealthy stock-broker, counting with care two pennies from amongst a handful of silver, was servant to the impulses of his nature. It crossed his mind that they must be only farthing candles--a penny, therefore, was a very profitable return--the

Church was too grasping. He would buy no more than two. Why should the Church profit seventy-five per cent. upon his faith? He gave generously to the collection. It may be questioned, too, why St. Joseph should give him what he had asked, a transaction which brought no apparent profit to St. Joseph at all? He did not appreciate that side of it. He had prayed that a speculation involving some thousands of pounds should prove successful. If his prayer were granted, he would be the richer by twenty per cent. upon his investment--but not seventy-five, oh, no--not seventy-five! And so those two pennies assumed the proportions of an exactment which he grudgingly bestowed. They rattled in his ear as they fell.

After him followed the charwoman. Crossing herself, she bobbed before the image. Her money was already in her hand. All through the service, she had gripped it in a perspiring palm, fearing that it might be lost. Three-penny-bits are mischievous little coins. She gave out a gentle sigh of relief when at last she heard it tinkle in the box. It was safe there. That was its destination. The three farthing candles became hers. She lit them lovingly. Three children there were, waiting in some tenement buildings for her return. As she put each candle in its socket, she whispered each separate name--John--Mary--Michael. There was not one for herself.

Then came the clerk. He lit four. They represented the sum of coppers that he had. It might have bought a packet of cigarettes. He looked pensively at the four candles he had lighted in the sconce, then turned, fatalistically, on his heel. After all, what good could four farthing candles do to poor St. Joseph? Perhaps he had been a fool--perhaps it was a waste of money.

Following him was the bank manager. Six candles he took out of the brown wooden box. Every year he lit six. He had never lit more; he had never lit less. He lit them hurriedly, self-consciously, as though he were ashamed of so many and, turning quickly away, did not notice that the wick of one of them had burnt down and gone out.

The first servant girl who came after him, lifted it out of the socket and lit it at another flame.

"I'm going to let that do for me," she whispered to the servant girl behind her. "I lit it--it 'ud a' been like that to-morrow if I 'adn't a' lit it."

Seeing her companion's expression of contempt, she giggled nervously. She must have been glad to get away down into the shadows of the church. There, she slipped into an empty pew and sank on to her knees.

"Please Gawd, forgive me," she whispered. "I know it was mean of me," and she tried to summon the courage to go back and light a new candle. But the courage was not there. It requires more courage than you would think.

At last all had gone but the lady in the heavy fur coat and the writer--the journalist--the driver of the pen. There was a flood of light from all the candles at the little altar, the church was empty, everything was still; but there these two remained, kneeling silently in their separate pews.

What need was there in the heart of her that kept her so patiently upon her knees? Some pressing desire, you may be sure--some want that women have and only women understand. And what was the need in him? Not money! Nothing that St. Joseph could give. He had no money. One penny was lying contentedly at the bottom of his pocket. That, at the moment, was all he had in the world. It is mostly when you have many possessions that you need the possession of more. To own one penny, knowing that there is no immediate possibility of owning another, that is as near contentment as one can well-nigh reach.

Then why did he wait on upon his knees? What was the need in the heart of him? Nature again--human nature, too--simply the need to know the need in her. That was all.

Ten minutes passed. He watched her through the interstices of his fingers. But she did not move. At last, despairing of any further discovery than that you may wear a fur coat costing thirty guineas and still be poor, still pray to St. Joseph, he rose slowly to his feet.

Almost immediately afterwards, she followed him.

He walked directly to the altar and his penny had jangled in the box before he became aware that there was only one candle left.

He looked back. The lady was waiting. The impulse came in a moment. He stood aside and left the candle where it was. Then he slowly turned away.

There are moments in life when playful Circumstance links hands with a light-hearted Fate, and the two combined execute as dainty an impromptu dance of events as would take the wit of a man some months of thought to rehearse.

Here you have a man, a woman, and a candle destined for the altar of St. Joseph, all flung together in an empty church by the playful hand of Circumstance and out of so strange a medley comes a fairy story--the story of the City of Beautiful Nonsense--a dream or a reality--they are one and the same thing--a little piece of colour in the great patchwork which views the souls still sleeping.

He knew, as he slowly turned away, that the matter did not end there. You must not only be a student of human nature in order to drive a pen. Circumstance must be anticipated as well. There may be nature in everything, but it is the playful hand of

Circumstance which brings it to your eyes. So, he slowly turned away--oh, but very slowly--with just so much show of action as was necessary to convey that he had no intention to remain.

But every sense in him was ready for the moment when her voice arrested him.

"You have not," said she, "taken the candle that you paid for." Her voice was low to a whisper.

He came round on his heel at once.

"No--it's the last. I didn't notice that when I dropped my penny in."

"But you ought to take it."

"I left it for you."

"But why should you?"

"It seemed possible that you might want to light it more than I did."

What did he mean by that? That she was poor, poorer than he? That the generosity of St. Joseph was of greater account to her? It was. It must be surely. No one could need more sorely the assistance of the powers of heaven than she did then.

But why should he know? Why should he think that? Had it been that poor charwoman--oh, yes. But--she looked at his serviceable blue serge suit, compared it instinctively with the luxury of her heavy fur coat--why should he think that of her?

"I don't see why I should accept your generosity," she whispered.

He smiled.

"I offer it to St. Joseph," said he.

She took up the candle.

"I shouldn't be surprised if he found your offering the more acceptable of the two."

He watched her light it; he watched her place it in an empty socket. He noticed her hands--delicate--white--fingers that tapered to the dainty finger nails. What could it have been that she had been praying for?

"Well--I don't suppose St. Joseph is very particular," he said with a humorous twist of the lip.

"Don't you? Poor St. Joseph!"

She crossed herself and turned away from the altar.

"Now--I owe you a penny," she added.

She held out the coin, but he made no motion to take it.

"I'd rather not be robbed," said he, "of a fraction of my offer to St. Joseph. Would you mind very much if you continued to owe?"

"As you wish." She withdrew her hand. "Then, thank you very much. Good-night."

"Good-night."

He walked slowly after her down the church. It had been a delicate stringing of moments on a slender thread of incident--that was all. It had yielded nothing. She left him just as ignorant as before. He knew no better why she had been praying so earnestly to poor St. Joseph.

But then, when you know what a woman prays for, you know the deepest secret of her heart. And it is impossible to learn the deepest secret of a woman's heart in ten minutes; though you may more likely arrive at it then, than in a life-time.

CHAPTER III

THE GREENGROCER'S--FETTER LANE

Two or three years ago, there was a certain greengrocer's shop in Fetter Lane. The front window had been removed, the better to expose the display of fruits and vegetables which were arranged on gradually ascending tiers, completely obstructing your vision into the shop itself. Oranges, bananas, potatoes, apples, dates--all pressed together in the condition in which they had arrived at the London docks, ballast for the good ship that brought them--carrots and cauliflowers, all in separate little compartments, were huddled together on the ascending rows of shelves like colours that a painter leaves negligently upon his palette.

At night, a double gas jet blew in the wind just outside, deepening the contrasts, the oranges with the dull earth brown of the potatoes, the bright yellow bananas with the sheen of blue on the green cabbages! Oh, that sheen of blue on the green cabbages! It was all the more beautiful for being an effect rather than a real colour. How an artist would have loved it!

These greengrocers' shops and stalls are really most picturesque, so much more savoury, too, than any other shop--except a chemist's. Of course, there is nothing to equal that wholesome smell of brown Windsor soap which pervades even the most cash of all cash chemist's! An up-to-date fruiterer's in Piccadilly may have as fine an odour, perhaps; but then an up-to-date fruiterer is not a greengrocer. He does not dream of calling himself such. They are greengrocers in Fetter Lane--greengrocers in the Edgware Road--greengrocers in old Drury, but fruiterers in Piccadilly.

Compared, then, with the ham and beef shop, the fish-monger's, and the inevitable oil shop, where, in such neighbourhoods as these, you buy everything, this greengrocer's was a welcome oasis in a desert of unsavoury smells and gloomy surroundings. The colours it displayed, the brilliant flame of that pyramid of oranges, those rosy cheeks of the apples, that glaring yellow cluster of bananas hanging from a hook in the ceiling, and the soft green background of cabbages, cauliflowers and every other green vegetable which chanced to be in season, with one last touch of all, some beetroot, cut and bleeding, colour that an emperor might wear, combined to make that little greengrocer's shop in Fetter Lane the one saving clause in an otherwise dreary scheme. It cheered you as you passed it by. You felt thankful for it. Those oranges looked clean and wholesome. They shone in the light of that double gas jet. They had every reason to shine. Mrs. Meakin rubbed them with her apron every morning when she built up that perilous pyramid. She rubbed the apples, too, until their faces glowed, glowed like children ready to start for school. When you looked at them you thought of the country, the orchards where they had been gathered, and Fetter Lane, with all its hawkers' cries and screaming children, vanished from your senses. You do not get that sort of an impression when you look in the window of a ham and beef shop. A plate of sliced ham, on which two or three flies crawl lazily, a pan of sausages, sizzling in their own fat, bear no relation to anything higher than the unfastidious appetite of a hungry man.

That sort of shop, you pass by quickly; but, even if you had not wished to buy anything, you might have hesitated, then stopped before Mrs. Meakin's little greengrocer's stall in Fetter Lane.

Mrs. Meakin was very fat. She had a face like an apple--not an apple just picked, but one that has been lying on the straw in a loft through the winter, well-preserved, losing none of its flavour, but the skin of which is wrinkled and shrivelled with age. On a wooden chair without any back to it, she sat in the shop all day long, inhaling that healthy, cleanly smell of good mother earth which clung about the sacks of potatoes. Here it was she waited for the advent of customers. Whenever they appeared at the door, she paused for a moment, judging from their attitude the likelihood of their custom, then, slapping both hands on her knees, she would rise slowly to her feet.

She was a good woman of business, was Mrs. Meakin, with a capable way of explaining how poor the season was for whatever fruit or vegetable her customers wished to purchase. It must not be supposed that under this pretence she demanded higher prices than were being asked elsewhere. Oh--not at all! Honesty was written in her face. It was only that she succeeded in persuading her customers that under the circumstances they got their vegetables at a reasonable price and, going away quite contented, they were willing to return again.

But what in the name, even of everything that is unreasonable have the greengrocery business and the premises of Mrs. Meakin to do with the City of Beautiful Nonsense? Is it part of the Nonsense to jump from a trade in candles before the altar of St. Joseph to a trade in oranges in Fetter Lane? Yet there is no nonsense in it. In this fairy story, the two are intimately related.

This is how it happens. The house, in which Mrs. Meakin's shop was on the ground floor, was three stories high and, on the first floor above the shop itself, lived John Grey, the journalist, the writer, the driver of the pen, the at-present unexplained figure in this story who offered his gift of generosity to St. Joseph, in order that the other as-yet-unexplained figure of the lady in the heavy fur coat should gratify her desire to light the last candle and place it in the sconce--a seal upon the deed of her supplication.

So then it is we have dealings with Mrs. Meakin and her greengrocery business in Fetter Lane. This little shop, with such generous show of brilliant colours in the midst of its drab grey surroundings, is part of the atmosphere, all part of this fairy-tale romance which began on the eighteenth of March--oh, how many years ago? Before Kingsway was built, before Holywell Street bit the dust in which it had grovelled for so long.

And so, I venture, that it is well you should see this small shop of Mrs. Meakin's, with its splashes of orange and red, its daubs of crimson and yellow--see it in your mind's eye--see it when the shadows of the houses fall on it in the morning, when the sun touches it at mid-day--when the double gas jet illuminates it at night, for you will never see it in real life now. Mrs. Meakin gave up the business a year or so ago. She went to live in the country, and there she has a kitchen garden of her own; there she grows her own cabbages, her own potatoes and her own beetroot. And her face is still like an apple--an older apple to be sure--an apple that has lain in the straw in a large roomy loft, lain there all through the winter and--been forgotten, left behind.

CHAPTER IV
WHAT TO CALL A HERO

John Grey is scarcely the name for a hero; not the sort of name you would choose of your own free will if the telling of a fairy story was placed unreservedly in your hands. If every latitude were offered you, quite possibly you would select the name of Raoul or Rudolfe--some name, at least, that had a ring in it as it left the tongue. They say, however, that by any other name a rose would smell as sweet. Oh--but I cannot believe that is true--good heavens! think of the pleasure you would lose if you had to call it a turnip!

And yet I lose no pleasure, no sense of mine is jarred when I call my hero--John Grey. But if I do lose no pleasure, it is with a very good reason. It is because I have no other alternative. John Grey was a real person. He lived. He lived, too, over that identical little greengrocer's shop of Mrs. Meakin's in Fetter Lane and, though there was a private side entrance from the street, he often passed through the shop in order to smell the wholesome smell of good mother earth, to look at the rosy cheeks of the apples, to wish he was in the country, and to say just a few words to the good lady of the shop.

To the rest of the inhabitants of the house, even to Mrs. Meakin herself, he was a mystery. They never quite understood why he lived there. The woman who looked after his rooms, waking him at nine o'clock in the morning, making his cup of coffee, lingering with a duster in his sitting-room until he was dressed, then lingering over the making of his bed in the bedroom until it was eleven o'clock--the time of her departure--even she was reticent about him.

There is a reticence amongst the lower classes which is a combination of ignorance of facts and a supreme lack of imagination. This was the reticence of Mrs. Rowse. She knew nothing; she could invent nothing; so she said nothing. They plied her with questions in vain. He received a lot of letters, she said, some with crests on the envelopes. She used to look at these in wonder before she brought them into his bedroom. They might have been coronets for the awe in which she held them; but in themselves they explained nothing, merely added, in fact, to the mystery which surrounded him. Who was he? What was he? He dressed well--not always, but the clothes were there had he liked to wear them. Three times a week, sometimes more, sometimes less, he donned evening dress, stuck an opera hat on his head and Mrs. Meakin would see him pass down the Lane in front of her shop. If she went to the door to watch him, which quite frequently she did, it was ten chances to one that he would stop a passing hansom, get into it, and drive away. The good lady would watch it with her eyes as it wheeled round into Holborn, and then, returning to her backless chair, exclaim:

"Well--my word--he's a puzzle, he is--there's no tellin' what he mightn't be in disguise--" by which she conveyed to herself and anyone who was there to listen, so wrapt, so entangled a sense of mystery as would need the entire skill of Scotland Yard to unravel.

Then, finally, the rooms themselves, which he occupied--their furnishing, their decoration--the last incomprehensible touch was added with them. Mrs. Meakin, Mrs. Brown, the wife of the theatre cleaner on the second floor, Mrs. Morrell, the wife of the plumber on the third floor, they had all seen them, all marvelled at the rows of brass candlesticks, the crucifixes and the brass incense burners, the real pictures on the walls--pictures, mind you, that were painted, not copied--the rows upon rows of books, the collection of old glass on the mantle-piece, the collection of old china on the piano, the carpet--real velvet pile--and the furniture all solid oak, with old brass fittings which, so Mrs. Rowse told them, he insisted upon having kept as bright as the brass candlesticks themselves. They had seen all this, and they had wondered, wondered why a gentleman who could furnish rooms in such a manner, who could put on evening dress at least three times a week--evening dress, if you please, that was not hired, but his own--who could as often drive away in a hansom, presumably up West, why he should choose to live in such a place as Fetter Lane, over a greengrocer's shop, in rooms the rent of which could not possibly be more than thirty pounds a year.

To them, it remained a mystery; but surely to you who read this it is no mystery at all.

John Grey was a writer, a journalist, a driver of the pen, a business which brings with it more responsibilities than its remuneration can reasonably afford. There is no real living to be made by literature alone, if you have any ambitions and any respect for them. Most people certainly have ambitions, but their respect for them is so inconsiderable when compared with their desire of reward, that they only keep them alive by talking of them. These are the people who know thoroughly the meaning of that word Art, and can discuss it letter for letter, beginning with the capital first.

But to have ambitions and to live up to them is only possible to the extreme idealist--a man who, seeing God in everything, the world has not yet learnt or perhaps forgotten to cater for.

So far everything is utilitarian--supplying the needs of the body which can only see God in consecrated wine, and so it is that wise men build churches for fools to pray in--the wise man in this world being he who grows rich.

This, then, is the solution to the mystery of John Grey. He was an idealist--the very type of person to live in a City of Beautiful Nonsense, where the rarest things in the world cost nothing and the most sordid necessities are dear. For example, the rent of number thirty-nine was a gross exactment upon his purse. He could ill afford that thirty pounds a year. He could ill afford the meals which sometimes hunger compelled him to pay for. But when he bought a piece of brass--the little brass man, for example, an old seal, that was of no use to anybody in the world, and only stood passively inert upon his mantel-piece--the price of it was as nothing when compared with the cheap and vulgar necessities of existence.

But it must not be supposed that Fetter Lane and its environs constitute the spires, the roofs and domes of that City of Beautiful Nonsense. It is not so. Far away East, on the breast of the Adriatic, that wonderful City lies. And we shall come to it--we shall come to it all too soon.

CHAPTER V
THE BALLAD-MONGER--FETTER LANE

In Kensington Gardens, you will find romance. Many a real, many a legendary, person has found it there. It will always be found there so long as this great City of London remains a hive for the millions of human bees that pass in and out of its doors, swarming or working, idling or pursuing in silent and unconscious obedience to a law which not one of them will ever live to understand.

Why it should be Kensington Gardens, more than any other place of the kind, is not quite possible of explanation. Why not Regent's Park, or St. James's Park? Why not those little gardens on the Embankment where the band plays in the late mornings of summer and romances certainly do find a setting? Why not any of these? But no--Kensington Gardens rule *par excellence*, and there is no spot in this vast acreage of humanity to touch them.

You will see there the romances that begin from both ends of a perambulator and, from that onwards, Romance in all its countless periods, infinitely more numerous than the seven ages of man; for Romance is more wonderful than just life. It has a thousand more variations, it plays a thousand more tricks with the understanding. Life is real, they tell us--Life is earnest; but Romance is all that is unreal besides; it is everything that is and is not, everything that has been and will be, and you will find some of the strangest examples of it under the boughs of those huge elms, on those uncomfortable little penny seats in Kensington Gardens.

When those rooms of his in Fetter Lane became unbearable, John Grey would betake himself to the Gardens, sitting by the round Pond where the great ships make their perilous voyages, or he would find a seat under the trees near that little one-storyed house which always shows so brave a blaze of colour in the flower beds that circle it round.

Who lives in that little house? Of course, everybody knows-- well, everybody? I confess, I do not. But the rest of the world does, and so what is the good of letting one's imagination run a-riot when the first policeman would cheerfully give one the information. But if your imagination did run riot, think of the tales you could tell yourself about the owner of that little house in Kensington Gardens! I have never asked a policeman, so I am at liberty to do what I like. It is really the best way in this world; so much more interesting than knowledge. Knowledge, after all, is only knowing things, facts, which next year may not be facts at all. Facts die. But when you imagine, you create something which can live forever. The whole secret of the matter being that its life depends on you, not on Circumstance.

One Friday, three weeks or more after the slender incident of the last candle in the Sardinia St. chapel, those rooms in number 39 Fetter Lane became unbearable. When they did that, they got very small; the walls closed in together and there was no room to move. Even the sounds in the street had no meaning. They became so loud and jarring that they lost meaning altogether.

Moreover, on Friday, the clarionet player came. It was his day; nothing could alter that. If the calendar had not been moved on for weeks together--and some calendars do suffer in that way-- John at least knew the Friday of the week. It is an ill wind, you know--even when it is that which is blown through the reed of a clarionet.

But on this particular morning, the clarionet player was insufferable.

There is a day in nearly every week on which the things which one has grown accustomed to, the sounds that one listens to without hearing, the sights that one looks at without seeing, become blatant and jarring. It is then that we hear these sounds twice as loudly as we should, that we see those things twice as vividly as they are. It is then that the word "unbearable" comes charged with the fullest of its meaning. And just such a day was this Friday in the middle of April--it does not matter how many years ago.

John had been working. He was writing a short story--a very tricksy thing to try and do. It was nearly finished, the room was getting smaller and smaller; the sounds in the street were becoming more and more insistent. A barrel organ had just moved away, leaving a rent of silence in all the noise of traffic, a rent of silence which was almost as unbearable as the confused clattering of sounds; and then the clarionet player struck up his tune.

"Oh, Charlie, he's my darling, my darling, my darling--
Oh, Charlie, he's my darling, my young Chevalier."

This was one of the only four tunes he knew. You may readily guess the rest. He always played them through, one after the other, in never-varying order. Charlie, he's my darling--the Arethusa-- Sally in our Alley and Come Lasses and Lads. He was a ballad- monger. He looked a ballad-monger--only he was a ballad-monger on the clarionet. John Leech has drawn him over and over again in the long ago pages of Punch; drawn him with his baggy trousers that crease where they were never intended to, with his faded black frock coat that was never cut for the shoulders it adorned, with every article of clothing, which the picture told you he would wear to the end of his days, inherited from a generous charity that had only disposed of its gifts in the last moments of decay.

"Oh, Charlie, he's my darling, my darling, my darling--"

He brought such a minor tone into it all; it might have been a dirge. It was as he sang it. For these ballad-mongers are sad creatures. Theirs is a hard, a miserable life, and it all comes out in their music.

The unhappy individual with a musical instrument who stands on the curbstone in the pouring rain can find some depressing note to dwell on in the liveliest of tunes. Art is most times only the cry of the individual.

When the clarionet player began, John shut up his book, rose from his chair, and went to the window. The windows wanted cleaning. It only costs a shilling for four windows--the difficulty is sometimes to find the man to do it--more often the difficulty is to find the shilling. There is generally a man at the first street corner, but never a coin of the realm.

Someone threw a penny into the street from an upper window. The music stopped with a jerk. The ballad-monger chased the rolling coin to the very edge of a drain, then stood erect with a red and grateful face.

He licked his lips, put the penny in his pocket and began again. That penny had insured another five minutes at least. The sun was burning down into the street. John got his hat, picked up his book and went downstairs. Kensington Gardens was the only place left in the world.

Outside, he passed the ballad-monger as he was shaking the moisture out of his reed. No wonder it is a thirsty business, this playing on the clarionet. John was not in the mood to appreciate that very necessary clearing of the instrument. At that moment all ballad-mongers were unnecessary, and their habits loathsome. He stopped.

"Do you know no other tunes," he asked, "than those four you play here every Friday?"

"No, sir." His voice was very deferential and as sad as his music.

"Well--don't you imagine we must all be very tired of them?"

"I often think that, sir. I often think that. But you only hear them every Friday."

"You mean you hear them every day of the week?"

"That is what I mean, sir."

There is always the other person's point of view. You learn that as you go along, and, in the street, you will learn it as quickly as anywhere. The man who runs into you on the pavement is going in his direction as well as you in yours, and it is always a nice point to decide whether you ran into him or he into you. In any case, you may be certain that he has his opinion on it.

John smiled.

"And you're sick of them too, eh?"

The ballad-monger fitted his mouthpiece carefully on to the instrument that played the golden tunes.

"Well, I've what you might call passed that stage, sir. They're in the blood, as you might say, by this time. They're always going on. When I'm asleep, I hear bands playing them in the street. If it isn't 'Arethusa,' it's 'Come Lasses and Lads,' or 'Sally in Our Alley.' They keep going on--and sometimes it's shocking to hear the way they play them. You almost might say that's how I earned the money that people give me, sir--not by playing them on this instrument here--I don't mind that so much. It's the playing them in my head--that's the job I ought to get paid for."

John looked at him. The man had a point of view. He could see the nicer side of a matter. There are not so very many people who can. The predominant idea when he came into the street, of telling the man he was a nuisance, vanished from John's mind. He felt in his pockets. There lay one sixpence. He fingered it for a moment, then brought it out.

"Buy yourself a penny score of another tune," he said, "and let's hear it next Friday. It may drive the others out."

The man took it, looked at him, but said no word of thanks. No words are so obsequious. No words can so spoil a gift. John walked away with a sense of respect.

At the top of the Lane he remembered that he had no penny to pay for his chair in Kensington Gardens. What was to be done? He walked back again. The ballad-monger was at the last bars of the "Arethusa."

He looked round when he had finished.

John stammered. It occurred to him that he was begging for the first time in his life and realised what an onerous profession it must be.

"Would you mind sparing me a penny out of that sixpence?" he asked; and to make it sound a little bit better, he added: "I've run rather short."

The man produced the sixpence immediately.

"You'd better take it all, sir," he said quickly. "You'll want it more than I shall."

John shook his head.

"Give me the penny," said he, "that you caught at the edge of the drain."

CHAPTER VI
OF KENSINGTON GARDENS

So strange a matter is this journey to the City of Beautiful Nonsense, that one cannot be blamed if, at times, one takes the wrong turning, finds oneself in the cul de sac of a digression and is compelled to retrace one's steps. It was intended with the best of good faith that the last chapter should be of Kensington Gardens. Quite honestly it began with that purpose. In Kensington Gardens, you will find Romance. What could be more open and above-board than that? Then up starts a ballad-monger out of nowhere and he has to be reckoned with before another step of the way can be taken.

But now we can proceed with our journey to that far city that lies so slumberously on the breast of the Adriatic.

If you live in Fetter Lane, these are your instructions. Walk straight up the Lane into Holborn; take your first turning on the left and continue directly through Oxford Street and Bayswater, until you reach Victoria Gate in the Park railings. This you enter. This is the very portal of the way.

'Twas precisely this direction taken by John Grey on that Friday morning in April, in such a year as history seems reticent to afford.

There is a means of travelling in London, you know, which is not exactly in accordance with the strict principles of honesty, since it is worked on the basis of false pretences; and if a hero of a modern day romance should stoop to employ it as a means of helping him on his journey to the City of Beautiful Nonsense, he must, on two grounds, be excused. The first ground is, that he has but a penny in his pocket, which is needed for the chair in Kensington Gardens; the second, that most human of all excuses which allows that, when Circumstance drives, a man may live by his wits, so long as he takes the risk of the whipping.

This, then, is the method, invented by John Grey in an inspired moment of poverty. There may be hundreds of others catching inspiration from the little street arabs, who have invented it too. Most probably there are, and they may be the very first to exclaim against the flippant treatment of so dishonest a practice. However that may be, out of his own wits John Grey conceived this felonious means of inexpensive travelling--absolutely the most inexpensive I ever knew.

You are going from Holborn to Victoria Gate in the Park railings--very well. You must mount the first 'bus which you see going in the direction you require; grasp the railings--and mount slowly to the top, having first ascertained that the conductor himself is on the roof. By the time you have reached the seat upstairs, if you have done it in a masterly and approved-of fashion, the 'bus has travelled at least twenty yards or so. Then, seeing the conductor, you ask him politely if his 'bus goes in a direction, which you are confident it does not. This, for example, is the conversation that will take place.

"Do you go to Paddington Station?"

"No, sir, we don't; we go straight to Shepherd's Bush."

"But I thought these green 'busses went to Paddington?"

"There are green 'busses as does, but we don't."

"Oh, yes, I think I know now, haven't they a yellow stripe-- you have a red one."

"That's right."

You rise slowly, regretfully.

"Oh, then I'm sorry," and you begin slowly to descend the stairs.

"But we go by the Edgware Road, and you can get a 'bus to Paddington there," says the conductor.

For a moment or two longer you stand on the steps and try ineffectually--or effectually, it does not matter which, so long as you take your time over it--to point out to him why you prefer the 'bus which goes direct to its destination, rather than the one which does not; then you descend with something like a hundred yards or so of your journey accomplished. Repeat this *ad lib* till the journey is fully complete and you will find that you still possess your penny for the chair in Kensington Gardens. The honesty which is amongst thieves compels you--for the sake of the poor horses who have not done you nearly so much harm as that conductor may have done--to mount and descend the vehicle while in motion. This is the unwritten etiquette of the practice. It also possesses that advantage of prohibiting all fat people from its enjoyment, whose weight on the 'bus would perceptibly increase the labour of the willing animals.

Beyond this, there is nothing to be said. The method must be left to your own conscience, with this subtle criticism upon your choice, that if you refuse to have anything to do with it, it will be because you appreciate the delight of condemning those who have. So you stand to gain anyhow by the possession of the secret. For myself, since John Grey told me of it, I do both--strain a sheer delight in a condemnation of those who use it, and use it myself on all those occasions when I have but a penny in my pocket for the chair in Kensington Gardens. Of course, you must pay for the chair.

By this method of progress, then, John Grey reached Kensington Gardens on that Friday morning--that Friday morning in April which was to prove so eventful in the making of this history.

The opening of the month had been too cold to admit of their beginning the trade in tea under the fat mushroom umbrellas--that afternoon tea which you and oh, I don't know how many sparrows and pigeons, all eat to your heart's content for the modest sum of one shilling. But they might have plied their trade that day with some success. There was a warm breath of the Spring in every little puff of wind that danced down the garden paths. The scarlet tulips nodded their heads to it, the daffodils courteseyed, bowed and swayed, catching the infection of the dancer's step. When Spring comes gladsomely to this country of ours, there is no place in the world quite like it. Even Browning, in the heart of the City of Beautiful Nonsense, must write:

"Oh to be in England,
Now that April's there."

From Fetter Lane to the flower-walk in Kensington Gardens, it is a far cry. Ah, you do not know what continents might lie between that wonderful flower-walk and Fetter Lane. Why, there are people in the darksome little alleys which lie off that neighbourhood of Fleet Street, who have never been further west than the Tottenham Court Road! Fetter Lane, the Tottenham Court Road, and the flower-walk in Kensington Gardens! It may be only three miles or so, but just as there is no such thing as time in the ratio of Eternity, so there is no such thing as distance in the ratio of Space. There is only contrast--and suffering. They measure everything.

John made his way first to the flower-walk, just for the sight and the scent of those wonderful growing things that bring their treasures of inimitable colour up out of the secret breast of the dull brown earth. Where, in that clod of earth, which does but soil the hands of him who touches it, does the tulip get its red? Has the Persian Poet guessed the secret? Is it the blood of a buried Cæsar? Enhance it by calling it a mystery--all the great things of the world are that. Wherever the tulip does get its red, it is a brave thing to look at after the dull, smoky bricks of the houses in Fetter Lane.

John stood at the top of the walk and filled his eyes with the varied colours. There were tulips red, tulips yellow, tulips purple and scarlet and mauve. The little hunchback was already there painting them, hugging up close to his easel, taking much more into the heart of him than he probably ever puts down upon his canvas.

He comes every season of every year, that little hunchback, and Spring and Summer, and Autumn and Winter, he paints in Kensington Gardens; and Spring and Summer, and Autumn and Winter, I have no doubt he will continue to paint the Gardens that he loves. And then one day, the Gardens will miss him. He will come no more. The dull brown earth will have taken him as it takes the bulb of a tulip, and perhaps out of his eyes--those eyes which have been drinking in the colours of the flowers for so long, some tulip will one day get its red.

Surely there cannot be libel in such a statement as this? We must all die. The little hunchback, if he reads this, will not approach me for damages, unless he were of the order of Christian Scientists or some such sect, who defy the ravages of Time. And how could he be that? He must have seen the tulips wither.

From the flower-walk, John made his way to the round pond. The ships were sailing. Sturdy mariners with long, thin, bamboo poles were launching their craft in the teeth of the freshening breeze. Ah, those brave ships, and those sturdy men with their young blue eyes, searching across that vast expanse of water for the return of the *Daisy* or the *Kittywake* or some such vessel with some such fanciful name!

John took a chair to watch them. A couple of hoary sailors--men who had vast dealings with ships and traffic on deep waters--passed by him with their vessels tucked up under their arms.

"I sail for 'Frisco in five minutes," said one--"for 'Frisco with a cargo of iron."

"What do you use for iron?" asked the other, with the solemnity that such cargo deserved.

"My sister gave me some of her hairpins," was the stern reply.

This, if you like it, is romance! Bound for 'Frisco with a cargo of iron! Think of it! The risk, the peril, the enormous fortune at stake! His sister's hairpins! What a world, what a City of Beautiful Nonsense, if one could only believe like this!

John spread out his short story on his knee, looked at the first lines of it, then closed it with disgust. What was the good of writing stories, when such adventures as these were afoot? Perhaps the little hunchback felt that too. What was the good of painting with red paint on a smooth canvas when God had painted those tulips on the rough brown earth? Why had not he got a sister who would hazard her hairpins in his keeping, so that he might join in the stern business of life and carry cargoes of iron to far-off parts?

He sat idly watching the good ship start for 'Frisco. One push of the thin bamboo pole and it was off--out upon the tossing of the waves. A breath of Spring air blew into its sails, filled them--with the scent of the tulips, perhaps--and bore it off upon its voyage, while the anxious master, with hands shading his eyes, watched it as it dipped over the horizon of all possible interference.

Where was it going to come to shore? The voyage lasted fully five minutes and, at the last moment, a trade wind seizing it--surely it must be a trade wind which seizes a vessel with a cargo such as this--it was born direct for the shore near where John was sitting.

The captain came hurrying along the beach to receive it and, from a seat under the elm trees, a girl came toward him.

"Do you think it's brought them safely?" she asked.

He looked up with a touch of manly pride.

"The *Albatross* has never heaved her cargo overboard yet," he said with a ringing voice.

So this was the sister. From that wonderful head of hair of hers had come the cargo of the good ship *Albatross*. She turned that head away to hide a smile of amusement. She looked in John's direction. Their eyes met.

It was the lady of the heavy fur coat who had prayed to St. Joseph in the Sardinia Street chapel.

CHAPTER VII
THE VOYAGE OF THE GOOD SHIP ALBATROSS

This is where Destiny and the long arm of Coincidence play a part in the making of all Romance. One quality surely there must be in such matters, far more essential than that happiness ever after which the sentimentalist so clamours for. That quality, it is, of Destiny, which makes one know that, whatever renunciation and despair may follow, such things were meant to be. Coincidence combines to make them so, and, you may be sure, for a very good reason. And is it so long a stretch of the arm from Sardinia Street Chapel to Kensington Gardens? Hardly! In fiction, and along the high-road, perhaps it might be; but then this is not fiction. This is true.

Romance then--let us get an entirely new definition for it--is a chain of Circumstances which out of the infinite chaos links two living things together for a definite end--that end which is a pendant upon the chain itself and may be a heart with a lock of hair inside, or it may be a cross, or a dagger, or a crown--you never know till the last link is forged.

When he looked into the eyes of the lady of St. Joseph--so he had, since that incident, called her in his mind--John knew that Destiny had a hand in the matter.

He told me afterwards----

"You only meet the people in this world whom you are meant to meet. Whether you want to meet them or not is another matter, and has no power to bribe the hand of Circumstance."

He was generalising certainly, but that is the cloak under which a man speaks of himself.

However that may be, and whether the law holds good or not, they met. He saw the look of recognition that passed across her eyes; then he rose to his feet.

The knowledge that you are in the hands of Destiny gives you boldness. John marched directly across to her and lifted his hat.

"My name is Grey," he said--"John Grey. I'm taking it for granted that St. Joseph has already introduced us and forgotten to tell you who I was. If I take too much for granted, say so, I shall perfectly understand."

Well, what could she say? You may tell a man that he's presumptuous; but hardly when he presumes like this. Besides, there was Destiny at the back of him, putting the words into his mouth.

She smiled. It was impossible to do otherwise.

"Do you think St. Joseph would be recognised in our society?" she asked.

"I have no doubt of it," said he. "St. Joseph was a very proper man."

They turned to a cry of the master mariner as the good ship *Albatross* touched the beach. Immediately she was unloaded and her cargo brought triumphantly to the owner.

"This," said John, "is the cargo of iron. Then I presume we're in 'Frisco.

"How did you know?" she asked.

"I heard the sailing orders given in the Docks at London ten minutes ago."

She looked down, concealing a smile, at her brother, then at John, lastly at the good ship *Albatross*--beached until further orders. He watched her. She was making up her mind.

"Ronald," said she, when the wandering of her eyes had found decision, "this is a friend of mine, Mr. Grey."

Ronald held out a horny hand.

"How do you do, sir."

Surely that settled matters? St. Joseph was approved of. She had said--this is a friend of mine.

They shook hands then with a heavy grip. It is the recognised way with those who go down to the sea in ships.

"When do you take your next voyage?" asked John.

"As soon as we can ship a cargo of gravel."

"And where are you bound for?"

"Port of Lagos--West Africa."

"Dangerous country, isn't it? Fever? White man's grave, and all that sort of thing?"

"Those are the orders," said Ronald staunchly, looking up to his sister for approval.

"I suppose you couldn't execute a secret commission for me," said John. He laid a gentle stress on the word secret. "You couldn't carry private papers and run a blockade?"

Private papers! Secret commission! Run a blockade! Why the good ship *Albatross* was just built for such nefarious trade as that.

John took the short story out of his pocket.

"Well, I want you to take this to the port of Venice," said he. "The port of Venice on the Adriatic, and deliver it yourself into the hands of one--Thomas Grey. There is a fortune to be made if you keep secret and talk to no one of your business. Are you willing to undertake it and share profits?"

"We'll do our best, sir," said Ronald.

Then the secret papers were taken aboard--off started the good ship *Albatross*.

The other mariner came up just as she had set sail.

"What cargo have you got this time?" he whispered.

Ronald walked away.

"Mustn't tell," he replied sternly, and by such ready confession of mystery laid himself open to all the perils of attack. That other mariner must know he was bound on secret service, and perhaps by playing the part of Thomas Grey on the other side of the round pond, would probably be admitted into confidence. There is no knowing. You can never be sure of what may happen in a world of romantic adventure.

John watched their departure lest his eagerness to talk to her alone should seem too apparent. Then he turned, suggested a seat under the elm trees and, in silence, they walked across the grass to the two little penny chairs that stood expectantly together.

There they sat, still in silence, watching the people who were promenading on the path that circles the round pond. Nurses and babies and perambulators, there were countless of these, for in the gardens of Kensington the babies grow like the tulips--rows upon rows of them, in endless numbers. Like the tulips, too, the sun brings them out and their gardeners take them and plant them under the trees. Every second passer-by that sunny morning in April was a gardener with her tulip or tulips, as the case might be; some red, some white, some just in bud, some fully blown. Oh, it is a wonderful place for things to grow in, is Kensington Gardens.

But there were other pedestrians than these. There were Darbys and Joans, Edwards and Angelinas.

Then there passed by two solemn nuns in white, who had crosses hanging from their waists and wore high-heeled shoes.

The lady of St. Joseph looked at John. John looked at her.

She lifted her eyebrows to a question.

"Protestant?" she said.

John nodded with a smile.

That broke the silence. Then they talked. They talked first of St. Joseph.

"You always pray to St. Joseph?" said he.

"No--not always--only for certain things. I'm awfully fond of him, but St. Cecilia's my saint. I don't like the look of St. Joseph, somehow or other. Of course, I know he's awfully good, but I don't like his beard. They always give him a brown beard, and I hate a man with a brown beard."

"I saw St. Joseph once with a grey beard," said John.

"Grey? But he wasn't old."

"No, but this one I saw was grey. It was in Ardmore, a wee fishing village in the county of Waterford, in Ireland. Ah, you should see Ardmore. Heaven comes nearer to the sea there than any place I know."

"But what about St. Joseph?"

"Oh, St. Joseph! Well, there was a lady there intent upon the cause of temperance. She built little temperance cafés all about the country, and had the pictures of Cruikshank's story of the Bottle, framed and put on all the walls. To propitiate the Fates for the café in Ardmore, she decided also to set up the statue of St. Daeclan, their patron saint in those parts. So she sent up to Mulcahy's, in Cork, for a statue of St. Daeclan. Now St. Daeclan, you know, is scarcely in popular demand."

"I've never heard of him," said the lady of St. Joseph.

"Neither had I till I went to Ardmore. Well, anyhow, Mulcahy had not got a statue. Should he send away and see if he could order one? Certainly he should send away. A week later came the reply. There is not a statue of St. Daeclan to be procured anywhere. Will an image of St. Joseph do as well? It would have to do. Very well, it came--St. Joseph with his brown beard.

"'If only we could have got St. Daeclan,' they said as they stood in front of it. 'But he's too young for St. Daeclan. St. Daeclan was an old man.'

"I suppose it did not occur to them that St. Daeclan may not have been born old; but they conceived of a notion just as wise. They got a pot of paint from Foley's, the provision store, and, with judicious applications, they made grey the brown beard of St. Joseph, then, washing out the gold letters of his name, they painted in place of them the name of St. Daeclan."

The lady of St. Joseph smiled.

"Are you making this up?" asked she.

He shook his head.

"Well, then, the café was opened, and a little choir of birds from the chapel began to sing, and all the people round about who had no intention to be temperate, but loved a ceremony, came to see the opening. They trouped into the little hall and stood with gaping mouths looking at that false image which bore the superscription of St. Daeclan, and the old women held up their hands and they said:

"Oh, shure, glory be to God! 'tis just loike the pore man--it is indeed. Faith, I never want to see a better loikeness of himself than that."

John turned and looked at her.

"And there he stands to this day," he added--"as fine an example of good faith and bad painting as I have ever seen in my life."

"What a delightful little story," she said, and she looked at him with that expression in the eyes when admiration mingles so charmingly with bewilderment that one is compelled to take them both as a compliment.

"Do you know you surprise me," she added.

"So I see," said he.

"You see?"

"In your eyes."

"You saw that?"

"Yes, you were wondering how I came to be praying-- probably for money--to St. Joseph--praying in an old blue serge suit that looked as if a little money could easily be spent on it, and yet can afford to sit out here in the morning in Kensington Gardens and tell you what you are so good as to call a delightful little story?"

"That's quite true. I was wondering that."

"And I," said John, "have been wondering just the same about you."

What might not such a conversation as this have led to? They were just beginning to tread upon that virgin soil from which any fruit may be born. It is a wonderful moment that, the moment when two personalities just touch. You can feel the contact tingling to the tips of your fingers.

What might they not have talked of then? She might even have told him why she was praying to St. Joseph, but then the master mariner returned, bearing papers in his hand.

"Are you one Thomas Grey?" said he.

"I am that man," replied John.

"These are secret papers which I am to deliver into your hands. There is a fortune to be made if you keep secret."

John took the short story.

"Secrecy shall be observed," said he.

CHAPTER VIII
THE FATEFUL TICKET-PUNCHER

The master of the good ship *Albatross* departed, chartered for another voyage to the Port of Lagos with his cargo of gravel, gathered with the sweat of the brow and the tearing of the finger nails from the paths in Kensington Gardens.

John hid the short story away and lit a cigarette. She watched him take it loose from his waistcoat pocket. Had he no cigarette case? She watched him take a match--loose also--from the ticket pocket of his coat. Had he no match-box? She watched him strike it upon the sole of his boot, believing all the time that he was unaware of the direction of her eyes.

But he knew. He knew well enough, and took as long over the business as it was possible to be. When the apprehension of discovery made her turn her head, he threw the match away. Well, it was a waste of time then.

"I thought," said she presently, "you had told me your name was John?"

"So it is."

"Then why did you tell Ronald to deliver the papers to Thomas Grey?"

"That is my father."

"And does he live in Venice?"

What a wonderful thing is curiosity in other people, when you yourself are only too ready to divulge! Loth only to tell her it all too quickly, John readily answered all she asked.

"Yes, he lives in Venice," he replied.

"Always?"

"Always now."

She gazed into a distance of her own--that distance in which nearly every woman lives.

"What a wonderful place it must be to live in," said she.

He turned his head to look at her.

"You've never been there?"

"Never."

"Ah! there's a day in your life yet then."

Her forehead wrinkled. Ah, it may not sound pretty, but it was. The daintiest things in life are not to be written in a sentence. You get them sometimes in a single word; but oh, that word is so hard to find.

"How do you mean?" she asked.

"The day you go to Venice--if ever you do go--will be one day quite by itself in your life. You will be alive that day."

"You love it?"

She knew he did. That was the attraction in asking the question--to hear him say so. There is that in the voice of one confessing to the emotion--for whatever object it may happen to be--which can thrill the ear of a sensitive listener. A sense of envy comes tingling with it. It is the note in the voice, perhaps. You may hear it sometimes in the throat of a singer--that note which means the passion, the love of something, and something within you thrills in answer to it.

"You love it?" she repeated.

"I know it," replied John--"that's more than loving."

"What does your father do there?"

"He's an artist--but he does very little work now. He's too old. His heart is weak, also."

"Then does he live there by himself?"

"Oh, no--my mother lives with him. They have wonderful old rooms in the Palazzo Capello in the Rio Marin. She is old, too. Well--she's over sixty. They didn't marry until she was forty. And he's about ten years older than she is."

"Are you the only child?"

"The only child--yes."

"How is it that they didn't marry until your mother was forty?"

She pattered on with her questions. Having accepted him as a friend, the next thing to do was to get to know all about him. It is just as well, in case people should ask; but in this huddle of houses where one knows more of the life of one's next-door neighbour than one ever does of one's friends, it really scarcely matters. She thought she wanted to know because she ought to know. But that was not it at all. She had to know. She was meant to know. There is a difference.

"Perhaps I'm being too inquisitive?" she suggested gently. This is only another way of getting one's question answered. You might call it the question circumspect and, by borrowing from another's wit, mark the distinction between it and the question direct. But it is not so much the name that matters, as its effectiveness.

In a moment, John was all apologies for his silence.

"Inquisitive? No! It's only the new sensation."

"What new sensation?"

"Somebody wanting to know something about oneself. On the other side of the street where I live, there resides a parrot; and every Sunday they put him outside on the window-sill, and there he keeps calling out--'Do you want to know who I am? Do you want to know who I am?' And crowds of little boys and little girls, and idle men and lazy women, stand down below his cage in the street and imitate him in order to get him to say it again. 'Do you want to know who I am, Polly?' they call out. And oh, my goodness, it's so like life. They never reply--'Who are you, then?' But every single one of them must ask him if he wants to know who they are, just when he's longing to tell them all about himself. It is like life you know."

"What nice little stories you tell. I believe you make them up as you go along--but they're quite nice. So that's the new sensation?"

"Yes--that's it. Someone, at last, has said 'Who are you, then?' And I hardly know where to begin."

"Well, I asked you why your father didn't marry till your mother was forty. You said she was forty."

"Yes, I know--yes, that's quite right. You see he was married before to a wealthy woman. They lived here in London. I'm afraid they didn't get on well together. It was his fault. He says so, and I believe it was. I can quite understand the way it all happened. You must love money very much to be able to get on with it when it's not your own. He didn't love it enough. Her money got between them. One never really knows the ins and outs of these things. Nobody can possibly explain them. I say I understand it, but I don't. They happen when people marry. Only, it would appear, when they marry. She never threw it in his face, I'm sure of that. He always speaks of her as a wonderful woman; but it was just there--that's all. Gold's a strange metal, you know--an uncanny metal, I think. They talk of the ill-luck of the opal, it's nothing to the ill-luck of the gold the opal is set in. You must realise the absolute valuelessness of it, that it's no more worth than tin, or iron, or lead, or any other metal that the stray thrust of a spade may dig up; if you don't think of it like that, if you haven't an utter contempt for it, it's a poison, is gold. It's subtle, deadly poison that finds its heavy way into the most sacred heart of human beings and rots the dearest and the gentlest thoughts they have. They say familiarity breeds contempt. In every case but that of gold, it's true. But in gold it's just the reverse. The only way with gold, to have contempt for it, is to have none and, when it does enter your possession, give it away. You keep it, you struggle for it, you give it a moment's place on your altar, and you'll find that your first-born must be the burnt offering you will have to make to assuage its insatiable lust."

The sense of humour saved him from saying more. Suddenly he turned and looked at her, and laughed. The only way with gold, to have contempt for it, is to have none and, when it does enter your possession, give it away.

Glorious words to say when you have only a penny in your pocket to pay for your chair in Kensington Gardens--such a fine sense of bravado in them. As for the chance of money falling from the heavens or the elm trees into your lap, it is so remote, that you can afford to voice your preachings without fear of having to put them into immediate practice.

Seeing all this and, seeing the solemn expression on her face, John laughed. All that fine parade of words of his was very human. He knew it. There is not one amongst us but who does it every day. There never is so fine an army of brave men as you will find in times of peace; never so lavish a man with money as he who has none. These are the real humours, the real comedies in this struggle for existence. And yet, it is the only philosophy for the poor man who has nothing, to say he wants less. So you cheat the little gods of their laughter, and whistle a tune to show how little you care.

But to see through it all--there are so many who do it unconsciously--that is a quality beyond philosophy. John laughed.

She looked up quickly.

"You laugh? Why?"

"You look so serious."

"I was. It's so true--quite true, all you said. But what is one to do when everybody around one sets their standard in gold--when people are only good-spirited when there is money to be had, and cross and inconsiderate when there is none? What is one to do then?"

"Must you follow their lead?" asked John.

"What else? The community governs, doesn't it?"

"So they say. But even government is a thing that must be taught, and someone must teach it to the community, so that the community may become proficient at its job. When you get into a community of people like that, all you have to do is to break away. It doesn't matter how universally good a wrong may be, you can't make it right for the individual."

"What did your father do?"

"Oh--he disobeyed the laws of the community. He went away. He deserted her."

She stole a hurried glance at his face.

"Don't you speak rather hardly?"

"No--conventionally--that's all. That is the technical term. He deserted her. Went and lived in the slums and worked. He was probably no paragon, either, until he met my mother. No man is until he meets *the* woman with the great heart and God's good gift of understanding."

"Have you ever met her yet?"

"No--I'm only twenty-six."

"Do you think you ever will meet her?"

"Yes--one day."

"When?"

"Oh, the time that Fate allots for these things."

"When is that?"

"When it's too late."

"Isn't that pessimistic?"

"No--I'm only speaking of Time. Time's nothing--Time doesn't count. You may count it--you generally do with a mechanical contrivance called a clock--but it doesn't count itself. As the community looks at these things it may be too late, but it's not too late to make all the difference in life. The point is meeting her, knowing her. Nothing else really matters. Once you know her, she is as much in your life as ever marriage and all such little conventional ceremonies as that can make her."

She looked up at him again.

"What strange ideas you have."

"Are they?"

"They are to me. Then your father didn't meet your mother too late? How soon did he meet her after--after he went away?"

"Two years or so."

"Oh--he was quite old, then?"

"No--quite young."

"But I thought you said they didn't marry until she was forty."

"Yes--that is so. He couldn't marry her till then. They were both Catholics, you see. Eighteen years went by before they married."

She made patterns on a bare piece of ground with the ferrule of her umbrella, as she listened. When he came to this point of the story, she carved the figure one and eight in the mould.

"Yes," said John, looking at them--"it was a long time to wait--wasn't it?"

She nodded her head and slowly scratched the figures out.

"So the secret papers were sent to your father?" she said.

"Yes."

She communed with herself for a few moments. She was very curious to know the secret of those papers; just as curious as that other mariner had been. But when you get beyond a certain age, they tell you it is rude to be curious--more's the pity! It takes away half the pleasure from life. She wanted so much to know. The mystery that surrounded John Grey in Fetter Lane was clinging to him here in Kensington Gardens. She felt just as curious about him as did Mrs. Meakin, and Mrs. Rowse; and Mrs. Morrell, and, like them, she was afraid to show it to him.

Presently she left off scratching her patterns in the mould and raised her head, looking out wistfully across the pond.

"Ronald was delighted to be carrying secret papers," she said pensively.

"Was he?"

"Yes--he's been reading Stevenson, and Henty, and all those books--the idea of secret papers was just what he loved."

John's eyes twinkled.

"Do you think he told that other boy?" he asked.

"Oh--no--I'm sure he wouldn't."

"Not if he got the other boy to play the part of Thomas Grey--and satisfied his conscience like that?"

"No--because he delivered them to you. I'm sure he never looked at them. You're the only one who knows the secret."

John's eyes twinkled again. She was so curious to know.

"It's a terrible thing to be the only possessor of a secret like that," he said solemnly.

She glanced quickly at his face.

"It is, if it's something you mustn't tell," said she. And you could hear the question in that; just the faint lingering note of it; but it was there. Of course, if he could not tell, the sooner she knew it the better. You can waste upon a person even so poor a sentiment as curiosity, and when a woman gets proud, she will give you none of it.

If he had kept his secret another moment longer, she would undoubtedly have got proud; but just then, there came into view the insignificant little figure of a man in faded, dirty livery, a peaked cap, a sleuth-like, watchful air and, hidden in the grasping of his hand, there was a fateful ticket puncher. Two seats, and John had only a penny! What can one do under such circumstances as these? He looked helplessly through his mind for a way out of the dilemma. He even looked on the ground to see whether some former charitable person had thrown away their tickets when they left--he always did as much for the cause of unknown humanity himself. You never know how many people there are in London with only a penny in their pockets. But he looked in vain. There were only the figures that she had carved and scratched out in the mould.

He thought of saying that he had bought a ticket and lost it. One of those little gusts of wind that were dancing under the elm trees would readily vouch for the truth of his story in such a predicament as this. But then this might be the only ticket puncher in the gardens at that time of the year, and he would know. He thought of going through all his pockets and simulating the despair of a man who has lost his last piece of gold. And the slouching figure of the chair man drew nearer and nearer. And oh, he came so cunningly, as if he had nothing whatever to do with this crushing tax upon the impoverished resources of those who seek Romance.

Yes, John rather liked that last idea. Anyone might lose their last piece of gold. It is not even a paradox to say it would be the first they would lose. But it would be acting the lie to her as well as to the chairman. Was that fair? The chairman would only look imperturbably at him with a stony eye--it was more than likely he would have heard that story before, and a chair man will not be baulked of his prey. Then she would have to pay. No--that would not be fair. Then----

"I'm going to pay for my seat," said the Lady of St. Joseph.

"Oh, no!" said John vehemently--"Why should you?"

Couldn't he get up and say he was only sitting there by accident; had never meant to sit down at all?

"Yes--I'm going to pay," she said--"I owe you a penny for the candle to St. Joseph."

Ah! That was the way out of it! You see, if you only pray earnestly enough, St. Joseph is bound to answer your prayer. This was his return for John's offer of generosity. There is not a doubt of it in my mind. There was not a doubt of it in his.

CHAPTER IX
THE ART OF HIEROGLYPHICS

The bell of the ticket-puncher rang, the tiny slips of paper were torn off the roll and exchanged hands. For that day, at least--so long as they chose to sit there--the little penny chairs belonged to them; indisputably to them.

You feel you have bought something when you pay for it with your last penny. John leant back with a breath of relief as the chair man walked away. It had been a terrible moment. In this life, you never lose that sense that it is only the one friend in the world who does not judge you by the contents of your pocket; and when an acquaintance is but of a few moment's standing--even if it be a Lady of St. Joseph--it is hazarding everything to have to admit to the possession of only one penny.

Do you wonder his breath was of relief? Would you wonder if, wrapped up in that breath, there had been a prayer of thanks to St. Joseph? Only a little prayer, not even spoken in the breath, hardly expressed in the thought that accompanied it--but still a prayer--as much a prayer in his heart, as you might say there was a butterfly in the heart of a cocoon. We know that there is only a chrysalis--sluggish, inert, incapable of the light and dainty flight of a butterfly's wings--but still it will be a butterfly one day. That was just about the relation of John's breath to a prayer.

Under his eyes, he stole a look at her. She was not thinking of pennies! Not she! Once you make a woman curious--pennies won't buy back her peace of mind. She was beginning her tricks again with the ferrule of her umbrella. Why is it that a woman can so much better express herself with the toe of an elegant shoe or the point of a fifteen and six-penny umbrella? Nothing less dainty than this will serve her. Give her speech and she ties herself into a knot with it like a ball of worsted and then complains that she is not understood. But with the toe of an elegant shoe--mind you, if it is not elegant, you must give her something else--she will explain a whole world of emotion.

She had begun scratching up the mould again. John watched the unconscious expression of her mind with the point of that umbrella. One figure after another she scratched and then crossed out. First it was a ship, rigged as no ship has ever been rigged before or since. The *Albatross*, of course. Then a dome, the dome of a building. He could not follow that. He would have had to know that she had once had a picture book in which was a picture of Santa Maria della Salute--otherwise the meaning of that dome was impossible to follow. He thought it was a beehive. Really, of course, you understood this from the first yourself, it meant Venice. Then she began carving letters. The first was G. The second was R. She thought she felt him looking, glanced up quickly, but he was gazing far away across the round pond. It is always as well not to look. Women are very shy when they are expressing their emotions. It is always as well not to look; but you will be thought a dullard if you do not see. John was gazing across the pond. But nevertheless, she scratched those first two letters out. When he saw that, he took pity.

"Shall I tell you what the secret papers are?" said he, with a smile.

Ah, the gratitude in her eyes.

"Do!" she replied.

"It's a short story."

"A short story! You write? Why didn't you tell me that before?"

"But it's only a short story," said John, "that no one'll ever read."

"Won't it be published?"

"No--never."

"Why?"

"Because people won't like it."

"How do you know?"

"I'm sure of it. I know what they like."

"Read it to me and I'll tell you if I like it."

Read it to her! Sit in Kensington Gardens and have his work listened to by the Lady of St. Joseph! He took it out of his pocket without another word and read it then and there.

This is it.

AN IDYLL OF SCIENCE

The world has grown some few of its grey hairs in search of the secret of perpetual motion. How many, with their ingeniously contrived keys, have not worn old and feeble in their efforts to open this Bluebeard's chamber: until their curiosity sank exhausted within them? You count them, from the dilettante Marquis of Worcester, playing with his mechanical toy before a king and his court, Jackson, Orffyreus, Bishop Wilkins, Addeley, with the rest of them, and, beyond arriving at the decision of the French Academy--"that the only perpetual motion possible ... would be useless for the purpose of the devisers," you are drawn to the conclusion that mankind shares curiosity with the beasts below him and calls it science lest the world should laugh.

You have now in this idyll here offered you, the story of one who found the secret, and showed it to me alone. Have patience to let your imagination wander through Irish country lanes, strolling hither and thither, drawn to no definite end, led by no ultimate hope, and the history of the blind beggar, who discovered the secret of perpetual motion, shall be disclosed for you; all the curiosity that ever thrilled you shall be appeased, feasted, satiated.

There was not one in the country-side who knew his name. Name a man in Ireland and you locate him; Murphy, and he comes from Cork--Power, and he comes from Waterford. Why enumerate them all? But this blind beggar had no name. There was no place that claimed him. With that tall silk hat of his which some parish priest had yielded him, with his long black coat which exposure to the sorrowful rains of a sad country had stained a faded green; with his long, crooked stick that tapped its wearisome, monotonous dirge and his colourless, red 'kerchief knotted round his neck, he was a figure well-known in three or four counties.

No village owned him. At Clonmel, they denied him, at Dungarvan, they disowned him; yet the whole country-side, at certain seasons of the year, had heard that well-known tapping of the crooked stick, had seen those sightless eyes blinking under the twisted rim of the old silk hat. For a day or so in the place, he was a well-known figure; for a day or so they slipped odd pennies into his sensitively opened palm, but the next morning would find him missing. Where had he gone? Who had seen him go? Not a soul! The rounded cobbles and the uneven pavements that had resounded to the old crooked stick would be silent of that tapping noise for another year, at least.

But had chance taken you out into the surrounding country, and had it taken you in the right direction, you would have found him toiling along by the hedges--oh, but so infinitely slowly!--his shoulders bent, and his hand nodding like some mechanical toy that had escaped the clutches of its inventor and was wandering aimlessly wherever its mechanism directed.

How it came to be known that he sought the secret of perpetual motion, is beyond me. It was one of those facts about him which seem as inseparable from a man as the clothes that belie his trade. You saw him coming up the road towards you and the words "perpetual motion" rushed, whispering, to your mind. About the matter himself, he was sensitively reticent; yet he must have told someone--someone must have told me. Who was it? Some inhabitant of the village of Rathmore must have spread the story. Whom could it have been? Foley, the carpenter? Burke, the fisherman? Fitzgerald, the publican--Troy, the farmer? I can trace it to none of these. I cannot remember who told me: and yet, when each year he came round for the ceremonies of the Pattern day, when they honoured the patron saint, I said as I saw him: "Here is the blind beggar who tried to invent perpetual motion." The idea became inseparable from the man.

With each succeeding year his movements became more feeble, his head hung lower as he walked. You could see Death stalking behind him in his footsteps, gaining on him, inch by inch, until the shadow of it fell before him as he walked.

There were times when I had struggled to draw him into conversation; moments when I had thought that I had won his confidence; but at the critical juncture, those sightless eyes would search me through and through and he would pass me by. There must have been a time when the world had treated him ill. I fancy, in fact, that I have heard such account of him; for he trusted no one. Year after year he came to Rathmore for the festival of the Pattern and, year after year, I remained in ignorance of his secret.

At last, when I saw the hand of Death stretched out almost to touch his shoulder, I spoke--straight to the pith of the matter, lest another year should bring him there no more.

He was walking down from the Holy Well where for the last hour, upon his tremulous knees, he had been making his devotions to a saint whose shrine his unseeing eyes had never beheld. This was the opportunity I seized. For a length of many moments, when first I had seen his bent and ill-fed figure, rocking to and fro with the steps he took, I had made up my mind to it.

As he reached my side, I slipped a shilling into his half-concealed palm. So do we assess our fellow-kind! The instinct is bestial, but ingrained. Honour, virtue and the like--we only call them priceless to ourselves; yet it takes a great deal to convince us that they are not priceless to others. I priced my blind beggar at a shilling! I watched his withered fingers close over it, rubbing against the minted edge that he might know its worth!

"That has won him," I thought.

Ah! What a brutal conception of God's handicraft! A shilling to buy the secret of perpetual motion! Surely I could not have thought that Nature would have sold her mysteries for that! I did. There is the naked truth of it.

"Who gives me this?" he asked, still fingering it as though it yet might burn his hand.

"A friend," said I.

"God's blessing on ye," he answered and his fingers finally held it tight. There he kept it, clutched within his hand. No pocket was safe in the clothes he wore to store such fortune as that. "You're leaving Rathmore after the Pattern, I suppose?" I began.

His head nodded as he tapped his stick.

"There's something I want to ask you before you go," I continued.

He stopped, I with him, watching the suspicions pass across his face.

"Someone has told me----" I sought desperately, clumsily, for my satisfaction now. "Someone has told me that you have found the secret of perpetual motion. Is that true?"

The milk-white, sightless eyes rushed querulously to mine. All the expression of yearning to see seemed to lie hidden behind them. A flame that was not a flame--the ghost of a flame burnt there, intense with questioning. He could not see; I knew he could not see; yet those vacant globes of matter were charged with unerring perception. In that moment, his soul was looking into mine, searching it for integrity, scouring the very corners of it for the true reason of my question.

I met his gaze. It seemed then to me, that if I failed and my eyes fell before his, he would have weighed and found me wanting. It is one of the few things in this world which I count to my credit, that those empty sockets found me worthy of the trust.

"Who told ye that?" he asked.

I answered him truthfully that I did not know.

"But is it the case?" I added.

He shifted his position. I could see that he was listening.

"There is no one on the road," I said--"We are quite alone."

He coughed nervously.

"'Tis a matter of fifteen years since I first thought the thing out at all. Shure, I dunno what made it come into me head; but 'twas the way I used to be working in a forge before I lost the sight of my eyes. I thought of it there, I suppose."

He stopped and I prompted him.

"What principle did you go on?" I asked--"Was it magnetism? How did you set to work to avoid friction?"

This time, as he looked at me, his eyes were expressionless. I felt that he was blind. He had not understood a word I had said.

"Are ye trying to get the secret out av me?" he asked at length. "Shure, there's many have done that. They all try and get it out av me. The blacksmith--him that was working at the forge where I was myself before I lost the sight in me eyes--he wanted to make the machine for me. But I'd known him before I was blind and I hadn't lost the knowledge with me eyesight."

"Are you making it yourself, then?"

He nodded his head.

"As well as I can," he continued--"but, shure, what can these fingers do with feeling alone--I must see what I'm doing. Faith, I've all the pieces here now in me pocket, only for the putting of 'em together, and glory be to God, I've tried and tried, but they won't go. Ye can't do it with feelin' alone."

Some lump threatened to rise in my throat.

"Good God!" I thought--"this is tragedy----" And I looked in vain for sight in his eyes.

"Would ye like to see the pieces?" he asked.

I assured him that the secret would be safe in my keeping were he so generous.

"No one about?" he asked.

"Not a soul!"

Then, from his pocket--one by one--he took them out and laid them down on a grass bank by our side. I watched each piece as he produced it and, with the placing of them on the bank of grass, I watched his face. These were the parts in the construction of his intricate mechanism that he showed to me--a foot of rod iron, a small tin pot that once perhaps had held its pound of coffee, a strip of hoop iron and an injured lock.

"There," he said proudly--"but if I were to give these to that blacksmith, he'd steal the secret before my face. I wouldn't trust him with 'em and I working these fifteen years."

I thanked God he could not see my face then. The foot of rod iron! The small tin pot! The injured lock! They stared at me in derision. Only they and I knew the secret--only they and I could tell it, as they themselves had told it me. His wits were gone. Perpetual motion! The wretched man was mad.

Perpetual motion out of these rusty old things--rusting for fifteen years in the corners of his pockets! Perpetual motion!

But here the reality of it all broke upon me--burst out with its thundering sense of truth. Mad the blind beggar might be; yet there, before my very eyes, in those motionless objects, was the secret of perpetual motion. Rust, decay, change--the obstinate metal of the iron rod, the flimsy substance of the tin pot, always under the condition of change; rusting in his pocket where they had lain for fifteen years--never quiescent, never still, always moving--moving--moving--in obedience to the inviolable law of change, as we all, in servile obedience to that law as well, are moving continually, from childhood into youth, youth to middle-age--middle-age to senility--then death, the last change of all. All this giant structure of manhood, the very essence of complicated intricacy compared to that piece of rod iron, passing into the dust from which the thousands of years had contrived to make it. What more could one want of perpetual motion than that?

I looked up into his face again.

"You've taught me a wonderful lesson," I said quietly.

"Ah," he replied--"it's all there--all there--the whole secret of it; if only I had the eyes to put it together."

If he only had the eyes? Have *any* of us the eyes? Have any of us the eyes?

When he had finished, he folded it slowly and put it back in his pocket.

"Well----?" he said.

His heart was beating with anticipation, with apprehension, with exaltation. With one beat he knew she must think it was good. It was his best. He had just done it and, when you have just done it, you are apt to think that. But with another beat, he felt she was going to say the conventional thing--to call it charming--to say-- "But how nice." It would be far better if she said it was all wrong, that it struck a wrong note, that its composition was ill. One can believe that about one's work--but that it is charming, that it is nice--never!

For that moment Destiny swung in a balance, poised upon the agate of chance. What was she going to say? It all depended upon that. But she was so silent. She sat so still. Mice are still when you startle them; then, when they collect their wits, they scamper away.

Suddenly she rose to her feet.

"Will you be here in the Gardens to-morrow morning at this time," she said--"Then I'll tell you how very much I liked it."

CHAPTER X
THE NEED FOR INTUITION

In such a world as this, anything which is wholly sane is entirely uninteresting. But--thank heaven for it!--madness is everywhere, in every corner, at every turning. You will not even find complete sanity in a Unitarian; in fact, some of the maddest people I have ever met have been Unitarians. Yet theirs is an aggravating madness. You can have no sympathy with a man who believes himself sane.

But anything more utterly irresponsible than this sudden, impulsive departure of the Lady of St. Joseph can scarcely be imagined. John did not even know her name and, what is more, did not even realise the fact until she and Ronald had crossed the stretch of grass and reached the Broad Walk. Then he ran after them.

Ronald turned first as he heard the hurrying footsteps. Anything running will arrest the attention of a boy, while a woman hears, just as quickly, but keeps her head rigid. Evidently, Ronald had told her. She turned as well. John suddenly found himself face to face with her. Then the impossible delicacy of the situation and his question came home to him.

How, before Ronald, to whom he had just been introduced as a friend, could he ask her name? Simplicity of mind is proverbial in those who traffic in deep waters; but could the master of the good ship *Albatross* ever be so simple as not to find the suggestion of something peculiar in such a question as this?

And so when he reached her side, he stood there despairingly dumb.

"You wanted to say something?" said she.

He looked helplessly at Ronald. Ronald looked helplessly at him. Then, when he looked at her, he saw the helplessness in her eyes as well.

"What is it you want?" said her eyes--"I can't get rid of him. He's as cunning as he can be."

And his eyes replied--"I want to know your name--I want to know who you are." Which is a foolish thing to say with one's eyes, because no one could possibly understand it. It might mean anything.

Then he launched a question at a venture. If she had any intuition, she could guide it safe to port.

"I just wanted to ask," said John--"if you were any relation to the--the----" At that moment the only name that entered his head was Wrigglesworth, who kept a little eating-house in Fetter Lane--"the--oh--what is their name!--the Merediths of Wrotham?"

He had just been reading "The Amazing Marriage." But where on earth was Wrotham? Well, it must do.

She looked at him in amazement. She had not understood. Who could blame her?

"The Merediths?" she repeated--"But why should you think----"

"Oh, yes--I know,"--he interposed quickly--"It's not the same name--but--they--they have relations of your name--they told me so--cousins or something like that, and I just wondered if--well, it doesn't matter--you're not. Good-bye."

He lifted his hat and departed. For a moment there was a quite unreasonable sense of disappointment in his mind. She was wanting in intuition. She ought to have understood. Of course, in her bewilderment at his question she had looked charming and that made up for a great deal. How intensely charming she had looked! Her forehead when she frowned--the eyes alight with questions. Anyhow, she had understood that what he had really wanted to say could not be said before Ronald and, into her confidence she had taken him--closing the door quite softly behind them. Without question, without understanding, she had done that. Perhaps it made up for everything.

Presently, he heard the hurrying of feet, and turned at once. How wonderfully she ran--like a boy of twelve, with a clean stride and a sure foot.

"I'm so sorry," she said in little breaths. "I didn't understand. The Merediths and the Wrotham put me all out. It's Dealtry--Julie Dealtry--they call me Jill. We live in Prince of Wales' Terrace."

She said the number. "Do they call you Jack? Good-bye--to-morrow." And she was off.

CHAPTER XI
A SIDE-LIGHT UPON APPEARANCES

He watched the last sway of her skirt, the last toss of her head, as she ran down the hill of the Broad Walk, then, repeating mechanically to himself:

Jack and Jill went up the hill
To fetch a pail of water,
Jack fell down and broke his crown
And Jill came tumbling after,

and, wondering what it all meant, wondering if, after all, those nursery rhymes were really charged with subtle meaning, he made his way to Victoria Gate in the Park Railings.

In the high road, he saw a man he knew, a member of his club, top-hatted and befrocked. The silk hat gleamed in the sunlight. It looked just like a silk hat you would draw, catching the light in two brilliant lines from crown to brim. The frock coat was caught with one button at the waist. Immaculate is the word. John hesitated. They were friends, casual friends, but he hesitated. There might be two opinions about the soft felt hat he was wearing. He found it comfortable; but one gets biased in one's opinions about one's hats. Even the fact that the evening before he had driven with this friend in a hansom for which he had paid as the friend had no money on him at the time--even this did not give him courage. He decided to keep to his, the Park side of the Bayswater Road.

But presently the friend saw him, lifted his stick, and shook it amicably in greeting. He even crossed the road. Well, after all, he could scarcely do anything else. John had paid for his hansom only the evening before. He remembered vividly how, on the suggestion that they should drive, his friend had dived his hand into his pocket, shaken his bunch of keys and said, with obvious embarrassment, that he had run rather short of change. It always is change that one runs short of. Capital is never wanting. There is always a balance at the poor man's bank, and the greater his pride the bigger the balance. But at that moment, John had been rich in change--that is to say, he had half a crown.

"Oh--I've got heaps," he had said. It is permissible to talk of heaps when you have enough. And he had paid for the whole journey. It was not to be wondered at then, that his friend came amicably across the road.

John greeted him lightly.

"Going up to town?"

"Yes--are you?"

John nodded. "Are you lunching at the Club?"

"No--I've got to meet some people at the Carlton--How's the time--my watch is being mended."

"I don't know," said John--"my watch is all smashed up. It's just on one I should think."

"As much as that? I must be moving on. Shall we get on a 'bus?"

The very thing. John acquiesced readily. He had nothing; a careful calculation of what he had spent that morning will account for that. But his friend could pay. It was his turn.

They mounted the stairs and took a front seat behind the driver.

"You'll have to pay for me to-day," said John. "My pockets are empty till I get a cheque changed."

The blood mounted to the face of his friend. For a moment he looked as though his beautiful hat were too tight for his head. He felt in his pocket. Then he produced a little stamp case, with gold mounted corners and one penny stamp inside.

"I'm awfully sorry," said he--"I--I've only got a penny stamp." He rose quickly to his feet.

John laughed--laughed loudly.

"What are you going to do?" said he.

"Well--get off," said his friend.

"Sit down," said John--"there's no hurry."

"Have you got twopence, then?"

"No--not a farthing. But we're getting into Town, aren't we? We've got nothing to grumble at."

When the 'bus had travelled another hundred yards or so, John stood up.

"Now, you come downstairs," said he. The friend followed obediently. The conductor was inside punching tickets. John looked in.

"Does this 'bus go to Paddington Station?" he asked inquiringly.

"No--Piccadilly Circus, Haymarket, and Strand."

"What a nuisance," said John--"Come on--we'd better get off."

They descended on to the road, and the friend, immaculate, top-hatted and befrocked, took his arm.

"I see," he said, and he looked back to measure the distance with his eye.

There are more people in London with only a penny in their pockets than you would imagine.

CHAPTER XII
THE CHAPEL OF UNREDEMPTION

The next morning was one of promise. For half an hour before the time appointed for his meeting, John was waiting, seated upon a penny chair, thinking innumerable thoughts, smoking innumerable cigarettes. Sometimes he felt the money that was in his pocket, running his finger nail over the minted edge of the half crowns and florins to distinguish them from the pennies. No woman, whatever franchise she may win, will ever understand the delight of this. You must have a pocket in your trousers and keep your money there--even gold when you possess it--to appreciate the innocent joy of such an occupation as this. Men have really a deal to be grateful for.

That morning, John had money. He even had gold. He had pawned his gold watch-chain, intending, if the opportunity arose, to ask Jill to lunch.

The watch, as you know, was smashed up. That is a technical term in use amongst all gentlemen and sensitive people, having this great advantage that it may be taken literally or not, at will. No one who uses the term has ever been so much in want of shame as to define it.

You may wonder why it is that the watch and not the chain should get smashed up first. It is the watch that tells the time. But then, it is the chain that tells you have got the watch that tells the time, and in this life one has always to be considering that there would be no maiden all forlorn if it were not for the house that Jack built. The chain will always be the last to go, so long as those three brass balls continue to hang over that suspicious-looking shop in the dingy side street.

John's watch had been smashed up for some weeks; but little boys and little girls in the street still flattered him by asking to be told the time.

With one eye searching for a distant clock while your hand pulls out the latch key which depends upon the chain, giving it the weight of a reason to stay in the pocket, you can easily deceive the eyes of these unsuspecting little people in the street. If you discover the distant clock, all well and good. If not, then a hundred devices are left open to you. You can guess--you can tell it by the sun, but, and if you are conscientious, you can apologise and say your watch has stopped. And last of all, if it is a nice little person with eyes in which a laugh is always a-tip-toe, you may dangle the key in front of their face, and with their merriment experience the clean pleasure of honesty.

A quality about John that was interesting, was his ability to anticipate possibilities. Perhaps a man's mind runs instinctively to the future, and it is the woman who lives in the past.

When Mrs. Rowse awakened him in the morning, he sat up in bed with the glowing consciousness that something was to happen that day. Something had been arranged; some appointment was to be kept; some new interest had entered his life which was to take definite shape that very day.

He asked Mrs. Rowse the time--not as one who really wishes to know it, but as it were a duty, which must sooner or later be accomplished. Directly she said a quarter to nine, he remembered. Jill! The Lady of St. Joseph! That morning she was going to tell him how much she liked his story.

He sat up at once in bed.

"Mrs. Rowse! I shall want my coffee in half an hour. Less! Twenty minutes!"

In twenty minutes, he was dressed. Allowance must be made if he chose a sock that matched a tie or spent a moment of thought upon the selection of a shirt to go with them. Vanity, it is, only to do these things for your own approval; but when all consciously, you stand upon the very threshold of romance, it may be excused you if you consider yourself in the reflexion of the door. It is the man who, wandering aimlessly through the streets in life, looks in at every mirror that he passes, who is abominable. That is the vanity of which the prophet spoke. The prophet, himself, would have been the first to set straight the tie, or rearrange the 'kerchief of the lover who goes to meet his mistress.

Even John smiled at himself. The socks matched the tie so absolutely; it was ludicrous how well they matched. There was no rough, blue serge suit that day. Out of the depths of the wardrobe came a coat well brushed and kept. Then he went in to breakfast.

During the meal, Mrs. Rowse lingered about in the sitting-room, dusting things that might easily have escaped notice. John, reading his paper, at last became aware of it with a rush of blood to his cheeks. She had paid the day before for the washing--three and elevenpence.

If you go to a laundry in the environment of Fetter Lane, it is like putting your clothes in pawn. You can't get them back again until the bill is paid, and there are times when that is inconvenient.

That was why Mrs. Rowse was lingering. She had paid for the washing. Whenever money was due to her, she lingered. It is a subtle method of reproach, a gentle process of reminder which at first scarcely explains itself.

On the first occasion when she had adopted it, John had thought she was losing her memory, that her wits were gathering. Out of the corner of his eye, he had nervously watched her going aimlessly about the room, dusting the same object perhaps six separate times. When a woman is paid seven shillings a week for keeping one's rooms tidy, such industry as this might well be a sign of madness.

At length, unable to bear it any longer, John had said that he thought she had done enough. Despairingly then, she had folded up the duster, put it away, taken an unconscionable time in the pinning on of that black, shabby hat, and finally, but only when at the door itself, she had said:

"Do you think you could spare my wages to-day, sir?"

Now she was lingering again. But he had come to know the signs and meanings of the process. This time, John knew it was the washing. He watched her covertly from behind his paper, hoping against hope that she might tire; for he had not got three and elevenpence, nor three halfpence in the world. But a master in the art of lingering does not know what it means to tire. Just when he thought she must have finished, when she had done all the glass on the mantel-piece for the second time, she went out of the room to the cupboard on the landing where John kept his two-hundredweight of coal and returned with all the rags and pots of paste necessary for the cleaning of the brass.

Here he gave in; the siege was over. Under cover of the newspaper, he detached the latch key from his watch-chain, slipped it into his pocket and rose, concealing the chain within his hand.

"I'm just going out," he said--"for a few moments. Can you wait till I get back?"

She looked as though she could not, as if it were rather encroaching upon the limit of her time to ask her to stay longer, but----

"I expect I can find one or two little things to do for a few moments," she said.

John left her doing them. They mainly consisted of putting the brass polish and the rags back again in the cupboard from which she had taken them.

It is here that you will see this quality interesting in John, this ability to anticipate possibilities. It was not really the victory of Mrs. Rowse that had impelled him to the sacrifice of his watch-chain. It is not consistent with human nature for any man to pawn an article of value--far less one which implies the possession of another--in order to pay his washing bill. Washing, like the income tax, is one of those indemnities in life which appear to have no justice in their existence. It would always seem that your integrity were still preserved, that you were still a man of honour if you could avoid paying them.

I know a man, who has eluded the income tax authorities for seven years, and he is held in the highest esteem as a man of acumen, ability, and the soul of honour. I admit that this opinion is only held of him by those who are endeavouring to do the same as he. A man, for instance, who belongs to the same club and pays his income tax to the last shilling, thinks him to be a hopelessly immoral citizen and would believe him capable of anything. But this is not fair. It would be far more just to say that the man who pays his income tax to the uttermost farthing is capable of nothing--invertebrate.

It was not, then, alone to pay his washing bill that John decided to part with the gold watch-chain. He had, in a moment of inspiration, conjured before him the possibility of asking Jill to lunch, and these two motives, uniting from opposite quarters of the compass of suggestion to one and the same end, he sacrificed the last pretentions he might have claimed to the opulence conveyed by a gold watch-chain and repaired to Payne and Welcome's.

With a bold and unconscious step, he strode into the little side entrance, which is a feature of all these jeweller's shops displaying the mystical sign of the three brass balls. Without the slightest sense of shame, he pushed open one of the small doors that give admittance to the little boxes--those little boxes where the confession of one's poverty is made. And to no sympathetic ear of a gentle priest are those terrible confessions to be whispered--the most terrible confession you can make in this world. The man to whom you tell your story of shame is greedy and willing to listen, eager and inexorable to make your penance as heavy as he may. A bailiff is, perhaps, more stony of heart than a pawnbroker; yet both are brothers in trade. The dearest things in the life of anyone are their possessions, and both these tradesmen deal in their heartless confiscation. The woman out at elbow, hollow-eyed, who comes to pawn her wedding ring, the man--shabby--genteel--wearing, until the nap is gone and the sleeves are frayed, the garment of his self-respect, who comes to put away his best and Sunday coat; they are all one to the pawnbroker. He beats them down to the last farthing, well knowing that, having once determined to part with their possessions, they will not willingly go away again without that for which they came. He has them utterly at his mercy. They are all one to him. The story in their faces is nothing to his eyes. He signs a hundred death warrants in the tickets that he writes every day--death warrants to possessions well-nigh as dear as life; but it means nothing to him.

The awful thought about it all, is to consider the ease with which one loses the sense of shame which, upon a first transaction of the kind, is a hot wind blowing on the face, burning the cheeks to scarlet.

On the first occasion that John was driven to such dealing, he passed that guilty side entrance many times before he finally summoned courage to enter. Every time that he essayed the fatal step, the street became full of people whom he knew. There was that editor who was considering his last short story! He turned swiftly, his heel a sudden pivot, and scrutinised the objects in the jeweller's window, then harried away up the street, as though he were ashamed of wasting his time. A glance over the shoulder, satisfied him that the editor was out of sight and back he slowly came. This time he had got within a foot of the door--a foot of it. One step more and he would have been in the sheltering seclusion of that narrow little passage! There was the girl who sold him stamps in the post-office--the girl who smiled at him and said she had read a beautiful story of his in one of the magazines! He had looked up quickly as though he had mistaken the number on the door, then marched into the next shop on the left, as if that were the one he had been looking for. When he had got in, he realised that it was a butcher's.

The butcher, in a blithe voice, had said:

"And what this morning, sir?"

"I want--can you tell me the time?" said John.

In about half an hour there came a moment when the street was empty. John had seized it and vanished up the little passage. But the ordeal was not over then. He had had to face the high priest of poverty--to tell to him the unforgivable, the mortal crime of penury. And there had been someone in the next confessional--someone hardened in sin--who could hear every single word that he said, and even so far over-stepped the bounds of decency as to look round the corner of their partition.

"How much will you give me for this?" said John, laying his watch upon the counter. It was the watch his mother had given him, the watch for which she had lovingly stinted herself of ten pounds in order to mark, with degree, his twenty-first birthday.

The high priest had picked it up superciliously.

"D'you want to sell it?"

"No--oh, no! Only--pawn it."

"Well, how much d'you want?"

"I'd rather you said," replied John meekly.

The high priest shrugged his shoulders. It was a wasting of his time, he said, to go on with nonsense like that.

"How much do you want?" he repeated.

"Five pounds," said John, and suddenly, without knowing how, found the watch back again in his possession. The high priest had turned to the hardened sinner in the next confessional, and he was left there looking at it blankly in the palm of his open hand. He scarcely knew how he had come by it again. In the midst of the other transaction, the pawnbroker presently addressed him over his shoulder--loudly, so that all in the shop could hear:

"I'll give you two pounds," he had said--"And that's about as much as I could sell it for myself."

Two pounds! It was an insult to that dear, little, old, white-haired lady who had scraped and saved to buy him the best she knew.

"It cost ten pounds!" John said boldly.

"Ten pounds!" The laugh he gave was like the breaking of glass. "The person who gave ten pounds for that must have wanted to get rid of money in a hurry."

Wanted to get rid of money in a hurry! If he could have seen the number of dainty shawls the thin white fingers had knitted and the trembling hands had sold in order to amass the fortune of that ten pounds, he would not have talked of hurry.

"I'll give you two pounds five," he had added. "Not a farthing more and if you take it away somewhere else and then bring it back here again, I'll only give you two pounds, what I said at first."

When the blood is mounting to your forehead, when it seems you are crushed about by those watching your discomfort till the warmth of their pressing, phantom bodies brings the perspiration out in beads upon your face, you will take anything to get away.

The pawnbroker had made out the ticket as John mumbled his name and address.

"Got a penny--a penny for the ticket?" said the man.

To be compelled to make this confession--the most unabsolvable of all--that he had nothing in his pocket, was the crisis to his suffering. The high priest sniffed, smiled and counted out two pounds four and elevenpence. Then John had turned and fled.

Out in the street again, he had breathed once more. The air was purer there. The passers-by, hearing the money jingle in his pocket, held him in higher esteem than did those devotees in the chapel of unredemption. He could even stop and look in the windows of the jeweller's shop--that open, smiling face of a shop window which, beneath its smug and shiny respectability, concealed all the secret, sordid crimes of poverty--the polished pledges unredeemed, that lay deceptively upon the glass shelves as though they had come just new from the maker's hands.

It was then, gazing in the window, on that memorable day when he had made his first confession, that John had seen the little brass man. He stood there on a glass shelf along with dozens of other unredeemed trinkets, his low-crowned top-hat, his long-tailed, slim-waisted, Georgian coat and many-buttoned vest, giving him an air of distinction which none of the other objects around him possessed. His attitude, his pose, was that of a *Chevalier d'honneur*--a chivalrous, courteous, proud old gentleman. The one hand resting on the hip, was full of dignity. The other stretched out as though to reach something, John came later, on acquaintance, to learn the fuller significance of that. But though all the features of his face were worn away by hands that had held him, gripping him as they pressed him down, a seal upon the molten wax, it had no power to lessen his undeniable dignity. For all his shapelessness of eyes and nose and mouth, there was not an inch thereby detracted from his stature. From the first moment that he had seen him, the little brass man had taken his stand in John's mind as the figure of all nobility, all honour, and all cleanliness and generosity of heart.

To see that little figure in brass was to covet him. John walked back without hesitation into the shop; but this time it was through the jeweller's entrance--this time it was with the confidence of one who comes to buy, not to sell, with the self-righteousness of the virtue of two pounds four and eleven-pence, not with the shame of the sin of poverty.

Ah, they treat you differently on this side of the counter. If you were ordering a High Mass to be sung, the priest of poverty could treat you with no greater deference. They may have thought he was mad--most probably they did. It is not characteristic of the man who comes without a penny to pay for the ticket as he pawns his watch, to immediately purchase, haphazard, a little trinket that is of no use to anyone. The high priest of poverty, himself, will tell you that the sin must weigh heavy with need upon the mind before the tongue can bring itself to confess.

They had looked at him in no little surprise as he re-entered; but when he had asked to be shown the little brass man, they cast glances from one to another, as people do when they think they are in the presence of a wandering mind.

"How much do you want for it?" John had asked.

"Seven and six. It's very good--an old seal, you know, quite an antique."

John considered the one pound fifteen which he owed out of that two pounds four and elevenpence.

"I'm afraid that's too much," said he.

"Ah--it's worth it. Why, that's over a hundred years old--quite unique."

"I'm afraid it's too much," John repeated.

"Well--look here--I'll tell you what we'll do. You can have it for seven shillings, and we'll give you six on it any day you like to bring it back."

They could have offered no greater proof than that of the value in which they held it. If a pawnbroker will buy back an article at almost the same price that he sells it, he must indeed be letting you have it cheap. This offering to take back the little brass man at only a shilling less than he was asking for it, was the highest expression of honesty with which he could defend his demands.

John accepted the conditions--paid out his seven shillings and bore the little *Chevalier d'honneur* in brass away.

It was three months later, he had only had breakfast for two days--breakfast, which consisted of toast made from a loaf that was ten days old, bloater paste which keeps for ever, and coffee which can--if you know where to get it--be obtained on credit. It was winter-time and the cold had made him hungry. Coals had run out. The last few scrapings of dust had been gathered out of that cupboard on the landing. Then depression set in. Depression is a heartless jade. She always pays you a visit when both stomach and pocket are empty. Putting his face in his hands, John had leant on the mantel-piece. There was nothing to pawn just then. Everything had gone! Suddenly, he became aware that he was gazing at the little brass man, and that the little brass man had got one hand aristocratically upon his hip, whilst the other was holding out something as though secretly to bestow it as a gift. John looked, and looked again. Then he saw what it was. The little brass man was offering him six shillings and a spasm of hunger creaking through him--he had taken it.

CHAPTER XIII
THE INVENTORY

All this had happened more than a year ago, and the sense of shame, accompanying that first confession, had been worn to the dull surface, incapable of reflecting the finer feelings of the mind. Under the very nose of that editor who was considering his last short story, John would have stepped boldly into the suspicious-looking little passage; returning the smile of the girl who sold him stamps in the post-office, he would have entered shamelessly the chapel of unredemption. Such is the reward of the perpetual sin of poverty. It brings with it the soothing narcotic of callousness, of indifference--and that perhaps is the saddest sin of all.

The watch-chain went that morning with the ease of a transaction constantly performed. There was no need to haggle over the price this time. The same price had been paid many times before. It came last but one on the list of things to be pawned. Last of all was the little brass man--the last to be pledged, the first to be redeemed. There is always an order in these things and it never varies. When pledging, you go from top to bottom of the list; when redeeming, it is just the reverse. And the order itself depends entirely upon that degree of sentiment with which each object is regarded.

The following was the list, in its correct order, of those things which from time to time left the world of John's possession, and were hidden in the seclusion of pledged retreat:--

FUR	COAT.
CUFF	LINKS.
CIGARETTE	CASE.
TIE	PIN.
MATCH	BOX.
WATCH.	
CHAIN.	
LITTLE BRASS MAN.	

Reverse the order of this and you arrive at the sequence in which they returned. And here follows a detailed account of the history of each object--detailed, where details are possible and of interest.

Fur Coat. This pretentious-looking article was bought by John as a bargain. One day, when paying his rent to the landlord--a man who smelted and refined the gold that has an acquaintance with false teeth--he was asked if he would like to buy something very cheap. Well--you know what a temptation that is. So great a temptation is it, that you ask first "How much?" and only when you have heard the price, do you inquire the nature of the article. Four pounds ten, he was told. Then what was it? A fur-lined overcoat with astrachan collar and cuffs! There must be a presumption on the part of the seller that you know nothing of fur coats, or he will not talk to you like this. Certainly it was cheap, but even then, it would not have been bought had John not overheard the former possessor offering to buy it back at four pounds five. Such a circumstance as this doubles the temptation. So seldom is it that one comes across a bargain when one has any money in one's pocket, that it is impossible, when one does, to let it go to another man. John bought it. It would be a useful thing to visit editors in when he had no money.

But you would scarcely credit the treachery of a fur-lined coat with astrachan collar and cuffs. John had no idea of it. It played fiendish tricks upon him. Just as he determined to mount upon a 'bus, it whispered in his ear--"You can't do this--you really can't. If you want to drive, you'd better get a hansom. If not, then you'd better walk."

It was of no avail that he complained of not being able to afford a hansom and of being in too great a hurry to walk. That heavy astrachan collar whispered again:

"You can't ride on a 'bus anyway--look at that man laughing at you already----"

And with a fiendish joy, it gave him sudden and magical insight into the jeering minds of all those people in the 'bus. He relinquished the 'bus then. He called a hansom; he was in a hurry and he drove away, while the astrachan collar preens itself with pride and delight as it looks in the little oblong mirror.

And this is not the only treachery which the fur coat played upon him. As he descended from the cab, a man rushed out of nowhere to protect that coat from the wheels, and overcome with pleasure, the fur coat whispered in his ear once more--"Give him twopence--you can't ignore him."

"I could have kept my coat off the wheel quite easily myself," John replied--"He was really only in the way."

"Never mind," exclaimed the astrachan collar--"If you're going to be seen about with me, you'll have to give him twopence."

Reluctantly John took the twopence out.

And then, all the while that he was fumbling in his pocket for the shilling which should have been more than his legal fare, seeing the distance he had come, only that it cannot be less, the astrachan collar was still at him.

"Can't you hear," it says suggestively--"can't you hear what the cabman is going to say when you only give him a shilling!"

Then it imitated his voice, just in the very way John knew he would say it, and he felt the blood tingling to the roots of his hair. Of course, he gave him one and six, for by this time he was the slave of that fur-lined coat. It dominated his life. It ran up bills in his name and he had to pay them. For myself, I would sooner live with an extravagant wife than with a fur-lined coat.

And so was it with John. That bargain he had purchased with the astrachan collar and cuffs treated him shamefully. It was insatiable in its demands, and all under false pretences; for there came one terrible day when John, who knew nothing about these things, learnt that it was only imitation astrachan. Then he asserted himself. He refused to take it out, and one freezing day in the month of February pawned it for two pounds five. Some three months later, on a blazing day in May, he received a notice from the pawnbroker, who said that he must redeem it immediately, for he could not hold himself responsible for the fur. Now, even an extravagant wife would have more consideration for you, more idea of the true fitness of things than that. Eventually that fur coat was pawned in order to save a lady from the last, the most extreme sentence that the law can pass upon the sin of poverty. There comes a time when the sin of poverty can be dealt no longer with by the high priest in the chapel of unredemption. Then it comes into the hands of the law. To save her from this, was a debt of honour and perhaps the most generous action that that fur coat ever did in its life, was to pay that debt: for the three months went by, and on one of the coldest days in winter, it passed silently and unwept into the possession of the high priest.

Cuff Links. No history is attached to these. They realised ten shillings many times, till the ticket was lost, and then, since, under these circumstances, an affidavit must be made, and cuff links not being worth the swearing about, they were lost sight of.

The Watch. For this is the next article on the inventory, of which any substance can be written, and its history is practically known already. John's mother had given it to him. It represented the many times those two bright eyes were tired with counting the stitches of the white lace shawls. It represented the thousands of times that those slender, sensitive fingers had rested in weariness from their ceaseless passing to and fro. It represented almost the last lace-work she had done, before those fingers had at length been held motionless in the cold grip of paralysis. But, above all, it stood for the love of that gentle heart that beat with so much pride and so much pleasure, to see the little boy, whose head her breast had fondled, come to the stern and mighty age of twenty-one. And two pounds five was the value they put upon it all.

The Little Brass Man,--the *Chevalier d'honneur*. His story has already been told--his life, so far as it concerns this history. But of what he had lived through in the hundred years that had gone before--nobody knows. One can only assume, without fear of inaccuracy, that it was the life of a gentleman.

CHAPTER XIV
THE WAY TO FIND OUT

These were the thoughts passing and re-passing idly through John's mind as he sat, waiting, upon the stiff little iron chair in Kensington Gardens, and felt the minted edge of the half-crowns and the florins that lay so comfortably at the bottom of his pocket.

And then came Jill. She came alone.

He saw her in the distance, coming up that sudden rise of the Broad Walk down which hoops roll so splendidly--become so realistically restive, and prance and rear beneath the blow of the stick in the circus-master's hand. And--she was walking alone.

Then, in a moment, the Gardens became empty. John was not conscious of their becoming so. They were--just empty. Down a long road, tapering to the infinite point of distance, on which her figure moved alone, she might have been coming--slowly, gradually, to their ultimate meeting.

He felt no wonder, realised no surprise at their sudden solitude. When in the midst of Romance, you are not conscious of the miracles it performs. You do not marvel at the wonders of its magic carpets which, in the whisk of a lamb's tail, transport you thousands of miles away; you are not amazed at the wizardry of its coats of invisibility which can hide you two from the whole world, or hide the whole world from you. All these you take for granted; for Romance, when it does come to you, comes, just plainly and without ceremony, in the everyday garments of life and you never know the magician you have been entertaining until he is gone.

Even John himself, whose business in life it was to see the romance in the life of others, could not recognise it now in his own. There were women he had met, there were women he had loved; but this was romance and he never knew it.

With pulses that beat warmly in a strange, quick way, he rose from his chair, thinking to go and meet her. But she might resent that. She might have changed her mind. She might not be coming to meet him at all. Perhaps, as she lay awake that morning--it was a presumption to think she had lain awake at all--perhaps she had altered her opinion about the propriety of an introduction afforded by St. Joseph. It were better, he thought, to see her hand held out, before he took it.

So he sat back again in his chair and watched her as she stepped over the railings--those little railings scarcely a foot high, over which, if you know what it is to be six, you know the grand delight of leaping; you know the thrill of pleasure when you look back, surveying the height you have cleared.

She was coming in his direction. Her skirt was brushing the short grass stems. Her head was down. She raised it and--she had seen him!

Those were the most poignant, the most conscious moments of all when, after their eyes had met, there were still some forty yards or so to be covered before they met. She smiled and looked up at the elm trees; he smiled and looked down at the grass. They could not call out to each other, saying--"How-do-you-do." Inexorably, without pity, Circumstance decreed that they must cross those forty yards of silence before they could speak. She felt the blood rising in a tide to her cheeks. He became conscious that he had hands and feet; that his head was set upon his shoulders and could not, without the accompaniment of his body, face round the other way. The correct term for these excruciating tortures of the mind--so I am assured--is platt. When there is such a distance between yourself and the person whom you are approaching to meet, you are known, if you have any sensitiveness at all, to have a platt.

Now, if ever people had a platt, it was these two. That distance was measured in their mind, yard by yard.

At last he held her hand.

"I was," she began at once, "going to write. But I didn't know your address."

"You were going to write----?"

He pulled forward a chair for her, near to his.

"Yes--I was going to write and tell you--I'm terribly sorry, but I can't come this morning----" and she sat down.

A look of deepest disappointment was so plainly written in his face as he seated himself beside her. He made no effort to render it illegible to those eyes of hers.

"Why not?" said he, despondently. "Why can't you come?"

"Oh--you wouldn't understand if I told you."

This was the moment for the ferrule of an umbrella, or the point of an elegant shoe. But she had not brought the umbrella, and her shoes, well--she was unable to come that morning, so it had scarcely mattered what she had put on. The toe of the shoe did peep out for a moment from under the skirt, but not being approved of for elegance, it withdrew. She was forced to fall back upon words; so she just repeated herself to emphasise them.

"You wouldn't understand if I told you," she said again.

"Is it fair to say that," said John, "before you've found me wanting in understanding?"

"No, but I know you wouldn't understand. Besides--it's about you."

"The reason why you can't come?"

"Yes."

"What is it?"

"I'll tell you another time, perhaps."

Ah, but that would never do. You can't tell people another time. They don't want to hear it then.

"You can tell me now," persisted John.

She shook her head.

"There's only one time to tell things," he said.

"When?"

"Now."

She just began. Her lips parted. She took the breath for speech. The words came into her eyes.

"No--I can't tell you--don't ask me."

But he asked. He kept on asking. Whenever there was a pause, he gently asked again. He began putting the words into her mouth, and when he'd half said it for her, he asked once more.

"Why do you keep on asking?" she said with a smile.

"Because I know," said John.

"You know?"

"Yes."

"Then why----"

"Because I want you to tell me, and because I only know a little. I don't know it all. I don't know why your mother objects to me, except that she doesn't approve of the introduction of St. Joseph. I don't know whether she's said you're not to see me again."

That look of amazement in her eyes was a just and fair reward for his simple hazard. Girls of twenty-one have mothers--more's the pity. He had only guessed it. And a mother who has a daughter of twenty-one has just reached that age when life lies in a groove and she would drag all within it if she could. She is forty-eight, perhaps, and knowing her husband as an obedient child knows its collect on a Sunday, she judges all men by him. Now, all men, fortunately for them, fortunately for everybody, are not husbands. Husbands are a type, a class by themselves; no other man is quite like them. They have irritating ways, and no wife should judge other men by their standards. When she would quarrel, theirs is the patience of Job. When she would be amiable, there is nothing to please them. They are seldom honest; they are scarcely ever truthful. For marriage will often bring out of a man the worst qualities that he has, as the washing-tub will sometimes only intensify the strain upon the linen.

In the back of his mind, John felt the unseen judgment of some woman upon him, and from this very standpoint. When he saw the look of amazement in Jill's eyes, he knew he was right.

"Why do you look so surprised?" he said, smiling.

"Because--well--why did you ask if you knew?"

"Do you think I should ask if I didn't know?"

"Wouldn't you?"

"Oh, no. It's no good asking a woman questions when you don't know, when you haven't the faintest idea of what her answer is going to be. She knows very well just how ignorant you are and, by a subtle process of the mind, she superimposes that ignorance upon herself. And if you go on asking her direct questions, there comes a moment when she really doesn't know either. Then she makes it up or tells you she has forgotten. Isn't that true?"

She watched him all the time he spoke. He might have been talking nonsense. He probably was; but there seemed to be some echo of the truth of it far away in the hidden recesses of her mind. She seemed to remember many times when just such a process had taken place within her. But how had he known that, when she had never realised it before?

"What do you do, then, when you don't know, if you don't ask questions?"

He took a loose cigarette from his pocket and slowly lit it.

"Ah--then you have recourse to that wonderful method of finding out. It's so difficult, so almost impossible, and that's why it's so wonderful. To begin with, you pretend you don't want to know. That must be the first step. All others--and there are hundreds--follow after that; but you must pretend you don't want to know, or she'll never tell you. But I am sure your mother's been saying something to you about me, and I really want to know what it is. How did she come to hear about me?"

He knew it would be easy for her to begin with that. No woman will tell unless it is easy.

"Did you tell her?" he suggested gently, knowing that she did not.

"Oh, no--I didn't. It was Ronald."

"Ah--he said something?"

"Yes--at lunch--something about the papers."

"And you had to explain?"

"Yes."

"Was she vexed?"

"Yes--rather. Well--I suppose it did sound rather funny, you know."

"You told her about St. Joseph?"

"I said where I'd met you, in the Sardinia St. Chapel." She smiled up at him incredulously. "You didn't think I'd tell her that St. Joseph had introduced us, did you?"

"Why not? St. Joseph's a very proper man."

"Yes--on his altar, but not in Kensington."

"Well--what did she say?"

"She asked where you lived."

"Oh----"

It is impossible to make comparison between Fetter Lane and Prince of Wales' Terrace without a face longer than is your wont--especially if it is you who live in Fetter Lane.

"And you told her you didn't know."

"Of course."

She said it so expectantly, so hopefully that he would divulge the terrible secret which meant so much to the continuation of their acquaintance.

"And what did she say to that?"

"She said, of course, that it was impossible for me to know you until you had come properly as a visitor to the house, and that she couldn't ask you until she knew where you lived. And I suppose that's quite right."

"I suppose it is," said John. "At any rate you agree with her?"

"I suppose so."

It meant she didn't. One never does the thing one supposes to be right; there's no satisfaction in it.

"Well--the Martyrs' Club will always find me."

This was John's club; that club, to become a member of which, he had been despoiled of the amount of a whole year's rent. He was still staggering financially under the blow.

"Do you live there?" she asked.

"No--no one lives there. Members go to sleep there, but they never go to bed. There are no beds."

"Then where do you live?"

He turned and looked full in her eyes. If she were to have sympathy, if she were to have confidence and understanding, it must be now.

"I can't tell you where I live," said John.

The clock of St. Mary Abbot's chimed the hour of midday. He watched her face to see if she heard. One--two--three--four--five--six--seven--eight nine--ten--eleven--twelve! She had not heard a single stroke of it, and they had been sitting there for an hour.

CHAPTER XV
WHAT IS HIDDEN BY A CAMISOLE

Add but the flavour of secrecy to the making of Romance; allow that every meeting be clandestine and every letter written sealed, and matters will so thrive apace that, before you can, with the children in the nursery, say Jack Robinson, the fire will be kindled and the flames of it leaping through your every pulse.

When, with tacit consent, Jill asked no further questions as to where John lived, and yet continued clandestinely to meet him, listening to the work he read aloud to her, offering her opinion, giving her approval, she was unconsciously, unwillingly, too, perhaps, had she known, hastening towards the ultimate and the inevitable end.

It must not be supposed that after this second interview in Kensington Gardens, when John had plainly said that he could not tell her where he lived, she had wilfully disobeyed the unyielding commands of her mother not to see him again. The fulfilment of destiny does not ask for disobedience. With the shuttles of circumstance and coincidence to its fingers, Destiny can weave a pattern in defiance of every law but that of Nature.

Jill had said that morning:

"Then we mustn't meet again."

"You mean that?" said John.

"I can't help it," she replied distressfully. "After all, I'm living with my people; I must respect their wishes to a certain degree. If you would only tell me----"

"But I can't," John had interposed. "It's no good. It's much better that I leave you in ignorance. Why won't the Martyrs' Club satisfy you? There are men at the Martyrs' Club who live on Carlton House Terrace. That is a part of their martyrdom. Is it beyond the stretch of your imagination for you to suppose that I might have an abode in--in--Bedford Park or Shepherd's Bush?"

She laughed, and then, as that stiff social figure of her mother rose before her eyes and she recalled to her mind remarks about a dressmaker who happened to live in Shepherd's Bush--"Poor thing--she lives at Shepherd's Bush--Life treats some people in a shameful way--" an expression of charity that went no further, for the dressmaker's work was not considered good enough or cheap enough, and she was given nothing more to do--when she remembered that, the laugh vanished from her eyes.

"Isn't it as good as Shepherd's Bush?" she had asked quite simply.

Well, when, in your more opulent moments, you have thought of such a thing as a better address at Shepherd's Bush, and have a question such as this put to you, you have little desire left to reveal the locality of the abode you do occupy. It takes the pride out of you. It silenced John. He recalled to his mind a remark of Mrs. Meakin's when, having invited him to take a rosy-cheeked apple from that little partition where the rosy-cheeked apples lay, she had thought by this subtle bribe to draw him into conversation about himself.

"Don't you find it very dull livin' 'ere all alone by yourself?" she had asked.

"Wherever you live," said John evasively, "you're by yourself. You're as much alone in a crowd as in an empty church."

She had nodded her head, picked up a large Spanish onion, and peeled off the outer skin to make it look more fresh.

"But I should have thought," she had added pensively--"I should have thought as 'ow you'd have found this such a very low-cality."

And so, perhaps it was--very low. And if Mrs. Meakin had thought so, and Jill herself could talk thus deprecatingly of Shepherd's Bush, where he had hoped to better his address, then it were as well to leave Fetter Lane alone.

"So you have made up your mind," he had said quietly. "You've made up your mind not to see me again?"

"It's not I who have made it up," she answered.

"But you're going to obey?"

"I must."

"You won't be here to-morrow morning, at this hour?"

"No--I can't--I mustn't."

"Not to tell me how you liked my short story?"

"You know I liked it--awfully."

"And you won't come and hear another that's better than that?"

"How can I? You don't understand. If you came and lived at Prince of Wales' Terrace, you'd understand then."

"Then it's no good my coming to-morrow?"

"Not if you want to see me."

"Then good-bye."

John stood up and held out his hand.

If you know the full value of coercion in renunciation; if you realise the full power of persuasion in the saying of good-bye, you have command of that weapon which is the surest and the most subtle in all the armament of Destiny. It is only when they have said good-bye that two people really come together.

"But why must you go now?" Jill had said regretfully.

John smiled.

"Well--first, because you said you couldn't come this morning, and we've been here for an hour and a half; and secondly, because if, as you say, we are to see no more of each other, then hadn't I better go now? I think it's better. Good-bye."

He held out his hand again. She took it reluctantly, and he was gone.

The next morning, Jill had wakened an hour earlier--an hour earlier than was her wont--an hour earlier, with the weight of a sense of loss pressing on her mind. It is that hour in bed before rising that a woman thinks all the truest things in her day; is most honest with herself, and least subtle in the expression of her thoughts. Then she gets up--bathes--does her hair and, by the time a dainty camisole is concealing those garments that prove her to be a true woman--all honesty is gone; she assumes the mystery of her sex.

In that hour earlier before her rising, Jill honestly admitted her disgust with life. Romance is well-nigh everything to a woman--for Romance is the Prelude, full of the most sonorous of chords, breathing with the most wonderful of cadences--a Prelude to the great Duty which she must inevitably perform. And this had been Romance. She had just touched it, just set in motion the unseen fingers that play with such divine inspiration upon the whole gamut of the strings, and now, it had been put away.

Mind you, she knew nothing of the evolution of the Prelude; she knew little of the history of the Duty to perform. It was not the conscious loss of these that brought the disgust of life into the complaining heart of her; for Romance, when first it comes to a woman, is like the peak of a mountain whose head is lifted above the clouds. It has nothing of this earth; means no such mundane phrase as--falling in love. To the girl of twenty-one, Romance is the spirit of things beautiful, and, therefore, the spirit of all things good. And Jill had lost it. They were not to meet again. She was never to hear another of his stories. He was not coming to Kensington Gardens any more.

But suppose he did come! Suppose there were the sense of regret in the heart of him, as it was with her, and suppose he came to see the place where they had sat together! If she could only know that he cared enough to do that! It would make the renunciation more bearable if she could only know that. How could she find out? Send Ronald to the Gardens at about that hour? He would say if he had seen him. But if Ronald went to the Gardens, he would be voyaging on the good ship *Albatross*, far away out at sea, out of sight of land, in the dim distance of make-belief. But if she went herself--just casually--just for a walk--just to see, only to see. And, if he were there, she could easily escape; she could easily creep away unnoticed. Well--not quite unnoticed, perhaps. He might see her in the distance, just before she passed out of sight.

She got up quickly from her bed. She bathed; she did her hair; she dressed; she put on that dainty camisole with its pale blue ribbon twined through intricate meshes and concealed those little garments which proved her to be a true woman--concealed them with the camisole and the mystery of her sex.

At breakfast, she talked of having her hair washed that morning. There was no gloss in it, she said. Ronald cast a glance at it, sniffed and then went on with his hasty mouthfuls of porridge. What fools were girls! As if it mattered! As if anyone noticed whether there were gloss or not! The good ship *Albatross* wanted a new spinnaker, and from whose under-linen that was to be stolen without detection was a far more delicate matter. He had petitioned for white linen shirts for himself for the last six months--white linen shirts are always valuable to a sailor--but he had not got them as yet. This deprivation naturally led to nefarious dealings with the tails of his father's old white shirts. It was impossible to use his own. You cannot have flannel sails to your ship, if she sails on the Round Pond. On the other waters--the Atlantic, for example--it doesn't matter so much. There were one or two things he had begun to fancy he would never be able to get.

Quite simply, quite pensively, he had said one day at dinner:

"I wonder if I shall ever eat the wing of a chicken."

They permitted him to wonder--he and his drumstick. One cannot be surprised, then, that he sniggered when Jill talked about the gloss of her hair.

"Well, don't go to this place in the High Street," said her mother. "They're terribly exorbitant."

"I shall go up to town," said Jill. And, up to town she started.

There are various ways of going up to town. She chose to cross the Broad Walk with the intention of going by Bayswater. She even made a detour of the Round Pond. It was nicer to walk on the grass--more comfortable under foot. It was not even an uncomfortable sensation to feel her heart beating as a lark's wings beat the air when it soars.

Then the rushing of the wings subsided. He was not there. From that mighty altitude to which it had risen, her heart began to descend--slowly, slowly, slowly to earth. He was not there!

But oh! you would never know, until you yourself had played there, the games of hide-and-seek that the big elms afford in Kensington Gardens. On the far side of a huge tree-trunk, she came suddenly upon him, and the slowly fluttering wings of her heart were struck to stillness. There he was, seated upon his chair with a smile upon his lips, in his eyes--spreading and spreading till it soon must be a laugh.

And--"Oh!" said she.

Then it was that the smile became a laugh.

"What are you doing here at this time in the morning?" he asked.

"I--I was just going up to town. I--I wanted to go to Bayswater first."

How much had he guessed? How long had he seen her looking here and there, and all about her?

"What are *you* doing?" She had as much a right to ask him.

"I've been waiting to see you go by," said he.

"But----"

"I knew you were coming."

"How?"

"We've been thinking just exactly the same things ever since I said good-bye yesterday. I woke up early this morning wondering what had happened."

"So did I," she whispered in an awed voice.

"Then--before I'd got my coat on, I came to the conclusion that I had to live somewhere, and that the only thing that mattered was whether I did it honestly--not where I did it. Then, I sort of felt you might come to the Gardens this morning."

She set her lips. Once that camisole is on, every woman has her dignity. It is a thing to play with, much as a child plays with its box of bricks. She makes wonderful patterns with it--noble ladies--imperious dames, who put dignity before humanity as you put the cart before the horse.

"Why should you think I would come to the Gardens?" she asked.

John steadied his eyes.

"Well, I presume you go up to town sometimes," he said.

"Yes--but one can get up to town by Knightsbridge."

"Of--course. I forgot that. But when you might be wanting to go to Bayswater first."

She looked very steadily into his eyes. How long had he seen her before she had seen him?

"Perhaps you're under the impression that I came to see you," she said, and she began walking towards the Bayswater Road.

He followed quietly by her side. This needed careful treatment. She was incensed. He ought not to have thought that, of course.

"I never said so," he replied quietly.

Then they fought--all the way over to the Bayswater side. Each little stroke was like velvet, but beneath it all was the passion of the claw.

"I expect it's as well we're not going to see each other any more," she said one moment and, when he agreed, repented it bitterly the next. He cursed himself for agreeing. But you must agree. Dignity, you know. Dignity before humanity.

And then he called her a hansom--helped her within.

"Are you going back to the Gardens?" she asked from inside, not shutting the doors.

"No--I'm going up to town."

"Well----" She pushed the bricks away. "Can't--can't I drive you up?"

He stepped inside, and the cab rolled off.

"Were you going to have walked?" she asked presently, after a long, long silence.

"No," said John. "I was going to drive--with you."

CHAPTER XVI
EASTER SUNDAY

One Easter Sunday, soon after his first clandestine meeting with Jill, John was seated alone in his room in Fetter Lane. The family of Morrell and the family of Brown--the plumber and the theatre cleaner--had united in a party and gone off to the country--what was the country to them. He had heard them discussing it as they descended the flights of uncarpeted wooden stairs and passed outside his door.

"As long as we get back to the Bull and Bush by five," Mr. Morrell had said emphatically, and Mr. Brown had said, "Make it half-past four." Then Mrs. Morrell had caught up the snatch of a song:

"I've a tickly feelin' in the bottom of me 'eart
For you--for you,"

and Mrs. Brown has echoed it with her uncertain notes. Finally the door into the street had opened--had banged--their voices had faded away into the distance, and John had been left alone listening to the amorous frolics on the stairs of the sandy cat which belonged to Mrs. Morrell, and the tortoise-shell, the property of Mrs. Brown.

Unless it be that you are an ardent churchman, and of that persuasion which calls you to the kirk three times within the twenty-four hours, Easter Sunday, for all its traditions, is a gladless day in London. There is positively nothing to do. Even Mass, if you attend it, is over at a quarter to one, and then the rest of the hours stretch monotonously before you. The oppressive knowledge that the Bank Holiday follows so closely on its heels, overburdens you with the sense of desolation. There will be no cheerful shops open on the morrow, no busy hurrying to and fro. The streets of the great city will be the streets of a city of the dead and, as you contemplate all this, the bells of your neighbourhood peal out in strains that are meant to be cheerful, yet really are inexpressibly doleful and sad. You know very well, when you come to think about it, why they are so importunate and so loud. They are only ringing so persistently, tumbling sounds one upon another, in order to draw people to the fulfilment of a duty that many would shirk if they dared.

The bells of a city church have need to be loud, they have to rise above the greater distractions of life. Listen to the bells of St. Martin's-in-the-Fields. The bell-ringers there know only too well the sounds they have to drown before they can induce a wandering pedestrian within. It was just the same in Fetter Lane. John listened to them clanging and jangling--each bell so intent and eager in its effort to make itself heard.

He thought of the country to which the families upstairs had departed; but in the country it is different. In the country, you would go to church were there no bell at all, and that gentle, sonorous note that does ring across the fields and down the river becomes one of the most soothing sounds in the world. You have only to hear it to see the old lych-gate swinging to and fro as the folk make their way up the gravel path to the church door. You have only to listen to it stealing through the meadows where the browsing cattle are steeping their noses in the dew, to see with the eye of your mind that pale, faint flicker of candle-light that creeps through the stained glass windows out into the heavy-laden air of a summer evening. A church bell is very different in the country. There is an unsophisticated note about it, a sound so far removed from the egotistical hawker crying the virtue of his wares as to make the one incomparable with the other. John envied Mrs. Brown and Mr. Morrell from the bottom of his heart--envied them at least till half-past four.

For an hour, after breakfast was finished, he sat staring into the fire he had lighted, too lonely even to work. That heartless jade, depression, one can not call her company.

Then came Mrs. Rowse to clear away the breakfast things and make his bed. He looked up with a smile as she entered.

"What sort of a day is it outside?" he asked.

"Cold, sir; and looks as if we was going to have rain."

She caught up the breakfast things, the china clattered in her fingers. He turned round a little in his chair and watched her clear away. This is loneliness--to find a sense of companionship in the woman who comes to look after one's rooms.

"Whenever a man is lonely," wrote Lamartine, "God sends him a dog." But that is not always so. Some men are not so fortunate as others. It happens sometimes that a dog is not available and then, God sends a Mrs. Rowse to clear away the breakfast things.

But Mrs. Rowse was in a hurry that morning. There was no money due to her. You would not have found the faintest suspicion of lingering in anything that she did then. Even the topic that interested her most--her daughters--had no power to distract her attention.

She was going to take them out to the country--they were going down to Denham to see her sister, as soon as her work was done--Lizzie, who stuck labels on the jam-jars in Crosse and Blackwell's, and Maud, who packed cigarettes in Lambert and Butler's.

There were those living in Peabody Buildings, who said that Lizzie would have a beautiful voice, if she'd only practise. She could sing, "Love Me and the World Is Mine." She could sing that lovely. And Maud--well, Mrs. Rowse had even got a piano in their little tenement rooms for Maud to learn on, but Maud would never practise neither. True, she could pick up just anything she heard, pick it up quite easy with the right hand, though she could only vamp, foolish-like, with the left.

Yet upon these portentous matters, Mrs. Rowse would say nothing that morning. They were going to catch a mid-day train from Marylebone down to Denham, and she had no time to waste.

"Would you mind me coming with you, Mrs. Rowse?" said John suddenly. As suddenly he regretted it, but only because of its impossibility.

There is some sort of unwritten law which says that when you accompany ladies on a journey by train, you must pay for their tickets, and all women are ladies if they do not swear or spit on the ground. You should take off your hat to everyone of them you know when in the street. It may be that they are charwomen, that they stick labels upon jam-jars in their spare hours, that they pack up little boxes of cigarettes when there is nothing else to do, but in the street, they are women--and all women, with the restrictions here mentioned, are ladies.

Now John could not possibly pay for their tickets. He could ill-afford to pay for his own. It would mean no meal the next day if he did. And here let it be said--lest any should think that his poverty is harped upon--John was always poor, except for five minutes after an excursion to the pawn-shop, and perhaps five days after the receipt of the royalties upon his work. You may be sure at least of this, that John will jingle the money in his pocket and run his finger-nail over the minted edge of the silver when he has any. If he has gold, you will see him take it out under the light of a lamp-post when it is dark, in order to make sure that the sovereign is not a shilling. On all other occasions than these, assume that he is poor,--nay, more than assume, take it for granted.

Accordingly, directly he had made this offer to accompany Mrs. Rowse and her daughters to Denham, he had to withdraw it.

"No," said he, "I wish I could come--but I'm afraid it's impossible. I've got work to do."

Quite soon after that Mrs. Rowse departed.

"Hope you'll enjoy yourselves," said he.

"We always do in the country," replied she as she put on her hat outside the door. And then--"Good-morning, sir,"--and she too had gone; the door into the street had banged again, and the whole house, from floor to roof, was empty but for the sandy cat, the tortoiseshell cat and John.

He sat on there in the stillness. Even the cats grew tired of play and were still. Then came the rain, rain that turned to sleet, that drove against the roofs outside and tried, by hiding in the corners of the chimneys, to look like snow. John thought of the tulips in Kensington Gardens. Spring can come gladsomely to England--it can come bitterly, too. Those poor people in the country! But would the country ever permit such weather as this? Even supposing it did, they would not be lonely as he was. Mr. Morrell had Mrs. Brown to talk to, and Mr. Brown had the company of Mrs. Morrell. There were Lizzie and Maud for Mrs. Rowse. Perhaps going down in the train, they would get a carriage to themselves and Lizzie would sing, "Love Me and the World Is Mine," and Maud would count cigarettes in her mind, and pack them up in her mind, or more probably forget that there ever were such things as cigarettes in the fresh delight of seeing the country with bread and cheese on all the hedges. Those young green buds on the hawthorn hedges are the pedestrian's bread and cheese. But you know that, every bit as well as I.

Well, it seemed that everyone had company but John. He took out of his pocket the last letter his mother had written him from Venice--took it out and spread it before him. If only she were there! If only her bright brown eyes were looking at him, what thousands of things there would be to say! What short stories and beginnings of new books would there not be to read her! And how sympathetically would she not listen. How frequently would she not place those dear paralysed hands of hers in his, as he read, at some new passage that she liked!

"*My darling boy----*"

He could hear that gentle voice of hers--like the sound you may hear in the ring of an old china tea-cup--he could hear it, as she had dictated it to his father to write----

"*This is where I begin counting the days to your visit. I dare not begin sooner--too many figures always bewildered me. It is now just about three months. Your father is much better than he was, and is doing a little work these days."*

And here was added in a quaint little parenthesis of his father's: *"She calls it work, my dear boy, just to please me--but when old men play, they like to hear it called work. You've got to do my work. And she is so quick--she has seen I have been writing more than she has said. I shall persuade her to let this stay in nevertheless."*

Then, uninterrupted for a space the letter continued.

"I'm so pleased that your work is going on so well. I thought your last story was too sad, though. Must stories end unhappily? Yours always seem to. But I think I guess. They won't always end like that. But your father says I am not to worry you on that point; that you can't paint in a tone of gold what you see in a tone of grey, and that what you see now in a tone of grey, you will as likely as not see one day in a tone of gold."

Then, here, another parenthesis.

"You will understand what I mean, my dear boy. I've read the story, and I don't think it ought to end sadly, and you will no doubt say, 'Oh, he's quite old-fashioned; he does not know that a sad ending is an artistic ending.' But that is not because I am old-fashioned. It is simply because I am old. When you are young, you see unhappy endings because you are young enough to bear the pain of them. It is only when you get older that you see otherwise. When you have had your sorrow, which, you know, only as an artist I wish for you, then you will write in another strain. Go on with your unhappy endings. Don't take any notice of us. All your work will be happy one day, and remember, you are not writing for but because of us. By the way, I think you spelt paregoric wrong."

Now again the dictation.

"Well, anyhow, though I know nothing about it, I feel you write as though you loved. You would tell me, would you not, if you did? I am sure it must be the way to write, the way, in fact, to do everything. Your father says the pictures he paints now lack strength and vigour; but I find them just as beautiful; they are so gentle."

Parenthesis.

"One can't always love as one did at twenty-six--T.G. That sounds like reverential gratitude for the fact, but you understand it is only my initials."

"He has written something again, John--and he won't tell me what it is. If he has said he is getting too old to love, don't believe him. He has just leant forward and kissed me on my forehead. I have insisted upon his writing this down. Your story about the girl in the chapel and the last candle amused us very much. It interested me especially. If it had been me, I should have fallen in

love with you then and there for being so considerate. What was she like? Have you ever seen her since? I can't feel that you were meant to meet her for nothing. I have tried to think, too, what she could have been praying to St. Joseph for, but it is beyond me. It is not like a woman to pray for money for herself. Perhaps some of her relations have money troubles. That is all I can imagine, though I have thought over it every day since I got your letter. God bless you, my darling. We are waiting eagerly for the reviews of your new book. When will it be out--the exact date? I want to say a novena for it, so let me know in good time. And if you meet the Lady of St. Joseph--as you call her--again, you must promise to tell me all about it. Your father wants the rest of the sheet of note-paper on which to say something to you--so, God bless you always."

"Don't read the reviews when they come out, John. Send them along to me, and I'll sort out the best ones and send them back to you to read. As far as I can see, there are so many critics who get the personal note into their criticisms, and to read these, whether praising or blaming, won't do you any good; so send them all along to me before you look at them. The first moment you can send me a copy, of course, you will. Your loving father."

Here the letter ended. Long as it was, it might well have been longer. They were good company, those two old people, talking to him through those thin sheets of foreign paper, one breaking in upon the other with all due courtesy, just as they might with a "Finish what you have to say, my dear," in ordinary conversation.

And now they had gone to the country, too--they had left him alone. When he had folded up the letter, it was almost as if he could hear the door bang again for the third time.

He leant back in his chair with an involuntary sigh. What a few people, after all, there were in the world whom he really knew! What a few people who would seek out his company on such a day as this! He stood up and stretched out his arms above his head--it was----

He stopped. A sound had struck to his heart and set it beating, as when the bull's-eye of a target is hit.

The bell had rung! His electric bell! The electric bell which had raised him immeasureably in station above Mrs. Morrell and Mrs. Brown, who had only a knocker common to the whole house--one, in fact, of the landlord's fixtures! It had rung, and his heart was beating to the echoes of it.

In another second, he had opened his door; in another moment, he was flying down the uncarpeted wooden stairs, five at a time. At the door itself, he paused, playing with the sensation of uncertainty. Who could it be? If the honest truth be known, it scarcely mattered. Someone! Someone had come out of nowhere to keep him company. A few personalities rushed to his mind. It might be the man who sometimes illustrated his stories, an untidy individual who had a single phrase that he always introduced into every conversation--it was, "Lend me half-a-crown till to-morrow, will you?" It would be splendid if it were him. They could lunch together on the half-crown. It might be the traveller from the wholesale tailor's--a man whom he had found begging in the street, and told to come round to Number 39 whenever he was at his wit's end for a meal. That would be better still; he was a man full of experiences, full of stories from the various sleeping-houses where he spent his nights.

Supposing it were Jill! A foolish, a hopeless thought to enter the mind. She did not know where he lived. She might, though, by some freak of

CHAPTER XVII
THE FLY IN THE AMBER

The sleet had driven honestly into snow by the time John had finished his lunch and, there being but two old original members in the Martyrs' Club, who were congratulating each other upon having put on their fur coats, stayed in town and not gone to the country, he left as soon as his meal was over.

The hall-porter stood reluctantly to his feet as he passed out,-- so reluctantly that John felt as though he should apologise for the etiquette of the club. In the street, he turned up the collar of his coat and set off with determination, intended to show the hall-porter that he had a definite destination and but little time in which to reach it.

Round the corner and out of sight, he began counting to himself the people he might go and see. Each name, as he reviewed it in his mind, presented some difficulty either of approval or of place. At last, he found himself wandering in the direction of Holborn. In a side street of that neighbourhood lived his little typewriter, who had promised to finish two short stories over Easter. She would be as glad of company as he. She would willingly cease from pounding the symphony of the one monotonous note on those lifeless keys. They would talk together of wonderful works yet to be typed. He would strum on her hired piano. The minutes would slip by and she would get tea, would boil the kettle on that miniature gas-stove, situated in her bedroom, where he had often imagined her saying her prayers in the morning while a piece of bacon was frying in the pan by her side--prayers, the Amen of which would be hastened and emphasised by the boiling over of the milk. Those are the prayers that reach Heaven. They are so human. And a burnt sacrifice of burnt milk accompanying them, they are consistent with all the ritual of the Old Testament.

To the little typewriter's, then, he decided to go. It did not matter so very much if his stories were not finished over Easter. They could wait.

He rang the bell, wondering if her heart was leaping as his had done but an hour or so before. His ears were alert for the scurrying of feet on her uncarpeted, wooden stairs. He bent his head sideways to the door. There was no sound. He rang again. Then he heard the creaking of the stairs. She was coming--oh, but so slowly! Annoyed, perhaps, by the disturbance, just as she was getting into work.

The door was opened. His heart dropped. He saw an old woman with red-rimmed eyes which peered at him suspiciously from the half-opened space.

"Is Miss Gerrard in?" he asked.

"Gone to the country--won't be back till Tuesday," was the reply.

Gone to the country! And his work would never be finished over Easter! Oh, it was not quite fair!

"Any message?" said the old housekeeper.

"No," said John; "nothing," and he walked away.

Circumstance was conspiring that he should work--circumstance was driving him back to Fetter Lane. Yet the loneliness of it all was intolerable. It was, moreover, a loneliness that he could not explain. There had been other Easter Sundays; there had been other days of snow and sleet and rain, but he had never felt this description of loneliness before. It was not depression. Depression sat there, certainly, as it were upon the doorstep, ready to enter at the faintest sound of invitation. But as yet, she was on the doorstep only, and this--this leaden weight at the heart, this chain upon all the energies--was loneliness that he was entertaining, a condition of loneliness that he had never known before.

Why had he gone to see the little typewriter? Why had he not chosen the man who illustrated his stories, or many of the other men whom he knew would be in town that day and any day--men who never went into the country from one year's end to the other?

It had been the company of a woman he had wanted. Why was that? Why that, suddenly, rather than the company he knew he could find? What was there in the companionship of a woman that he had so unexpectedly discovered the need of it? Why had he envied Mr. Brown who had Mrs. Morrell to talk to, or Mr. Morrell who could unburden himself to Mrs. Brown? Why had he been glad when Mrs. Rowse came and unutterably lonely when she left? Why had he suggested going to the country with her, pleased at the thought that Lizzie would sing, "Love Me and the World Is Mine," and that Maud would be counting and packing cigarettes in her mind?

The questions poured into his thoughts, rushing by, not waiting for an answer, until they all culminated in one overwhelming realisation. It was Jill.

Morning after morning, for a whole week, they had met in secret, not in Kensington Gardens alone, but in the most extraordinary of places--once even at Wrigglesworth's, the obscure eating-house in Fetter Lane, she little knowing how near they were to where he lived. He had read her his stories; he had given her copies of the two books that bore his name upon their covers. They had discussed them together. She had said she was sure he was going to be a great man, and that is always so consoling, because its utter impossibility prevents you from questioning it for a moment.

Then it was Jill. And all the disappointment, all the loneliness of this Easter Sunday had been leading up to this.

Common sense--except in that mad moment when he had hoped the bell had been rung by her--had debarred him from thinking of seeking her out. But away in the deep corners of his mind, it was her company he was looking for--her company he had sought to find, first in Mrs. Rowse and then in the little typewriter.

Shutting the door of his room, he went across to the chair by the fire. What did it mean? What did it mean? Here and there he had fallen in love; but this was not the same sort of thing. This was not falling in love. Falling in love was quick, sudden, a flash that burnt up all desire to work, flared out in a moment, obliterating everything else. But this was slow, stealthy, a growing thing that asked, not for sudden satisfaction, but for wonderful, untellable things.

All the attributes common to love, as he had understood it, had no place in this sensation. As he had thought of it, love found its expression in the gratification of the need with which it had begun, or it ended, like his stories--unhappily. Then this could not be love. There was no ending of gratification and no ending of unhappiness to this. It was unending. Was that what his mother had meant he would learn?

Then, as he sat before the fire, wondering what new thing he had found, the bell rang again. It found no echo on this occasion. He slowly turned his head. They were not going to deceive him a second time. He rose quietly from his chair, crossed to the window, silently raised it and, as silently, looked out. There, below him, he saw a woman's hat--a hat with fur in it, cunningly twined through grey velvet,--a hat that he knew, a hat that he had often seen before.

He closed the window quietly and slowly made his way downstairs. Before he reached the end of the passage, the bell rang again. Then he opened the door.

It was the lady on whose behalf the fur coat had discharged the debt of honour.

She stepped right in with a little laugh of pleasure at finding him there; turned and waited while he closed the door behind them, then linked her arm in his as they mounted the stairs.

"I came," said she, "on chance. Aren't you glad to see me?"

There was just that fraction's pause before he replied--that pause into which a woman's mind leaps for answer. And how accurately she makes that leap, how surely she reaches the mental ground upon which you take your place, you will never be able truly to anticipate.

"Yes," said John, "I'm very glad."

"Then what is it?" she said quickly. "Are you writing?"

"No, I'm not. I've tried to, but I can't."

"Then are you expecting someone?"

He looked up at her, smiled, opened the door of his room, and bid her pass through.

"And is all this," said he, "because I paused a moment when you asked me if I was glad to see you?"

She seated herself easily in the chair to which she was accustomed. She began drawing the pins out of her hat, as a woman does when she feels at home. When the hat was free of her heaps of brown-red hair, she threw it carelessly upon the table, shook her head and lifted the hair from her forehead with her fingers. And John stood by with a smile, thinking how the faintest shadow of a word of question would make that hat fly back on to the head of brown-red hair, the hat-pins pierce the crown with hasty pride, and the little purse that lay upon the table alongside of them be clutched in an eager, scornful hand, as she would rise, full of dignity, to depart.

He let the smile fade away, and repeated his question.

"Yes," she said. "I thought when you didn't answer at once that you weren't very keen to see me."

"And if I said I wasn't very keen, would you go at once?"

Her eyebrows lifted high. She made a movement in her chair. One hand was already beginning to stretch out for the grey velvet hat.

"Like a shot!" she answered.

He nodded his head.

"That's what I thought," said John.

She rose quickly to her feet.

"If you want me to go, why don't you say so?"

He put his hands on her shoulders and seated her gently back again in the chair.

"But I don't want you to go," he replied. "I've got a lot of things I want to say to you."

"If you're going to talk evolution----" she began.

He laughed.

"It's something very like it," said he.

She gave a sigh of resignation, took out a packet of cigarettes, extracted one, lit it and inhaled the first breath deep--deep into her lungs.

"Well, go on," she said.

"Have you got plenty of cigarettes?"

"Yes, plenty to-day."

"Hadn't you yesterday?"

"No, Mother and I raked up all the cigarette ends out of the fireplaces, and I just had a penny for a packet of cigarette papers." She laughed.

This is the honesty of poverty. She would take no money from any man. For just as the virtue of wealth will bring out the evil of avarice, so will the evil of poverty bring out the virtue of self-respect. In this world, there is as much good that comes out of evil as ever stands by itself alone. This, in fact, is the need of evil, that out of it may lift the good.

"Well, what have you got to say?" she continued. "Get it over as quick as you can. I shan't understand half of it."

"You'll understand it all," said John. "You may not admit it. You don't admit your own honesty--you probably won't admit mine."

She screwed up her eyes at him. He said the most incomprehensible things. Of course, he was a crank. She knew that--took it for granted--but what did he mean by her honesty?

"I don't steal," she said. "But I owe fifteen pounds to my dressmaker, and thirteen to Derry & Toms, and six somewhere else, and I don't suppose they'll ever get paid. Do you call that honest?"

"I don't mean that sort of honesty. That's the sort of honesty that a dishonest man shields behind. You'd pay them if I gave you the money to pay them, or if anybody else gave you the money, or if you made the money. You meant to pay them, you probably thought you could pay them when you ordered the things."

She looked up at him and laughed.

"You poor old dear! I don't suppose you've got twopence in your pocket. You couldn't give it to me."

"I've got one and nine," said John. "But the point is, if I could give it you, you wouldn't take it. That's the honesty I'm talking about. From the standard at which you rate life, that's honesty, and you never depart from it. And, in a way, my standard has been much about the same--till now."

"Till now?" She echoed it in a little note of apprehension.

"Yes--till now. I thought these things were honest--now I've changed my standard, and I find them different, too."

"What do you mean?"

Her eyes looked far into his, and he stood there looking far back into hers.

"You don't love me, do you?" he said presently.

A pause preceded her answer.

"No," she said.

"And I've never told you I loved you?"

"No--never."

"And yet, does it strike you that there may be such a thing?"

"Oh, I suppose there is. Some people pretend they know all about it. I think you're the kindest and the best person I've ever met--that's enough for me."

"Would you marry me?" said John.

"No--never."

"Why not?"

"Because directly people marry--directly they find themselves bound, they look at each other in a different light. The question of whether it can last begins to creep in. With us, it doesn't matter. I come and see you whenever you want me to. If it doesn't last, then nobody's hurt by it--if it does, let it last as long as it can. I don't want it to end to-day--I might to-morrow. I might see someone I liked better."

"And then you'd go?"

"Most certainly."

"Well--suppose you came across someone with whom you knew it must last; from whom you expected to find those things which go on past time and all measuring of clocks, would you marry them?"

She came up close to him and laid her hands upon his shoulders.

"You can tell me straight out," she said gently. "One of us was bound to find it one of these days. I only hoped it would be me. You can tell me who she is. Go on."

John told her. This was what he had wanted the woman for--first his mother, then Mrs. Rowse, then the little typewriter, then even Jill herself. For it is a woman to whom a man must tell these things--nobody else will do; nobody else will understand.

And when she had heard it all, she looked up with the suspicion of tears in her eyes and smiled.

"Then I guess I'm the fly in the amber," she said. "It won't be a clear bit of stone till I'm gone. Isn't that what you mean?"

And, taking his face in her hands, she kissed his forehead. "You're a funny little boy," she said with a wry smile.

This was the box of bricks, the playing at her dignity. Every woman has them, and while some throw them at your head, the best make patterns--patterns of fine ladies and noble dames. It was a fine lady who would call him a funny little boy. It was a noble dame who would show him that she was not hurt. He had wanted her in his way, in their way--the way she wanted him as well. All men want some woman like that, and there are as good women to supply the need as there are bad ones who would shrink from it. And now, he wanted her no longer. She knew she had to bow her head to something that she could not understand, something that she could not supply. He loved. And they had so easily avoided it.

"Are you going to be married?" she enquired. She longed to ask what the other one was like.

John shrugged his shoulders.

"You don't know?"

"No, I don't know."

"Does she love you?"

"I couldn't tell you."

"You haven't asked her?"

"No--we haven't said a word about it."

She smiled.

"Then why do you send me away?"

"Because--I know, myself. There comes a time--I didn't know it--when you know--a time when you don't excuse yourself with the plea of humanity--when you wish to offer no excuse--when there is only one way, the way I'm choosing. I'm a crank, of course. I know you've called me that before. To you I'm a crank,--to heaps of other people as well. But in the back of this muddled head of mine, I've got an ideal--so has everyone else--so have you. But now I've found a means of expressing it. You say I'm in love-- that's what you call it. I prefer just to say, I love--which is another matter altogether. People fall in and out of love like an india-rubber ball dancing on a spray of water. But this sort of thing must be always, and it may be only once or twice in your life that you find a means of expressing it. But it's there all the time. And one time it's a woman with dark hair and another it's a woman with gold--but the emotion--the heart of it is just the same. It's the same love--the love of the good--the love of the beautiful--the love of the thing which is clean through and through and through. And when you meet it, you'll sacrifice everything for it. And if you don't meet it, you'll go on hunting for it your life through--unless you lose heart, or lose character, or lose strength--then this wonderful ideal vanishes. You come to look for it less and less and less till at last you only seek for the other thing--what you call--falling in love."

"Do you think we all have this ideal?" she asked.

"Yes, every one of us."

"Then have I lost it?"

"No, I don't believe so. I saw tears in your eyes just now."

CHAPTER XVIII
THE NONSENSE-MAKER

John took a box at the opera. There is some sense in taking a box at the opera when you owe two quarters of your rent of thirty pounds a year. To have a box all the year round with your visiting-card pinned to the door, that is needless, unforgiveable extravagance, for it does not then belong to you, but to your friends.

When John took the stage-box on the third tier, it was bread and butter, dinners and teas, that he laid down in payment for the little slip of paper. They did not know that. The clerk at the office thought it was three guineas. He brushed off the money carelessly into the palm of his hand without thinking that it could be anything but coin of the realm. Who ever would go to the box-office of Covent Garden, and, tendering ingenuously bread and butter, expect to get a ticket for the stage-box on the third tier in return? But they are not observant, these box-office clerks, for heaps of people do it.

There was an old lady just behind John, who handed in all her warm spring under-clothing and a nice little embroidered lace cap that would have looked delightful on her white head in the evenings of the summer that was to come.

"I want a stall," said she, "for Tuesday night."

And in just the same inconsequent and unobservant way, the clerk, without the slightest embarrassment, swept all the warm spring under-clothing and the little lace cap into his hand and gave it her without a word, but heavens! how insulted he would have been if you had told him that he was simply a dealer in second-hand under-linen! It would not have appeased him a bit, to tell him that the under-linen had never been worn, that, in fact, it had never even been bought.

Just in this way, he took John's bread and butter, and gave him the stage-box on the third tier. It was for the night of *La Bohéme*.

On that same night, Jill was going to a dance, chaperoned by an older school-friend of hers--one who had married--a Mrs. Crossthwaite. And Mrs. Crossthwaite knew everything; not because she had been told it. That is not the way amongst women. They tell each other what they are pretending to believe, and both of them know all about it all the time.

There was the invitation to the dance--one known as a subscription. Mrs. Dealtry could not go. She had a dinner party. Jill nominated Mrs. Crossthwaite as her chaperon, and went to tea with her that day, having seen John in the morning.

First, she spoke of the dance. Mrs. Crossthwaite was delighted. She had been stepping it in the heart of her ever since she was married; but only in the heart of her, and the heart of a woman is an impossible floor to dance upon. It makes the heart, not the feet, tired.

Having won her consent--an easy matter, not lasting more than five minutes--Jill began gently, unobtrusively, to speak of the work of an author called John Grey. Mrs. Crossthwaite had read one of the books, thought it distinctly above the average, but very sad. She did not like sad books. There was quite enough sadness in real life, and so on. All of which is very, very true, if people would only realise it, as well as say it.

From there, with that adroitness which only women have the fine fingers for, Jill led on the conversation to her acquaintance with John. Oh, it was all very difficult to do, for a school-friend, once she has married, may have become a very different sort of person from the girl who was ready to swarm down the drain-pipe to meet the boy with the fair hair and the cap far on the back of his head, who passed her a note concealed between the pages of the Burial Service in the Prayer-book. Marriage is apt to rob your school-friend of this courage; for, though she never did climb down the drain-pipe, she made you think she was going to. She had one leg on the window-sill and would soon have been outside, only that she heard the voice of the mistress in the corridor just in time. And she sometimes loses this courage when she marries. Jill, therefore, had to proceed with caution.

They merely talked about his work. He was very interesting. His ideas were strange. Of course, it was a terrible pity that he would not say where he lived, but Mrs. Crossthwaite did not seem to consider that. For a moment, she had expressed surprise and approval of Mrs. Dealtry's action; but he was a member of the Martyrs' Club, and Mr. Crossthwaite's greatest friend was a member there as well, and Mr. Crossthwaite's greatest friend was naturally nearly as wonderful a person as Mr. Crossthwaite himself. So what did it really matter where he lived? The position of man was his club. She even had no curiosity about his residence.

Again, Jill had never seen *Bohème*. Her people were not musical. They hated it. She loved it. This was the opportunity of her life. He would bring her back to the dance, of course, and no one need ever know that she had not been there all the time. And in the intervals of the opera they would talk about his work. That was all they ever did talk about. She knew all his ambitions, all his hopes. Once or twice he had accepted her suggestions, when really she knew nothing about it. It was only what she felt; but he had felt it too, and the alteration had been made. He said she helped him, and that was all that was between them. The main fact of importance was that she had never seen *La Bohème*, and might never see it, if she refused this opportunity.

All these specious arguments she put forward in a gentle, enticing, winning way--full of simplicity--full of honesty; but the principal reason that Mrs. Crossthwaite consented to become a party to this collusion was that she did not believe a single word of it.

Romance! it is a word in itself, a thing in itself--a piece of fine-worked lace that must catch the eye of every woman, and which every woman would stitch to the Garment of maternity if she could.

So it was arranged. In the vestibule of the rooms where the dance was held, John was formally introduced to the chaperon before he bore her charge away. Then they stepped into a hansom.

"The Opera," said John, through the trap-door, carelessly, as though he went there most evenings of his life; for when you give your bread and butter to get a box at Covent Garden, hunger makes you talk like that. This is all part of the delight which you miss in having a box all the year round.

And when they had got far away into the traffic--that passing to and fro of people, which is all a thumb-nail illustration of the stream of life--and when her heart had begun to beat a little less like a lark's wings in a six-inch cage, Jill broke the silence.

"What did Mrs. Crossthwaite say to you while I went to get my cloak?" she asked.

"She was good enough to hope that I would call on her."

"Oh! I'm so glad she's asked you. Did she say anything else?"

"She asked me if I lived in London all the year round. I said I did--except for a month in the year, when I went to Venice. Then she asked me what part of London I lived in."

"She asked you that?"

"Yes."

Jill was silent for a few moments. It is always an interesting moment in a woman's life when she learns something about her sex.

"And what did you say?" she asked.

John laughed. He thought he had said it rather neatly.

"Oh, I've got rooms," he had said, "just between St. Paul's and the Strand." Which might be the Inner Temple, if you had a nice mind with which to look at it. He told Jill this answer. She smiled.

"And is it between St. Paul's and the Strand?" she asked.

"Roughly speaking--yes--but very roughly speaking."

Again she was silent. Could it be that he was poor--at least, not well enough off to live at a good-sounding address? Could that have been why he was praying to St. Joseph on the eighteenth of March? Yet he was a member of the Martyrs' Club, and here he was taking her to a box at Covent Garden. She looked up quickly into his face. This was more mystery than her desire for knowledge could afford.

"Do you remember what you said to me once," she began, "about the woman with the gift of understanding?"

"Yes--the first day that we met in Kensington Gardens."

"Well--do you think I am absolutely ungifted that way?"

John closely searched her eyes. Did she remember all he had said about the woman with God's good gift of understanding? Did she realise the confession it would entail if he admitted--as he believed--that she was? She was young, perhaps--a girl, a child, a baby--just twenty-one. But the understanding which is the gift of God, comes independently of experience. Like genius, it is a gift and of just such a nature. Absolute simplicity is the source of it, and with it, it brings the reward of youth, keeping the heart young no matter the years. Experience will show you that the world is full of evil--evil motives and evil deeds; it will teach you that evil is said of everyone, even the best. But with God's good gift of understanding, you have the heart of a child, knowing nothing yet finding the good in everything.

To such a one, no secrets are possible, no deeds can lie hid; for no man does evil because he would, but because it rises stronger against the innermost will of him. And so few are there with the gift to understand this, that confession is seldom made.

And for John to tell her that she had this gift, was to make admission of all he had learnt that Easter Sunday. Could it be that she asked for that reason? Did she wish to know? In his own way, he had meant to tell her; but not like this. And so he searched her eyes; but searched in vain.

"Why do you ask?" he said at length.

"Because--if you think I have any understanding at all, don't you think I should understand, even if you told me you lived at----" She could not think of a poor enough neighbourhood where people might live. She scarcely knew any.

"Shepherd's Bush?" he suggested.

"Well--yes--Shepherd's Bush."

"And so you want to know where I do live?"

"Yes."

"Why?"

She looked up at him quite honestly.

"Well--pride, I suppose. We're good friends. I hope we are. I've never had a friend before. I think I should tell you everything, and I expect I feel hurt because you don't tell me. I'm sure you have a good reason for not letting my people know, but that hasn't prevented me from keeping you as my friend against all their wishes. They don't understand, I admit. But I believe I should. I'm sure I should."

Her hand in its white glove was resting on the door of the hansom in front of her. For a moment he looked at it, and then, with heart beating, in fear, joy, apprehension--a thousand emotions all flowing into one--he took it in his and pressed it reverently, then let it go.

"I know you would," he replied in his breath. And then he told her.

Did she remember Wrigglesworth's? Would she ever forget it? Those high-backed seats, the sawdust on the floor, the poll-parrot in its cage in the middle of the room! And, then, who could forget the name of Wrigglesworth?

Did she remember the little greengrocer's shop he had pointed out to her, and how she had said she would love one of the rosy-cheeked apples that were piled up in their little partitions--and his reply, rather reluctant, evidently none too eager that one of the rosy-cheeked apples should be hers? Yes, she remembered. She remembered, too, that nothing more had been said about the apples, and that he had not reminded her of them again when they came away from lunch.

Exactly--because over that very little greengrocer's shop in Fetter Lane--the two windows above the shop itself--was where he lived.

For a moment she gazed at him in astonishment; then she stared out into the traffic before her. Back through her mind raced the sensations she had experienced that day when she had lunched with him. The secrecy, the novelty, the stuffy little eating-house, it had all seemed very romantic then. The tablecloth was not as clean as it might be, but the high-backed seats had been there for nearly two hundred years. One thing weighed with another. The waiter was familiar; but, as John had explained to her, the waiters knew everybody, and you might feel as much annoyed at their familiarity as you had reason to at the age of the poll-parrot and the remarks that he made about the cooking. They all combined to make Wrigglesworth's--Wrigglesworth's; and she had taken it for granted in the halo of romance. But to live there! To sleep at night within sight and sound of all the things which her unaccustomed eyes and cars had seen and heard! She suddenly remembered the type of people she had seen coming in and out of the doorways; then she looked back at John.

"Then you're very poor?" she said gently.

"If you mean I haven't a lot of money," he said.

"Yes."

"Then poor is the word."

He sat and watched her in silence. She was thinking very fast. He could see the thoughts, as you see cloud shadows creeping across water--passing through her eyes. Even now, he knew that she would understand in the face of all upbringing, all hereditary ideas. But he waited for her to speak again. The moment was hers. He trusted her to make the best of it.

"Why didn't you ask me to come and see your rooms after we'd had lunch at Wrigglesworth's?" she said presently and, expecting simplicity, counting upon understanding, even he was surprised.

"Ask you there? To those rooms? Over the little greengrocer's shop? Up those uncarpeted wooden stairs?"

And then they found themselves under the portico of the Opera House; in another moment in the crush of people in the vestibule; then making their way round the cheaply-papered boxes along the ugly little passages to the stage-box on the third tier.

The attendant threw open the door. Like children, who have been allowed down to the drawing-room after dinner, they walked in. And it was all very wonderful, the sky of brilliant lights and the sea of human beings below them. It was real romance to be perched away up in a little box in the great wall--a little box which shut them in so safely and so far away from all those people to whom they were so near. Her heart was beating with the sense of anticipation and fear for the fruit which their hands had stolen. For the first ten minutes, she would scarcely have been surprised had the door of the box opened behind them and her mother appeared in a vision of wrath and justice. Some things seem too good to be true, too wonderful to last, too much to have hoped for. And Romance is just that quality of real life which happens to be full of them.

From the moment that the curtain rose upon the life of these four happy-go-lucky Bohemians, to the moment when it fell as Rudolfo and Mimi set off to the *café*, these two sat in their third-tier box like mice in a cage, never moving a finger, never stirring an eye. Only John's nostrils quivered and once or twice there passed a ripple down Jill's throat.

At last fell the curtain, one moment of stillness to follow and, shattering that stillness then into a thousand little pieces, the storm of the clapping of hands.

Music is a drug, a subtle potion of sound made liquid, which one drinks without knowing what strange effect it may or may not have upon the blood. To some it is harmless, ineffectual, passing as quietly through the veins as a draught of cool spring water; to others it is wine, nocuous and sweet, bringing visions to the senses and pulses to the heart, burning the lips of men to love and the eyes of women to submission. To others again, it is a narcotic, a draught bringing the sleep that is drugged with the wildest and most impossible of dreams. But some there are, who by this philtre are imbued with all the knowledge of the good, are stirred to the desire to reach forward just that hand's stretch which in such a moment but separates the divine in the human from the things which are infinite.

This was the power that music had upon John.

While the applause was still vibrating through the house, while the curtain was still rising and falling to the repeated appearances of the players, he slipped his hand into his pocket, took something quickly out, and when she turned after the final curtain fall, Jill beheld, standing upon the velvet railing of the box, a little man all in brass, with one hand resting aristocratically upon his hip and the other stretched out as though to take her own.

Surprise and question filled her eyes. She looked up at John. She looked back at the little brass man, and the little brass man looked back at her. It may not have been that he raised his hat; but he had all the appearance of having just done so.

"Did you put that there?" she asked.

John nodded. She picked him up, and once her fingers had touched him, the spell of his dignity was cast.

"What is he? Where did you get him? What does he mean?" One question fell fast upon another.

"He's my little brass man," said John. "He's an old seal, over a hundred years old----" And he told her the whole story.

When he had finished, the curtain rose once more--outside the *Café* Momus with the babel of children and the hum and laughter of a crowd that only a city southeast of the Thames can know or understand. Through all the act, Jill sat with the little brass man standing boldly beside her. When it was over, she turned to him again.

"Aren't you very miserable when you have to--to part with him?" she asked.

"Very.--He comes back as soon as possible. But I've made a resolve."

"What's that?"

"I'm going to put him out of reach of the indignity. He's never going to the chapel of unredemption any more."

"What are you going to do?"

"Give him to you. You are the only person I know of, who has the gift of understanding poverty."

"To me?" Instinctively her fingers tightened round him. "To me?" she repeated.

He smiled and bent his head. "He seals our friendship," said he.

This was his way of telling her that he knew she understood. The perfect nonsense of the gift--a figure in brass that cost seven' shillings and had been pledged and redeemed for six, times out of number--this had little or nothing to do with it. Everything in this world is nonsense; the whole of life is a plethora of ludicrous absurdities, one more fanciful than another. The setting upon the head of a man a fantastic piece of metal and calling in a loud voice that he is king--the holding aloft of another piece of metal, crossed in shape, studded with precious stones, and exhorting those who behold it to fall upon their knees--the placing on the finger of a little circular band--of metal too--and thereby binding irrevocably the lives and freedom of two living beings in an indissoluble bondage, all these things are nonsense, childish, inconsequent nonsense, but for their symbolism and the inner meaning that they hold.

The crown is nothing, the cross is nothing, the ring is nothing, too. A goldsmith, a silversmith, a worker in brass, these men can turn them out under the hammer or upon the lathe; they can scatter the earth with them and have done so. From the crown in finest gold and rarest jewels to the crown in paper gilt, the difference can only be in value, not in truth. From the great cross in Westminster Cathedral to the little nickel toy that hangs from the cheapest of rosary beads, the difference is only the same. From the massive ring that the Pope must wear to the tinsel thing that the cracker hides in its gaudy wrappings at Christmas-time, the difference is just the same. Each would serve the other's purpose. Each would mean nothing but nonsense and empty foolishness except to the eyes which behold the symbolism that they bear.

Yet they, because of their meanings, dominate the world. Little pieces of metal of the earth's reluctant yield--for the highest symbolism always takes form in metal--they govern and command with a despotism that is all part of the chaos of nonsense in which we live.

Only one form of metal there is, which is a meaning in itself; before which, without nonsense and without symbolism, a man must bow his head--the sword. The only thing in this world of ours in which nonsense plays no part; the only thing in this world of ours which needs no symbolism to give it power. Yet in times of peace, it lies idly in the scabbard and there are few to bring it reverence.

For the present, nonsense must content us then. The greatest intellects must admit that it is still in the nature of them to sprawl upon the floor of the nursery, making belief with crowns, with crosses and with rings--making belief that in these fanciful toys lies all the vast business of life.

Until we learn the whole riddle of it all, the highest profession will be that of the nonsense-maker. The man who can beat out of metal some symbolical form, earns the thankfulness of a complete world of children. For with baubles such as these, it is in the everlasting nature of us to play, until the hours slip by and the summons comes for sleep.

So played the two--children in a world of children--in their stage-box on the third tier. She knew well what the gift of the little brass man must mean--the *Chevalier d'honneur*. John might have sworn a thousand times that he knew the great power of her understanding; yet such is the nature of the child, that in this little symbol of brass--as much a nonsense thing as any symbol of its kind--she understood far clearer the inner meaning of that word friendship.

"Will you accept him?" said John gently.

She looked back in his eyes.

"On one condition."

"What is that?"

"That if ever we cease to be friends, he must be returned to you."

CHAPTER XIX
THE MR. CHESTERTON

It was always a strain when July came round, for John to amass those seventeen odd pounds for the journey to Venice. But it was a greater strain when, having amassed it, he had some days before him in which to walk about the streets before he departed--it was a greater strain, then, not to spend it. For money, to those who have none, is merely water and it percolates through the toughest pigskin purse, finds it way somehow or other into the pocket and, once there, is in a sieve with as broad a mesh as you could need to find.

It was always in these few days before his yearly exodus, that John ran across the things that one most desires to buy. Shop-keepers had a bad habit of placing their most alluring bargains in the very fore-front of the window. Everything, in fact, seemed cheaper in July, and seventeen pounds was a sum which had all the appearance of being so immense, that the detraction of thirty shillings from the hoard would make but little material difference to the bulk of it.

But John had learnt by experience that if you take thirty shillings from seventeen pounds, it leaves fifteen pounds ten, an odd amount, demanding that those ten shillings be spent also to equalise matters. Then the fifteen pounds which is left is still immense and the process beginning all over again, there is finally left but a quota of what had been at first. With fifteen pounds in bank notes in his letter-case and two pounds in gold in his pocket, he found himself looking in the window of Payne and Welcome's, where a little Nankin milk jug of some unimpeachable dynasty was standing in all expectation, just waiting to catch the eye of such a person as himself who might chance to pass by.

That afternoon, Jill was coming to tea--her first visit to Fetter Lane, made, as he thought, simply in honour of his departure. And that little milk jug was begging to come, too.

He stood for a while and stared at it. It would not be more than fifteen shillings--expensive, too, at that. Fifteen shillings would make no impression upon so vast a sum as seventeen pounds. A voice whispered it in his ear, from behind his back,--just over his shoulder.

"You want a milk jug," said the voice, "and it's a beautiful blue. It will go wonderfully with the teapot and the little blue and white cups and saucers. Get it, man! Get it!" and it reminded him in a joking way, with a subtle, cunning laugh, of his philosophy when he was a boy. "What are sweets for, but to eat?" "What is money for, but to spend?"

With sudden decision, he walked in; but it was not through the entrance of the jeweller's shop. He marched into the confessional box in the chapel of unredemption. There, pulling out his three five-pound notes and his two sovereigns, he planked them down upon the counter.

"I want ten shillings on those," said he.

They were used to John's eccentricities there, but they never thought him so mad as this.

"Why, it's seventeen pounds," said the man.

"That's quite right," said John. "I counted it myself. And I want ten shillings on it."

Ten shillings would feed him for a week. He strode out of the shop again with the ten shillings in his pocket and the seventeen pounds safe in the keeping of the high priest. There was a man who owed him fourteen shillings, and who, when the time came to go to Venice, might possibly be induced to part with that necessary ten, if he were asked for it as a loan. A man will willingly lend you ten shillings if he owes you fourteen; it is the paying you back that he does not like.

As he passed out into the street, John kept his face rigidly averted from the little Nankin milk jug. He had played that milk jug a sly, and a nasty trick. It was really nothing to be proud about.

When he returned to Number 39, there was a man waiting outside his door, a man dressed in a light-brown tweed, the colour of ripening corn. He had on a shiny-red silk tie, adorned with a pin--a horseshoe set with pearls. His face was round, fat and solemn--the solemnity that made you laugh. He put John in good spirits from the loss of the Nankin milk jug, the moment he saw him. Someone had left the door into the street open and so he had come upstairs.

"Who are you?" asked John.

"Well--my name's Chesterton, sir, Arthur Chesterton."

John opened his door with the innocence of a babe, and the man followed him into the room, closely at his heels.

"And what do you want?" asked John.

Mr. Chesterton handed him a paper. John looked it through.

"Yes--of course--my two quarter's rent. They shall be paid," he said easily. "There's money due to me next month."

Mr. Chesterton coughed behind his hand.

"It must be now," he said quietly. "That is to say--I must wait here till I get it."

A bailiff! And Jill was coming to tea! In another half hour she would be there! She knew he was poor; she thought Fetter Lane a terrible neighbourhood; but with all her imagination, she had not conceived anything as terrible as this.

There was only one way; to explain everything. He had a lady coming to tea with him that afternoon--a lady--did he understand? Anyhow, he nodded his head. Well--it was quite impossible for her to find him there--a bailiff! It was not his fault, of course, that he was a bailiff, but he must see how impossible the position was. The little man nodded his head again. Well, would he go away; just for a short time, till they had had tea. He could return then, John promised he would let him in. He knew that once a bailiff was out of possession, he was powerless; but this was a matter of honour. On his honour he would let him in again.

Mr. Chesterton blinked his eyes.

"Sometimes," he replied quietly--"Sometimes they tell me it's their father as is comin'--then again, if it's a woman, she says her husband'll be back in a minute and her husband's always a man with an 'orrible bad temper what's liable to do dangerous things. And sometimes, they say it's a girl they're sweet on--same as you."

"But I'll swear it's true!" cried John wildly.

Mr. Chesterton smiled.

"Wouldn't payin' the money be better than swearin'?" said he. "It's only fifteen pounds. Sometimes they gets rid of me that way-- and it's the only successful way of doin' it. You see I'm inside now. I'm the nine points of the law now. If I was outside, I'd be only one--you'd be the nine, then--see. You'd be able to lock your door and make a long nose at me out of the window. Lord! the times I've said that to people--and they don't seem to see the truth of it-- not they."

John had every sympathy with their obtuseness. If he saw the point of it himself, it was only because he knew it would not be so in his instance.

"Then you won't go?" he said.

Mr. Chesterton shook his head, quite patiently.

"Do you ever get kicked out of a place into the street?" asked John. The man was so small that the question would rise naturally to the minds of quite a lot of people.

He smiled amiably.

"Yes--they do that sometimes. But two months, without the option, for assault ain't pleasant, you know. I shouldn't care for it myself. I'd sooner 'ave the assault, it's over quicker."

There are some tragedies in life in which, if you do not find place for laughter, you become melodramatic--a sin which is unforgivable.

John just saved the position in time. He sat down in a chair and laughed aloud.

"And till I've paid this money," he said. "I've got to put you up. Where are you going to sleep? I've only got a bedroom besides this and a cupboard that holds two hundredweight of coal on the landing."

Mr. Chesterton looked about him.

"That settle looks comfortable enough," said he. "I've slep' worse than that." He crossed the room and felt the springs of it with his fist. "But it's a small place. I'm afraid I shall be a bit in the way."

"My Lord!" John jumped up again. "You will this afternoon." He was to have told Jill many things that afternoon. Now this ruined everything. They would have to go out to tea, because there was no paying of the money. He could not redeem his seventeen pounds and settle it with that. There would be nothing left with which to go to Venice and the calculations of that little old white-haired lady who was waiting for him to put his arms about her neck had become so small, so infinitely small, that he had not the heart to add to them by so much as a figure of seven.

"And you don't believe that a lady's coming to tea with me?" he said excitedly.

Mr. Chesterton spread out a pair of dirty hands.

"I know that lady so well," he said. "She's always every inch a lady who wouldn't understand the likes of me. But I'm quite easy to understand. Tell her I'm a friend of yours. I won't give the game away."

Oh! It was ludicrous! The laugh came again quickly to John's lips, but as soon it died away. So much was at stake. He had pictured it all so plainly. She would be disappointed when she heard he was going. He would ask her why that look had passed across her eyes. Her answer would be evasive, and then, word by word, look by look, he would lead her to the very door of his heart until the cry--"I love you"--the most wonderful words to say--the most terribly wonderful words to mean, would be wrung from his lips into her ears.

And now this imperturbable fiend of a bailiff, with his very natural incredulity and his simple way of expressing it, had come to wreck the greatest moment of his life.

John looked him up and down.

"What sort of a friend do you think I could introduce you as?" he asked. "Do you think you look like a friend of mine?"

The little man glanced down at his boots, at the light-brown tweed trousers, upturned and showing a pair of woollen socks not far removed in colour from that of his tie.

"Well--you never know," said he, looking up again. "I'm stayin' here, aren't I? They said you was a writer--that you wrote books. Well, have you never seen a person who wrote books, like me? Why there was a woman I 'ad to get the rent from once--a journalist, she called herself. She'd got a bit of a beard and a fair tidy moustache--and by gum, she dressed queerer than anything my old woman would ever put on. I felt quite ashamed to be stoppin' with her."

John laughed again; laughed uproariously. Mr. Chesterton was so amused at the remembrance of it, that he laughed as well. Suddenly their laughter snapped, as you break a slate pencil. There came a gentle, a timid knock on the door.

"This is she," whispered John. "The door below was open. She's come upstairs. What the devil am I going to do?"

At last the little man believed him. He really was going to see the lady this time, the lady who would never understand the likes of him, and he began to feel quite nervous. He began to feel ashamed of being a bailiff.

"Introduce me as a friend," he whispered--"It'll be all right--introduce me as a friend."

"Sit down there, then--on that settle."

Then John opened the door and Jill stepped hesitatingly into the room. Mr. Chesterton rose awkwardly to his feet.

This was the lady, materialised at last. From long habit of summing up in a glance the people with whom he had to deal, he made his estimation of Jill in a moment. The quietness of her voice as she said--"I was rather afraid to knock, for fear I had made a mistake"--that gentleness in the depth of the eyes which admits of no sudden understanding, yet as gently asks for it--the firm repose of the lips already moulded for the strength which comes with maturity, and all set in a face whose whole expression was that innocence of a mind which knows and has put aside until such moment when life shall demand contemplation. This--there was no doubt of it--was the lady who would not understand the likes of him.

John shook hands with her. Mr. Chesterton took it all in with his little solemn eyes. He was in the way. Never had he been so much in the way before. As their hands touched, he felt that John was telling her just how much in the way he was.

"May I introduce you," said John, turning, when that touching of the hands was done with. "This is my friend--Mr. Chesterton. Miss----" he paused. It seemed sacrilege to give her name to a bailiff, and the little man felt sensitively, in his boots every moment of that pause. His red socks were burning him. He could see the colour of his tie in every reflection. It was even creeping up into his cheeks.

"Miss Dealtry."

He was going to come forward and shake hands, but she bowed. Then, when she saw his confusion, out, generously, came her hand.

"Are you a writer, too?" she asked.

John was about to interpose; but the little man wanted to stand well with her. He felt that his socks and his tie and his corn-coloured suit ought all to be explained, and what more lucid or more natural explanation than this.

"Oh, yes, I'm a writer," he said quickly. "Books, you know--and a little journalism--just to--to keep me goin'--to amuse myself like. Journalism's a change, you know--what you might call a rest, when your always writin' books----" Then he remembered a quotation, but where from, he could not say, "Of the writin' of books, you know--at least, so they say--there's no end." And he smiled with pleasure to think how colloquially he had delivered the phrase.

"Why, of course, I know your work," said Jill--"Aren't you *the* Mr. Chesterton?"

The little man's face beamed. That was just what they all called him--*the* Mr. Chesterton.

"That's right," said he delightedly, "the one and only." And under the mantle of genius and celebrity his quaintnesses became witticisms, his merest phrase a paradox.

CHAPTER XX
WHY JILL PRAYED TO ST. JOSEPH

Little as you might have imagined it, there was a heart beneath that corn-coloured waistcoat of Mr. Chesterton's. His old woman, as he called her, would have vouched for that.

"He may have to do some dirty tricks in his job," she had said of him. "But 'e's got a 'eart, 'as my young man, if you know where to touch it."

And seemingly, Jill had known; tho' the knowledge was unconscious. It was just that she had believed--that was all. She had believed he was the Mr. Chesterton, presumably a great writer, a man to command respect. He had never commanded respect before in his life. Abuse! Plenty of that! So much of it that his skin had become hardened and tough. But respect--never.

Ah! She was a lady, certainly--a delightful, a charming young lady. He could quite believe that she would not understand the likes of him. He would even dare to swear, and did, when eventually he went home to his old woman, that she had never heard of a bailiff in her life.

And while John laid out the tea things, she talked to him all the time as if he were a great man--bless her little heart! He was a fine fellow, whoever this Chesterton was, and he seemed to have said some mighty smart things. Anyhow, if writing books was not a paying game, as, judging by this young Mr. Grey, it would not seem to be, it certainly brought one a deal of credit. The little bailiff basked in the light of it, feeling like a beggar who has awakened in the King's bed-chamber, ensconced in the King's bed. Only when, occasionally he caught sight of the expression on John's face, did he realise how abominably he must be in the way.

At last, when tea was ready, the kettle spitting on the little spirit stove in the grate, Mr. Chesterton rose to his feet. A look had passed between those two, a look unmistakable to his eyes--a look of mute appeal from her, an answering look of despair from John. Had it been John alone, he would have taken no notice. John had been making grimaces to himself for the last quarter of an hour; besides, he had brought it on himself. Young men should pay their rent up to time. He had little or no sympathy for John. But when he saw that look in Jill's eyes, realising that it was only her gentle politeness which made her talk to him so nicely--only her gentle politeness and the kudos which he had stolen from the name of Chesterton--then, he felt he could stay there no longer. He had always had a tender heart for women, so long as they were not unsexed by journalism, by a bit of a beard and a fair tidy moustache. He had no sympathy for them then if their rents were overdue. But now, this was a different matter. That look in Jill's eyes had cut him to the quick.

"I've got to be goin' now, Mr. Grey," he said.

John's mouth opened in amazement. He had just decided in his mind that Kensington Gardens was the only place left to them from this abominable interloper.

"Going?" he echoed. It might almost have seemed as if he were intensely sorry, his surprise was so great.

"Yes--goin'," said Mr. Chesterton with a look that meant the absolute certainty of his return. "Good-bye, Miss Dealtry--you'll excuse me runnin' away, won't you? Time and tide--they won't wait, you know--they're just like a pair o' children goin' to a circus. They don't want to miss nuthin'."

Now that was his own, his very own! He had been determined all through their conversation to work in something of his own. *The great* Mr. Chesterton had never said that! This credit of being another man, and gleaning all the approbation that did not belong to him, had brought with it its moments of remorse, and he longed to win her approval for something that was truly, really his.

He looked proudly at John as he said it. He laughed loudly at the thought of the two children dragging at their mother's hands all the way to the circus. It was a real picture to him. He could see it plainly. He had been one of those children himself once. Time and tide--like a pair o' children goin' to a circus! He thought it excellent--good, and he laughed and laughed, till suddenly he realised that John was not even smiling. Then wasn't it funny after all? Wasn't it clever? Yet the things which this Mr. Chesterton was reputed to have written, were quite unintelligible to him.

"The apple which Eve ate in the Garden of Eden was an orange and the peel has been lying about ever since."

Where was the sense in that? How could an apple be an orange. But Time and Tide, like a pair o' children going to a circus! Oh--he thought it excellent.

Then, with a pitiable sensation of failure, he turned in almost an attitude of appeal to Jill. But she was smiling. She was amused. Then there was something in it after all! It had amused her. He held out his hand, feeling a wild inclination to grip it fiercely and bless her for that smile.

"Good-bye," said he in his best and most elaborate of manners. "I'm very pleased to have made your acquaintance," and he marched, with head erect, to the door.

John followed him.

"I'll just come down with you," he said.

As soon as they were outside and the door was closed, he caught the little man's hand warmly in his.

"You're a brick," said he. "You're a brick. I'll let you in whenever you come back--you needn't be afraid."

Mr. Chesterton stopped on the stairs as they descended.

"I wouldn't have done it," he said emphatically--"if it wasn't that she was a lady as wouldn't understand the likes of me. I tell you, she's a sort of lady as I shall never come across again,--not even in my line of business,--bless her heart." He descended another step or so, then stopped once more. "See the way she smiled at that what I said. I tell you, she's got a nicer sense of understandin' than what you have."

John smiled.

"I know she has," said he.

"I suppose you didn't think that clever, what I said?"

"Oh, yes, I do--I do. I don't even think *the* Mr. Chesterton would have thought of that."

"Don'tcher really, now? Don'tcher really?"

John had not smiled; but this--well, of course, this made up for everything. *The* Mr. Chesterton would not have thought of Time and Tide being like a pair of children goin' to a circus! Now, if he were to write that and a few other things like it, which he dared say he could think of easily enough, he, too, might be a great man whose name would be on the lips of such women as that perfect little lady upstairs. Then she *would* understand the likes of him.

"Then you think I suited the part?" he said cheerfully at the door.

"I think, under the circumstances and everything being considered, you did it wonderfully," said John. "And as for your being good enough to trust me--well--it's finer than all the epigrams in the world."

He wrung his hand once more and the little man departed happily down the Lane, thinking of all the clever things that he would say to his old woman when eventually he got home. But-- Time and Tide, like a pair of children--he knew he'd never beat that. She had smiled at it. She had thought it clever. The other things that came laboriously into his mind as he walked down the Lane, were not a patch on it.

The moment John had closed the door, he flew upstairs.

"Well--what do you think of *the great* Mr. Chesterton?" he asked with a laugh.

"I do not think his conversation is nearly as good as his writing," said Jill.

"But you smiled at that last thing he said."

"Yes, I know." She explained it first with her eyes and then, "He was going," she added--"and I think it must have been relief."

John's heart thumped. A light of daring blazed in his eyes. It was relief! She was glad to be alone with him! This meant more than the look of disappointment. He had crossed the room, found himself beside her, found her hand gripped fiercely in his before he realised that he had obeyed the volition to do so.

"You wanted us to be alone?" he whispered.

"Yes--I've got a lot I want to say."

Had the moment not been such as this, he would have caught the note of pain that vibrated in her voice; but he was in the whirlwind of his love. It was deafening in his ears, it was blinding in his eyes; because then he knew she loved him also. He heard nothing. He saw nothing. Her hand was to his lips and he was kissing every finger.

Presently he held her hand to him and looked up.

"You knew this," he said--"didn't you? You knew this was bound to be?"

She bent her head.

"I don't know what it means," he went on passionately. "I haven't the faintest idea what it means. I love you--that's all. You mean everything to me. But I can't ask you to marry me. It wouldn't be fair." A thought of Mr. Chesterton rushed across his mind. "I--I can barely keep myself in rooms like these. I couldn't keep you. So I suppose I haven't a moment's right to say one of these things to you. But I had to say them. You knew I was going to say them--didn't you--Jill--my Jill--you knew--didn't you?"

She let him take both her hands in his; she let him drag them to his shoulders and press them there. But she bent her head forward. She hid her face from his. There was that which she had to tell him, things which she had to say, that must be told before he could blame himself any more for the love he had offered. She had known it was coming. He was quite right; she had known all he was going to say, realised it ever since that day when they had quarrelled in Kensington Gardens. All the moments between until this, had been a wonderful anticipation. A thousand times her breath had caught; a thousand times her heart had thumped, thinking he was about to speak; and through it all, just these few weeks or so, the anxious longing, the tireless praying that what she had now to say need never be said.

For a little while she let him hold her so. It would be the last time. God had been talking, or He had been sleeping, and St. Joseph--perhaps he had taken John's gift of generosity rather than that last candle of her's, for the petition she had made on that 18th of March in the Sardinia St. Chapel had not been answered.

Presently she looked up into his eyes.

"You mustn't blame yourself, John," she said gently. "It is I who deserve all the blame."

"Why?" he said--"why?"

"Because--not for the reason you said--but for something else, this is all impossible. I know it is the most wonderful thing that will ever be in my life. I know that. I'm sure of it. But something has happened since I saw you last, which makes it impossible for us to see each other again."

"Your people have found out? They forbid it?"

She shook her head.

"No--no--it's not that. They know nothing. I must go back in order to explain it to you."

Still holding his hand, she slipped into a chair, motioning him to draw up another beside her.

"You remember when we first met?"

He nodded.

"Did you ever wonder why I was praying to St. Joseph?"

"Wonder?" he echoed. "I've thought of a thousand different things."

"I don't suppose you've thought of the right one," said Jill. "My father's not rich, you know; not so rich as you might expect from his position and the house where we live. At one time we were better off, but they still try to live on at Prince of Wales' Terrace, though they can't really afford it. Father lost money in speculation, and, before that, he had put down Ronald's name for Eton. Then the chances of his ever going there seemed to dwindle to nothing. It was when it almost seemed as if we must leave the house in Kensington, that a friend of father's asked me to marry him. He was over forty--some years older than me and I----"

"You refused him, of course," said John quickly. At twenty-six, forty years can seem the millennium when they stand in your way.

"Yes--I--I refused. But he did not take my refusal. He asked me to think about it; that he would wait--would even wait a year. Then, I believe, he must have said something to father, besides telling him that I had refused, because father talked for a long while to me afterwards and mother, too. They showed me as plainly as they could, though, from their point of view alone, what an excellent match it would be. Father told me exactly what his financial position was--a thing he had never done before. I had always thought him to be quite rich. Then, at the end, he said he had invested in some speculation which he believed was going to set him quite right again, enable us to stay on in Kensington and make it quite possible for Ronald to go to Eton. But that if this failed, as he did not believe it would, then he hoped that I would reconsider my refusal to his friend. I say he hoped; but he did not put it in that way. He showed me that it would be my duty--that I should be spoiling Ronald's chances and mother's life and his, if I did not accept."

She paused. She waited for John to say something; but he sat there beside her with his lips set tight and his eyes unmoving.

"It was on the 18th of March, he told me that," she continued--"the day that I went to pray to St. Joseph that his speculation might not fail--the day I met you. Then--only the day before yesterday--they told me. The prayer had been no good. I always said poor St. Joseph was no good to me."

"He's lost his money?" said John hoarsely. He let her hand fall and moved away.

"Yes. I--I've got to accept."

CHAPTER XXI
THE CITY OF BEAUTIFUL NONSENSE

"Then you'll never know my people in Venice," said John presently. He had suddenly remembered that there was nothing to tell the little old white-haired lady now. To all the thousand questions which she would whisper into his ears, only evasive answers could be given her.

"I told my mother about you," he went on slowly. "I told her how we met. I told her that you were praying to St. Joseph and she's been wondering ever since--like me"--the emotion rose in his throat--"she's been wondering what you could have had to ask."

He came back to the arm-chair--the arm-chair in which he did his work--and quietly sat down. Then, as quietly, as naturally as if she had done it a thousand times before, Jill seated herself on the floor at his feet and his arm wound gently round her neck.

"Did your mother know we met again?" she asked presently.

"Yes--I told her about the first time in Kensington Gardens. I haven't told her any more. I dared not."

"Dared not?" She looked up quickly.

"No--it's the hope of her life to see me happy--to see me married. They think I make more money than I do, because I won't take anything from them. They believe I'm in a position to marry and, in nearly every letter she writes, she makes some quaint sort of allusion to it. I believe already her mind is set on you. She's so awfully cute. She reads every single word between the lines, and sometimes sees more what has been in my mind when I wrote to her, than I even did myself."

Jill's interest wakened. Suddenly this old lady, far away in Venice, began to live for her.

"What is she like?" she asked--"Describe her. You've never told me what she's like."

Diffidently, John began. At first it seemed wasting their last moments together to be talking of someone else; but, word by word, he became more interested, more absorbed. It was entering Jill into his life, making her a greater part of it than she would have been had she gone away knowing nothing more of him than these rooms in Fetter Lane. At last the little old white-haired lady, with those pathetically powerless hands of hers, was there, alive, in the room with them.

Jill looked up at him with such eyes as concealed their tears.

"She means a lot to you," she said gently.

"Yes--she means a great deal."

"And yet, do you know, from your description of her, I seemed more to gather how much you meant to her. She lives in you."

"I know she does."

"And your father? Thomas Grey--of the port of Venice?" She tried to smile at the remembrance which that brought.

"Yes--he lives in me, too. They both of them do. He, for the work I shall do, carrying on where he left off; she, for the woman I shall love and the children I know she prays I may have before she dies. That is the essence of true fatherhood and true motherhood. They are perfectly content to die when they are once assured that their work and their love is going on living in their child."

She thought of it all. She tried in one grasp of her mind to hold all that that meant, but could only find herself wondering if the little old white-haired lady would be disappointed in her, would disapprove of the duty she was about to fulfil, if she knew.

After a long pause, she asked to be told where they lived; to be told all--everything about them; and in a mood of inspiration, John wove her a romance.

"You've got to see Venice," he began, "you've got to see a city of slender towers and white domes, sleeping in the water like a mass of water lilies. You've got to see dark water-ways, mysterious threads of shadow, binding all these flowers of stone together. You've got to hear the silence in which the whispers of lovers of a thousand years ago, and the cries of men, betrayed, all breathe and echo in every bush. These are the only noises in Venice--these and the plash of the gondolier's oar or his call--'Ohé!' as he rounds a sudden corner. You've got to see it all in the night--at night, when the great white lily flowers are blackened in shadow, and the darkened water-ways are lost in an impenetrable depth of gloom. You've got to hear the stealthy creeping of a gondola and the lapping of the water against the slimy stones as it hurries by. In every little burning light that flickers in a barred window up above, you must be able to see plotters at work, conspirators planning deeds of evil or a lover in his mistress' arms. You've got to see magic, mystery, tragedy, and romance, all compassed by grey stone and green water, to know the sort of place where my mother and father live, to know the place where I should have taken you, if--if things had been different."

"Should we have gone there together?" she said in a breath.

"Yes--I've always sort of dreamed, when I've thought of the woman with God's good gift of understanding, I've always sort of dreamed of what we should do together there."

She looked up into his face. The picture of it all was there in his eyes. She saw it as well. She saw the vision of all she was losing and, as you play with a memory that hurts, as a mother handles the tiny faded shoe of the baby she has lost, she wanted to see more of it.

"Should we have gone there together?" she whispered.

He smiled down at her--mock bravery--a smile that helped him bear the pain.

"Yes,--every year--as long as they lived and every year afterwards, if you wished. Every morning, we'd have got up early--you know those early mornings when the sun's white and all the shadows are sort of misty and the water looks cleaner and fresher than at any other time because the dew has purged it. We'd have got up early and come downstairs and outside in the little Rio, the gondolier would be blowing on his fingers, waiting for us. They can be cold those early mornings in Venice. Then we'd have gone to the Giudecca, where all the ships lie basking in the sun--all the ships that have come from Trieste, from Greece, from the mysterious East, up through the Adriatic, threading their way through the patchwork of islands, past Fort San Nicolo and Lido till they reach the Giudecca Canal. They lie there in the sun in the early mornings like huge, big water-spiders, and up from all the cabins you'll see a little curl of pale blue smoke where the sailors are cooking their breakfasts."

"And how early will that be?" asked Jill in a whisper.

"Oh--six o'clock, perhaps."

"Then I shall be awfully sleepy. I never wake up till eight o'clock and even then it's not properly waking up."

"Well, then, you'll put your head on my shoulder and you'll go to sleep. It's a wonderful place to sleep in, is a gondola. We'll go away down towards Lido and you can go to sleep."

"But the gondolier?"

"Oh"--he laughed gently. "The hood's up--he stands behind the hood. He can't see. And if he can, what does that matter? He understands. A gondolier is not a London cabby. He plies that oar of his mechanically. He's probably dreaming, too, miles away from us. There are some places in the world where it is natural for a man to love a woman, where it isn't a spectacle, as it is here, exciting sordid curiosity, and Venice is one of them. Well, then, you'll go to sleep, with your head on my shoulder. And when we're coming back again, I shall wake you up--how shall I wake you?"

He leant over her. Her eyes were in Venice already. Her head was on his shoulder. She was asleep. How should he wake her? He bent still lower, till his face touched hers.

"I shall kiss you," he whispered--"I shall kiss your eyes, and they'll open." And he kissed her eyes--and they closed.

"We'll go back to breakfast, then," he went on, scarcely noticing how subtly the tense had changed since he had begun. "What do you think you'd like for breakfast?"

"Oh--anything--it doesn't matter much what one eats, does it?"

"Then we'll eat anything," he smiled--"whatever they give us. But we shall be hungry, you know. We shall be awfully hungry."

"Well," said Jill under her breath--"I'm sure they'll give us enough. And what do we do then?"

"After breakfast?"

"Yes."

"Well--I finish just one moment before you do, and then I get up, pretending that I'm going to the window."

She looked up surprised.

"Pretending? What for?"

"Because I want to get behind your chair."

"But why?"

"Because I want to put my arms round your neck and kiss you again."

He showed her how. He showed her what he meant. She took a deep breath, and closed her eyes once more.

"When, without complaint, you take whatever is given you, that's the only grace for such a meal as that. Well--when we've said grace--then out we go again."

"In the garden?"

"Yes--to the Palazzo Capello in the Rio Marin."

"That's where your people live?"

"Yes. Well, perhaps, we take them out, or we go and sit in the garden. I expect father will want us to go and sit in the garden and see the things he's planted; and mother of course'll consent, though she'll be longing to go out to the Piazza San Marco and look at the lace in the shops under the Arcade."

"Well, then, I'll go out with her----" said Jill.

"If you go, I go," said John.

She laughed, and forced him to a compromise. He would stay in the garden for half an hour; it need not be more.

"There might be things we wanted to buy in the shops," she said--"shops where you might not be allowed to come." So he could understand that it ought to be half an hour. But it must not be more.

"And then--what then?" she asked.

"Well, then, directly after lunch, we'd take a gondola once more and set off for Murano."

"Directly after? Wouldn't it be cruel to leave them so soon? If we only go for a month every year, wouldn't it be cruel?"

This is where a man is selfish. This is where a woman is kind. It was natural enough, but he had not thought so much of them.

He consented that they should stay till tea-time was over--tea in those little, wee cups without any handles, which the little old white-haired lady could just manage to grasp in her twisted hands, and accordingly, loved so much because they did not jeer at her powerlessness as did the many things which she had once been able to hold.

"You didn't want not to come out with me--did you?" he asked when the tea-time picture had passed before his eyes.

"Not--not want--but you'd get tired, perhaps, if you saw too much of me alone."

"Get tired!"

Three score years and ten were the utmost that a man might hope for in this life. Get tired!

Well, then, tea was over at last. The light of a pearl was creeping into the sky. That was the most wonderful time of all to cross the Lagoon to Murano.

"Then it was much better we stayed to tea," she whispered.

Much better, since the shadows were deepening under the arches, and he could take her head in his hands and kiss her--as he kissed her then--without being seen. Oh--it was much better that they had stayed to tea.

Now they had started, past the Chiesa San Giacomo into the Grand Canal, down the broad waterway, past the Ca' d'Oro, which the Contarini built, to the narrow Rio di Felice; then out into the Sacca della Misericordia, and there, before them, the broad stretch of the silent Lagoon--a lake of opal water that never ended, but as silently became the sky, with no line of light or shade to mark the alchemy of change.

"And across this," said John,--"with their hour glasses spilling out the sand, come the gondolas with the dead, to the cemetery that lies in the water in the midst of the Lagoon. They churn up the water with the speed they go, and if you ask a gondolier why they go so fast, he will tell you it is because the dead cannot pay for that last journey of theirs. That is their humour in the city they call *La citta del riso sangue*. But we shall creep through the water--we can pay--at least----" he thought of his two quarters' rent--"I suppose we can. We shall steer through the water like the shadow of a little cloud gliding across the sea. Oh----" he pressed his hands to his eyes--"but it would be wonderful there with you! And at night, when the whole city is full of darkness--strange, silent, mysterious darkness--where every lighted taper that burns and every lamp that is lit seems to illuminate a deed of mystery, we would go out into the Grand Canal, when we had said good-night to those dear old people of mine and we'd listen to them singing--and, oh,--they sing so badly, but it sounds so wonderful there. At last--one by one, the lights would begin to flicker out. The windows that were alive and awake would close their eyes and hide in the mysterious darkness; a huge white lamp of a moon would glide up out of the breast of the Adriatic, and then----"

"Then?" she whispered.

"Then we should turn back to the little room amongst all those other little rooms in the great darkness--the gondolier would row home, and I should be left alone with my arms tight round you and my head resting on the gentlest place in the world."

He lifted his hands above his head--he laughed bitterly with the unreality of it all.

"What beautiful nonsense all this is," said he.

She looked up with the tears burning in her eyes. She looked up and her glance fell upon a picture that his father had painted and given him--a picture of the Rialto lifting with its white arches over the green water. She pointed to it. He followed with his eyes the white line of her finger.

"Then that," said Jill, and her voice quivered--"that's the City--the City of Beautiful Nonsense."

BOOK II
THE TUNNEL
CHAPTER XXII
THE HEART OF THE SHADOW

Ideals in the human being are as the flight of a swallow, now high, now sinking to earth, borne upwards by the bright light of air, pressed downwards by the lowering of a heavy sky.

When John had said his last good-bye to Jill, when it seemed to both of them that the Romance was finished--when the City of Beautiful Nonsense had just been seen upon the horizon, like a land of promise viewed from a height of Pisgah, and then faded into the mist of impossible things, John turned back to those rooms in Fetter Lane, with his ideal hugging close to earth and all the loneliness of life stretching out monotonously before him.

But not until he had seen the empty tea-cups in their position upon the table just as they had left them, the little piece of bread and butter she had half eaten, upon her plate; not until he had seen the empty chairs standing closely together as though repeating in whispers all the story of the City of Beautiful Nonsense which he had told her, did he come actually to realise that he had lost her--that he was alone.

The minutes ticked wearily by as he sat there, staring at it all as though it were an empty stage at the end of a play, which the players had deserted.

At the sound of footsteps mounting the stairs, he looked up. Then, as a knock fell upon the door, he started to his feet. She had come back! She could bear the parting no more than he! They were never to be parted! This loneliness was too unendurable, too awful to bear. In hurried strides, he reached the door and flung it open.

There stood the little bailiff--*the great* Mr. Chesterton--with a smile spreading agreeably over his solemn face. In those two hours of his absence, he had thought of three clever things--three! which, having just invented, he found to be in every way as good as that famous simile of Time and Tide. He was longing to say them.

But when he saw the look on John's face, he stopped.

"Yer not expecting another young lady are yer?" he asked.

John turned back despairingly into the room, making way for him to enter. He offered no reply to the little man's remark.

Mr. Chesterton closed the door behind him.

"'Ave you 'ad a scrap?" he asked sympathetically.

Now, sympathy from a bailiff, may be a very beautiful thing, but when the mind of a man is floundering in the nethermost pit, he has no need of it. John turned on him, his face changed, his whole expression altered.

"You've come here to do your work, haven't you?" he said thickly--"you've come here to take possession of any confounded thing you like. Well--take it! Take the whole blessed show! I don't want to see a single thing in this room again." He strode to the door. The little man stood staring at him amazed. "You can rip every damned thing off the walls----" he went on wildly. "Make up your fifteen pounds whatever you do. Don't stint yourself! For God's sake don't stint yourself!--Take every damned thing!"

The door slammed. He was gone.

It was half-past six. Payne and Welcome were just beginning to put up their shutters. John hurried into the side entrance and threw his ticket down on the counter.

"I want that seventeen pounds," he said, and the ten-shilling-piece twisted a giddy dance on the counter by the side of the ticket, then sank down with a gentle ringing sound.

The pawnbroker looked at him in amazement, then went to a little pigeon-hole and produced the packet of money. John snatched it up and went.

They stared after him; then stared at one another.

"He ain't so far off it this time," said one.

"Next thing I'll do," said the high priest--"I'll cut 'is throat in a barber's shop."

But supremely unconscious of all these gentle remarks, John was hurrying on through the streets, scarcely conscious of where he was going, or why he had redeemed the money that was now gripped fiercely in his hand.

For what did anything matter now? There must be some colour of reality about the ideal, some red lamp burning before an altar to light up that utter darkness into which the mind inevitably falls, blindly and stumblingly, without such actual guiding flame as this. Where would be the wonderful reality of the Host in the Tabernacle, if it was not for the dim red lamp that burnt silently by day and night before the altar? Who could pray, who could believe in utter darkness?

And in utter darkness Jill had surely left him now. It might have been that they could not have married for some years; it might have been that they could never have married at all; but to see her no more--never to feel again the touch of understanding in her hands, the look of understanding in her eyes--that was the gale of the wind which had obliterated the red light of the lamp that burnt before his altar. And now--he was in darkness. Neither could he pray, nor believe.

For an hour, he wandered through the streets, then, as a clock struck the half-hour after seven, he turned into a fashionable restaurant and took a table in a corner alone.

A waiter came with the menu of the dinners--five shillings, seven and six, ten shillings. He chose the last as it was handed to him. The mere action of spending money needlessly seemed a part of the expression of that bitterness which was tainting all his thoughts.

The waiter handed him the wine list with a bow.

John shook his head.

"Water," he said.

This was not his way of seeking oblivion. In even the blackest moments of his mind, he must have his senses wide-eyed and awake. The man who drinks to forget, forgets Remorse as well. Remorse is a thing to be learnt of, not to drown.

This, if John had known it, was what his father meant by wishing for the sorrow in his life. By such moments as these, he was to come to learn the value of optimism; by such moments as these, he was to come to know, not that there is too much sadness in life already, but that there is too little of the contrast of real happiness to appreciate it.

All through the meal, sending away one course after another unfinished, he gave way voluntarily to the passion of bitterness, made no effort to steady the balance of his mind.

In a balcony, at the far end of the room, a band of string instruments played the worst of meanings into bad music--the music one hears without listening to. It was not long in finding its way into John's mind, not long in exerting its influence upon his mood. One by one, crowding quickly upon each other, he permitted its suggestions to take a hold upon his thoughts. What did it matter how he thought? What did it matter how low his ideal should fall? He could see nothing beyond the moment, nothing further than that he was alone, deprived of the greatest, the highest hope with which his whole being had associated itself? What did anything matter now that he had lost that.

And then, out of a stillness that had fallen since the last playing of the band, the musicians began a selection from *La Bohème*. He laid his knife and fork upon the plate. He sat back in his chair and listened.

Why did it sound so different? What had changed in it since that night when he had heard it at the Opera? Now there was sensuality in every note of it. It maddened him. The very passages that he had once found beautiful--found wonderful as he had listened to them with Jill--became charged with the vilest imaginations. Thoughts, the impurest, surged into his mind. The wildest and most incomprehensible desire beat in his brain. Was it the players? Was it their rendering of the music, or was it himself?

He called the waiter, ordered his bill, paid--thinking no loss in it--out of the seventeen pounds he had redeemed, and strode out of the place into the street.

There was nowhere to go, no friend whom he cared at such a moment to see. At last, without consciously determining upon it, he found himself making his way back to Fetter Lane.

With steps almost like those of an old man, he climbed up the stairs, passing the sandy cat without notice--not so much as a good-evening.

When he opened the door of his room, there was Mr. Chesterton, comfortably ensconced in his armchair and only saving his presumptuousness of its occupation, by reading one of John's books.

But Mr. Chesterton was a man with a certain amount of humility. He rose to his feet as John entered; because there was no doubt as to its being John's particular arm-chair. It was the only armchair in the room. The little bailiff had observed that. In fact, for that very reason, he had considerately omitted it in the making of his inventory.

"I--I just been reading one of your books, Mr. Grey," he said, "an' if yer don't mind my sayin' so, I've read many a story what was worse. I 'ave, indeed. I like this story first rate. It's no more like a thing you'd hear of in life than I'm like the photograph my son took of me last week with a five-shilling camera. 'Ow on earth you manage to do it is a marvel to me. Do you get a plot in yer 'ead like and just stick it down just as it comes to yer--what my old woman calls when the spirit moves? 'The spirit moves,' she says, and then she goes out and gets a jug of beer. But that's only figurative, of course. What I mean is, do you go on writing what's in your 'ead, or do you get bits of it out of other books? 'He threw his arms around her neck and held her in a passionate embrace.' I've read that in 'eaps of books. I suppose they get it from each other."

"Did you find it in mine?" asked John.

"Well, no--I can't say as I 'ave yet. But then, they've only just been introduced. I expect you'll 'ave to come to it sooner or later. They all do."

"That's quite right," said John--"we all do. There's something inevitable about it. Have you had a meal yet?"

"No--but I've got a little something here in a basket. I'll eat it on the landing if you like."

"Oh, no," said John--"eat it here. It makes no difference to me."

So Mr. Chesterton pulled out the basket with the little something inside. Two cold sausages and some bread and butter were the extent of his meal which he ate with evident relish, and table manners that, perhaps, a fastidious person might have objected to. You could, for example, hear him eating. Sometimes he exclaimed how excellent were sausages when they were cold. He went so far as to say he loved them. He also expanded on the way his old woman cooked tripe; but when he talked about the brains of certain animals being cheap and at the same time a great delicacy, John found that his hands wanted washing and went into the other room.

"They've had a tiff," said the little man as he bit into the second sausage--"they've 'ad a tiff. He's that down in the mouth, there's nothin' I can say as'll buck him up. Why, if I talk about sheep's brains to my old woman, she gets as chirpy as a cock-sparrer."

When John came back, Mr. Chesterton had finished; the basket was put away and he was doing things with his teeth and a bent pin in a far corner of the room.

"'Ave yer got a box of draughts, Mr. Grey?" he asked, when he was at liberty. John nodded his head.

"Then come along," said the little man--"let's have a game!"

CHAPTER XXIII
AMBER

But there is no oblivion to be found in a game of draughts. For some days, John bore with the society of the amiable Mr. Chesterton. He listened to his stories of visits that he had paid in other establishments, where they had prevailed upon him to do odd jobs about the house, even to the cleaning of the knives and boots.

The only time when he seemed to have resolutely refused to do anything, was on the occasion he had spent seven days with the lady journalist who had a beard and a fair tidy moustache.

"I wouldn't even have shaved her if she'd asked me to," he said.

This sort of thing may be amusing; but it needs the time, it needs the place. In those rooms of his, where only a few days before, Jill had been sitting--at that period of his life when hope was lowest and despair triumphant, John found no amusement in it at all.

He wanted his oblivion. His whole desire was to forget. The life that had held all promise for him, was gone--irrevocably broken. He sought for that, which would, by contrast, close the memory of it, as you shut a book that is read. It was not to be done by playing draughts with Mr. Chesterton. It was not to be done in the ways that the crowd of men will choose. He had attempted that--found it impossible and flung it aside.

It was then that he thought of Amber. She had had a rightful place once, a place that had accorded with his ideas of the cleanliness of existence. Only that he had met Jill--only that he had loved--only that he had found the expression of his ideal in her, Amber would still have been there. And now--now that he had lost everything--why not return? It was the most human thing in the world. Life was not possible of such ideals.

So he argued, the darkness slowly diminishing--the light of some reason creeping again into his mind. But the bitterness was still there. He still did not care and, as yet, his mind did not even rebel against such callousness.

One evening, then, he left Mr. Chesterton finishing the reading of his book. He hailed the first hansom he saw and, screwing himself into the corner of the seat, took a deep breath of relief as he drove away.

Then began the fear as he drove, the fear that he would not find Amber, that since she had gone out of his life, she would have readjusted her mind, found other interests, or even that she might not be there when he arrived. And now, once his destination was made, he dreaded the thought that Circumstance should balk his desire.

Jumping quickly out of the hansom, he paid his fare, hurried up the steps and rattled the flap of the letter-box. This was the knocker of friends. All those who used the proper means were creditors, not answered until inspected carefully from behind lace curtains.

For a few moments, his heart beat tentatively. There was no sound, no light from within. Then came the quick tapping of high-heels. He took a breath. The door opened. He saw her face of amazement in the darkness.

"You!" she exclaimed. The door opened wider to her hand. "Come in."

He took off his hat and stepped in. His manner was strange. He knew it was strange; he understood the look of question in her eyes as she stared at him--it reflected the look in his own mind.

"Are you alone?" he asked.

She nodded her head.

"My aunt is staying with me," she explained, "but she's gone to bed. She's got my bedroom. The mater's gone to bed. I'm sleeping on the floor in the drawing-room. I was sitting there. Come in."

He followed her into the drawing-room. There was her bed upon the floor--a mattress, sheets and blanket. That was all.

"You're sleeping there?" he said.

She said--"hm" with a little jerk of the head, in the most natural way in the world. If he thought he knew what it was to be poor, he flattered himself. He had been without meals, but he had never slept on the floor.

"Isn't it hard?" he questioned. "Do you go to sleep at all?"

She laughed gently under her breath.

"Good heavens, yes! I'm used to it. But what have you come for?"

She sat down in a heap, like a journeyman tailor, upon her bed, and gazed up at him. At first, he did not know how to say it. Then he blurted it out.

"I want you to come back again to see me in Fetter Lane."

She smiled with pride. Her mind reached for its box of bricks. He had sent her away from Fetter Lane. That was all over--past--done with.

"That's rather unexpected--isn't it?"

"I can't help that," he exclaimed, with a moment of wildness.

"But after all you've said?"

"I can't help what I've said. It holds good no longer. I take it all back. It means nothing."

She knelt up quickly on her knees. Dignity comes often before humanity with a woman, but pity will always outride the two. Something had happened to him. He was in trouble. The old appeal he had once made to her rose out of the pity that she felt. She stretched up her hands to his shoulders.

"What's happened?" she asked--"tell me what's happened."

He dropped on to the mattress on the floor. He told her everything. He told her how far his ideals had fallen in those last few days. He stripped the whole of his mind for her to lash if she chose; he stripped it, like a child undressing for a whipping.

When he had finished, she sat back again in her former position. She stared into the empty grate.

"I wonder," said she--"I wonder does the man exist who can bear disappointment without becoming like that."

That was the only lash that fell from her. And she did not direct it upon him, but it whipped across the nakedness of his mind with a stinging blow. He winced under it. It made him long to be that man. Yet still, there was his desire; still there was the fear, that circumstance would balk him of his oblivion.

"Why do you say that?" he asked.

"Because, I thought you would be different," she said.

"I'm as human as the rest," said he. "I'm the crank, of course-- but I'm a human crank. Will you come back to me again?"

She rose to her knees again. She was trembling, but she took his hand in hers and gripped it hard to hide it from him.

"What will you say afterwards?" she asked gently. "What will you feel? You'll be full of remorse. You'll hate me. You'll hate yourself. What about your ideal?"

"I have none," he exclaimed blindly.

"I said that once," she whispered--"and you said I was wrong, that I had an ideal, that everybody had, only they lost sight of it."

He remembered all that. He remembered the reasoning of his mind. He knew it was true. He knew it was true even then.

"Now you've lost sight of yours," she continued. "But you'll see it again, you'll realise it again to-morrow, and then--heavens! How you'll hate me! How you'll hate yourself."

He stared at her. Were women as good, as fine as this? Was he the only vile thing in existence then? What would Jill think if she could see into the pit of his mind now? So low had he fallen that he thought it impossible to struggle upwards; so low, that it seemed he must touch the utmost depth before he could get the purchase to regain his feet. And if he touched the lowest, he might rise again, but it would not be so high as before.

Amber watched all the thoughts in his face. She had done her utmost. She could not do more. If he did not fight it out from this, then, what must be, must be.

Yet one more thing she could do. If she spoke of Venice. But why should she say it? It was his battle, not hers. She had given him every weapon to wage it but this. Why should she say it? The battle was against herself. Yet she answered to the best. There was her ideal as well, however unconscious it may have been.

"When are you going to Venice?" she asked hoarsely.

He told her how he had spent some of the money--more than a pound of it was gone.

She pulled out her purse, quickly, fiercely, feverishly.

"Then won't you be able to go?" she asked.

"Not for a while."

"Won't your mother be disappointed,--the little old white-haired lady?"

He tried to beat back the emotion in his throat, then felt something cold and hard in his hand. He looked down. It was a sovereign.

"You must take that," she said breathlessly. "Pay it back some other time and go--go to Venice to-morrow."

John looked full in her eyes.

"And you called yourself the fly in the amber," he said. Then he tightened her fingers round the coin--kissed them and walked to the door.

"I'll go to Venice," he said--"I'll go--somehow or other. I'll be the man who can bear things without becoming like that. You shan't be disappointed."

He came back again and seized her hand. Then he hurried out.

She listened to the door slamming. She heard his footsteps in the quiet street, then she dropped down on the mattress on the drawing-room floor.

"Oh, you fool!" she whispered under her breath. "Oh, you fool!"

But wisdom and folly, they are matters of environment. Behind it all, there was the most wonderful satisfaction in the world in saying--"Oh, you fool!"

BOOK III
THE CITY
CHAPTER XXIV
THE PALAZZO CAPELLO

They tell you--come to Venice by night; that then you will drift silently into the marvellous mystery of it all; that then you will feel the weight of the centuries in every shadow that lurks in the deep set doorways; that then you will realise the tragedies that have been played, the romances woven, and the dark deeds that have been done in the making of its history--all this, if you come to Venice by night.

They tell you, you will never see Venice as the tourist sees it, if you will but do this; that the impression of mystery will outlast the sight of the Philistines crowding in the Square of St. Mark's, will obliterate the picture of a fleet of gondolas tearing through the Grand Canal, led by a conductor shouting out the names of the Palaces as they pass. Your conception of the city of mystery will last for ever, so they tell you, if you do but come to Venice by night.

But there is another Venice than this, a Venice you see as you come to it in the early morning--a city of light and of air, a city of glittering water, of domes in gossamer that rise lightly above the surface, finding the sun, as bubbles that melt all the prisms of light into their liquid shells.

Come to Venice in the early morning and you will see a city bathed in a sea of light; for it is not only that the sun shines upon it, but that, like the white shoulders of a mermaid, glittering with the water drops as she rises out of the sea, this wonderful city is not illuminated only, but is drenched in light itself. It is no city of shadow and mysteries then. There are no dark water-ways, no deepening gloom beneath the bridges. In the early morning, it lies, as yet unwakened, blinking, flashing, burning--a rose opal, set clear against the sun.

Then the deepest shadow is in a tone of gold, the highest light in a mist of glittering silver. The domes of San Marco and Santa Maria della Salute are caught up in the brilliancy and melt shapelessly into the glow.

Come to Venice in the early morning and you will see a smelter's furnace into which has been cast the gold and silver from a boundless treasure hoard. You will see all that white and yellow metal running in molten streams of light; you will see the vibrating waves of air as the flames leap upward, curling and twisting to the very gates of heaven itself. You will see a city of gold and silver, of light and air all made liquid in one sea of brilliance, if you do but come to Venice in the early morning.

*   *   *   *   *

In the Grand Canal, just at the corner of the *Palazzo Babarigo*, there appears the entrance to one of those myriad little ways that shoot secretly away from the great, wide water street. Turning into this, the *Rio San Polo*, following its course under the bridges and taking the second turning on the left, an obedient gondolier will swing you round with one sweep of his long oar into the *Rio Marin*.

Being human, assuming your love of the beautiful, taking time also as his perquisite, he will probably choose more devious ways than this. But, everyone will tell you that, by the *Rio San Polo*, it is the shortest.

On each side of the *Rio Marin*, there runs a narrow little pathway. Here, the houses do not dip down to the water's edge, the space of light is wider, and the hurrying of the pedestrian on the footway seems to concentrate life for a moment and give it speech, in a place where everything is mute, where everything is still.

Idlers gather lazily on the bridges to watch the swaying gondolas as they pass beneath. Here, even the mystery you will find by night, is driven away. The sun, the broad stretch of heaven, no longer a ribbon-strip of blue tying together the house-tops, these combine to defy mystery in the *Rio Marin*. Rose trees and flowering bushes top the grey walls; lift up their colours against a cloudless sky and smile down to you of gardens concealed on the other side.

Towards the end of this little water-way, almost opposite the *Chiesa Tedeschi*, stands the *Palazzo Capello*, a broad and somewhat unbeautiful house, looking placidly down upon the quiet water. No great history is attached to it. No poet has ever written there, seated at its windows; no tragedy has been played that the guide books know of, no blood has been splashed against its walls. You will not find it mentioned in any of the descriptions of Venice, for it has no history to detain the ear; it bears no show of ornament without to attract the eye. Yet, with that pomp and vanity that breathed in Venice in the middle centuries, it was called--a palace--and only to those who know it from within, can this dignity of name seem justified.

A great, wide door divides the front of grey stone, up to which lead steps from the pathway--steps, in the crevices of which a patch of green lies here and there in a perfect harmony of contrast to the well-worn slabs. This door is always closed and, with no windows on either side, only the broad stretch of masonry, there is a stern appearance about the place, suggesting a prison or a barracks in its almost forbidding aspect. But when once that wide, wooden gate is opened, the absence of windows upon the ground floor is partly explained and the mind is caught in a breath of enchantment. It does not give entrance to a hall, but to an archway--an archway tunnelling under the house itself, at the end of which, through the lace-work of wonderful wrought-iron palings, you see the fairy-land of an old Italian garden, glittering in the sun.

The shadows that lie heavily under the archway only serve to intensify the brilliance of the light beyond. Colours are concentrated to the essence of themselves and the burst of sunshine, after the darkness, brings a haze, as when you see the air quivering over a furnace.

But, having gained entrance and passed that doorway, you are not yet within the house. On either side of this cool damp tunnel, making way to the right and left on the palace, which is divided into two houses, there are smaller archways cut into the wall. Taking that on your left, and before your eyes have grown accustomed to the confusion of lights and shadows, you might think it was a passage burrowing down into some secret corners of the earth. Your feet stumble, you feel your way, fingers touching the cold walls, suddenly realising that there are steps to mount, not to descend and, groping onwards, you reach another door confronting you impassably in the blackness.

There is a bell here, but it is by chance you find it--a long chain, like that at a postern gate, which depends from somewhere above your head. As you pull it, there is a clanging and a jangling quite close to your ear, shattering in a thousand little pieces the stillness that reigns all round.

After a moment or so, a small door opens within the bigger door, a curtain is pulled and, stepping through the tiny entrance for which your head must be bent low, you find yourself in a vast, big room--a room stretching from back to front of the whole house--a room that makes the meaning of the word palace seem justified a thousand times.

At either end are windows, so broad, so high, that the great stretch of this vast chamber, with its lofty ceiling, is flooded by one swift stream of light. Upon the polished floor of wood, the generous sunlight is splashed in daring brightness, throwing all near it into comparative shade, yet reflecting from the shining surface of the ground a glow that fills the air with a mist of light.

Along the walls of a dull, cool grey, big pictures are hung. Many there are, yet so spacious is the room, that they do not appear crowded; there is no suggestion of a well-stocked gallery. And on each side of the room two rich, warm-coloured curtains hang, concealing behind them silent, heavy, doors, deep set within the wall.

One of these, if you open it, will give you admittance to a tiny little room--so tiny, so small, that its smallness laughs at you, as for the moment it peers through the open space into the vast chamber beyond.

Close the door and the smallness seems natural enough then. For there, sitting perhaps over their afternoon tea, or their cups of coffee in the evening, chatting and gossiping as tho' they had just met to keep each other company, are two small figures; small because they are old--one, that of an old man, whose eyes are somewhat dimmed behind the high cheek bones and the shaggy eyebrows, the other, crumpled and creased like a silk dress that has lain long-folded in a camphor-scented drawer, the figure of a little old white-haired lady.

CHAPTER XXV
THE LETTER--VENICE

In the daily affairs of those two old people in the Palazzo Capello, there was one undeviating ceremony, performed with the regularity and precision of those mechanical figures that strike the great bell on the clock tower in the square of St. Mark's.

As the bells of the churches rang out the hour of ten at night, Claudina, the old dame who looked after all the wants of this worthy pair, entered the little room, carrying a large box in her hands.

Whatever their occupation may have been, whether they were playing at cribbage, or merely writing letters, up went their white heads together and one or the other would say--in Italian--"You don't mean to say it's ten o'clock, Claudina?"

And Claudina would bend her head, with a sudden jerk, like a nodding mandarin, her big earrings would swing violently in her ears, and she would plant the box down gently upon the table.

"Si, signora," she said--always in the same tone of voice, as though she had suddenly realised that her nod of the head was not quite as respectful as it ought to be.

One cannot describe this as a ceremony; but it was the prelude to all the serious business that followed. Claudina was the mace bearer. Her entrance with the wooden box was the heralding of the quaint little procession of incidents that followed.

It was an evening in July, in that self-same year which has so successfully hidden itself in the crevices of our calendar. The *jalousies* had not long been closed upon a sky of primrose, in which the stars were set like early drops of dew. Claudina had just brought in a letter by the post. It was half-past nine.

"A letter, signora," Claudina had said and, knowing quite well who the letter was from, she had not laid it down upon the table as ordinary letters were treated, but had given it directly into her mistress's hand.

If the old Italian servant knows curiosity, she does not show it. Claudina, once the letter was delivered, discreetly left the room. The moment the door had closed, there followed as pretty a play of courtesy as you might have wished to see.

The old gentleman laid down his book.

"It is from John?" he said quickly.

She nodded her head and passed it across to him. Had she rolled the world to his feet, it could not have been more generously done. And had it been the world, he could not have taken it more eagerly.

His finger was just trembling inside the flap of the envelope, when he read the address.

"Why--it's written to you, my dear," said he, slowly withdrawing his finger.

She smiled. She nodded her head again. It was addressed to her; but in the rightful order of things, it was really his turn. For some unknown reason, John had addressed the last two letters to her. He never did do that. He was always most scrupulously fair in this tacit understanding that he should address his letters alternately, first to his father, then to his mother. This was the only time he had broken the unwritten law. It was really not her letter at all. That was why she had passed it across at once to her husband. He would never have dreamed of asking for the letter out of his turn. His fingers often twitched while her poor hands fumbled with the envelope, but he had never moved an inch to take it, until, of her own accord, she had handed it to him.

Now--knowing that it was his turn, his hand had stretched out for it naturally the moment Claudina had closed the door, and she had as readily given it. But there was a secret exultation in the heart of her. John had addressed it to her. There was no getting away from that.

For a moment, the old gentleman sat fingering it in dubious hesitation. Then he passed it back again.

"It's your letter, my dear," he said. "You open it." And picking up his book, he pretended to go on reading. Of course he did not see a single word on the page before him. Every sense in his body was strained to catch the sound of the tearing paper as she broke open the envelope. But there was no sound at all. Another moment of silence and she was bending over him from behind his chair, her arms round his neck and the letter held before his eyes.

"We'll open it together," she said.

It was her way of letting him do it without knowing that he had given way. To be sure, it was his finger that finally broke the flap of the envelope; but then, he retained all the dignity of the sacrifice. And so, as she leant over his shoulder, they read it together, with little exclamations of delight, little interruptions of pleasure, that need a heart for their purer translation, and cannot be written here because of that great gulf which is fixed behind the mind and the pen--because of that greater gulf which lies between the word and the eye that reads it.

"*My dearest----*"

Just those two words beginning; but they were almost the entire letter to her. They set her little brown eyes alight, her heart beating quickly behind the stiff bodice.

"*I have left writing to you until the last moment for fear I should be unable to come on the day that you were expecting me. But it is all right. I am starting to-morrow morning, and shall be with you the usual time the day following, just about sunset. I can't tell you how glad I shall be to get away from here. You know what London can be like in July, and I suppose I want a change as well. I can't work these days at all--but I don't mean to worry you. I expect I am depressed and want different air in my lungs. I shall go up to the bows of the steamer crossing to-morrow, stand there with my mouth open, and get it forced down my throat like a dose.*

"*God bless you, dearest. Give my love to father, but don't tell him I can't work. I know he understands it well enough, but I believe it depresses him as much as it does me.*"

He looked up simply into her face as he handed back the paper.

"You see, I wasn't meant to read it," he said quietly.

Impulsively, she put her arm round his neck. She knew so well how that had hurt. There had been letters sometimes that she was not meant to see. Of course, she had seen them; but that touch of intimacy which, when you are a lover, or a mother, makes letters such wonderful living things, had been utterly taken from them. They had contained loving messages to her. But the writing itself, that had been meant for another eye to read.

"But it was only because he was thoughtful about you," she whispered--"not because he didn't want you to see. He'll tell you himself quickly enough that he can't work when he comes. You see if he doesn't. He can't keep those sort of things to himself. He can do it in a letter, because he thinks he ought to. But he won't be here five minutes before he's telling you that he can't write a line. And think! He'll be here the day after to-morrow. Oh--he is such a dear boy! Isn't he? Isn't he the dearest boy two old people ever had in the world?"

So she charmed the smile back into his eyes; never pausing until she saw that passing look of pain vanish completely out of sight. And so Claudina found them, as she had often found them before, poring once again over the letter as she brought in the big box.

Up went the two white heads in amazement and concern.

"You don't mean to say it's ten o'clock, Claudina?"

For to old people, you know, the hours pass very quickly; they are scarcely awake, before they are again being put to bed. Time hurries by them with such quiet feet, stepping lightly on the tips of its toes lest it should disturb those peaceful last moments which God gives to the people who are old.

Claudina laid down the big box upon the table. She nodded her head; her earrings shook.

"Si, Signora," she replied, as always.

The little old white-haired lady crumpled the letter into her dress; concealed it behind the stiff black bodice. Then they both stood to their feet, and the procession, of which Claudina was the herald, began.

First of all the big wooden box was opened, and out of it were taken numbers and numbers of little white linen bags of all shapes and sizes. White? Well, they were white once, but long obedience to the service for which they were required had turned their white to grey.

Each one of them was numbered, the number stitched in thread upon the outside; each one of them had been made to fit some separate little ornament in the room, to wrap it up, to keep the dust from it through the night--a night-cap for it, in fact. At ten o'clock the ornaments were put to bed; after the ornaments, then these two old people--but first of all their treasures. They stood by, watching Claudina tuck them all up, one by one, and it gave them that delicious sensation which only old people and young children know anything about--the sensation that they are sitting up late that others are going to bed before them.

Of course they never knew they had that sensation; they were not aware of it for a moment. But you might have known by the way they turned and smiled at each other when the big Dresden-china shepherdess was popped into her bag, you might have known that in the hearts of them, that was what they felt.

This evening in particular, their smiles were more radiant than ever. The old lady forgot to make her little exclamations of terror when Claudina could not get the night-cap over the head of the Dresden-china shepherdess, and was in danger of dropping them both together; the old gentleman forgot his quiet--"Be careful, Claudina--be careful." For whenever his wife was very excited, it always made him realise that he was very quiet, very self-possessed. But they felt none of their usual anxiety on this evening in July. In two days--in less--John would be with them. They had waited a whole year for this moment and a whole year, however quickly the separate moments may pass, is a long, long time to old people.

"There is one thing," the old gentleman said, presently, as the last ornaments were being ranged upon the table, standing in readiness for their nightcaps to go on. "There is one thing I don't quite know about."

She slipped her arm into his and asked in a whisper what it was. There was no need to talk in a whisper, for Claudina did not know a word of English; but she guessed he was going to say something concerning John and about him, she nearly always spoke in a whisper.

"It's the--the shop," he replied--"I--I don't like to tell John."

"Oh--but why not?" She clung a little closer to him.

"It isn't that I don't think he would understand--but it's just like that sentence in his letter about me. I feel it would hurt him if he thought I couldn't sell my pictures any more. I believe he would blame himself and think he ought to be giving us money, if he knew that I had had to start this curio shop to make things meet more comfortably."

She nodded her head wisely. She would have been all for telling her son everything. But when he mentioned the fact of John thinking he ought to support them, and when she considered how John would need every penny that he earned to support the woman whom she longed for him to make his wife--it was a different matter. She quite agreed. It was better that John should be told nothing.

"You don't think he'll find out--do you?" she said, and her eyes looked startled at the thought.

"No--no--I shouldn't think so. It isn't as if I had to be there every day. Foscari looks after it quite well. Though I'm always afraid he'll sell the very things I can't bear to part with. He sold the old brass Jewish lamp the other day, and I wouldn't have parted with it for worlds. But I dare say if I tell him to be careful--I dare say----"

It was rather sad, this curio shop. It would have been very sad if his wife had not appreciated the need for it; if she had not made it easier by telling him how brave he was, by sharing with him the sense of shame he felt when it became apparent that his pictures were no longer saleable.

For when he had reached the age of seventy-three, that was what they had told him. If he had not been a landscape painter, it might have been different; but at seventy-three, when one's heart is weak, it is not possible, it is not wise, to go far afield, to tramp the mountains as once he had done, in search of subjects new. So, he had been compelled to stay at home, to try and paint from memory the pictures that lay heaped within his mind. Then it was that they began to tell him that they could not sell his work; then he came to find that there must be other means of support if they were not to appeal to John for aid. And so, having a collection of treasures such as artists find, picked up from all the odd corners of Europe, he bethought him of a curio shop and, finding a little place to let at a quiet corner in the *Merceria*, he took it, called it--The Treasure Shop--and painting the name in a quaint old sign which he hung outside, obliterated his identity from the public eye.

For weeks beforehand, they had discussed this plan. Some of their own treasures, of course, would have to be sacrificed; in fact, Claudina carried many little grey night-caps away with her in the wooden box--night-caps that no longer had Dresden heads to fit them. But the money they were going to make out of the Treasure Shop would make up for all these heart-rending sacrifices. They would even be able to send John little presents now and then. There was nothing like a curio-shop for minting money, especially if the curios were really genuine, as were theirs.

But that was the very rub of it. When he came to open the shop, the old gentleman found it was the very genuineness of the things he had to sell that made it impossible for him to part with them. He loved them too well. And even the most ignorant collectors, British sires with check-cloth caps and heavy ulsters, old ladies with guide books in one hand and cornucopias of maze for the pigeons in the other, even they seemed to pitch upon the very things he loved the most.

He asked exorbitant prices to try and save his treasures from their clutches and mostly this method succeeded; but sometimes they were fools enough to put the money down. For there was one thing he could never do; he could not belittle the thing that he loved. If it was good, if it was genuine, if it really was old, he had to say so despite himself. Enthusiasm would let him do no otherwise. But then, when he had said all he could in its praise, he would ask so immense a sum that the majority of would-be purchasers left the shop as if he had insulted them.

So it was that the Treasure Shop did not fulfil all the expectations they had had of it. It made just enough money for their wants; but that was all.

And now came the question as to whether they should let John know of it. Long into the night they discussed the question, their two white heads lying side by side on the pillows, their voices whispering in the darkness.

"And yet--I believe he would understand," said the little old lady on her side--"he's such a dear, good boy, I'm sure he would understand."

"I don't know--I don't know," replied the old gentleman dubiously--"It will be bad enough when he sees my last pictures. No--no--I don't think I'll tell him. Foscari can look after the place. I need hardly be there at all while he's with us."

And then, making the sign of the cross upon each other's foreheads--saying--"God bless you"--as they had done every night their whole lives long, they fell asleep.

CHAPTER XXVI
THE RETURN--VENICE

It was sunset when John arrived. The gondolas were riding on a sea of rose; the houses were standing, quietly, silently, as you will see cattle herd, knee-deep in the burning water. Here and there in the distance, the fiery sun found its reflection in some obscure window, and burnt there in a glowing flame of light. Then it was a city of rose and pink, of mauve and blue and grey, one shading into the other in a texture so delicate, so fine that the very threads of it could not be followed in their change.

John took a deep breath as he stepped into his gondola. It needed such colour as this to wash out the blackness of that night in London. It needed such stillness and such quiet to soothe the rancour of his bitterness; for the stillness of Venice is the hushed stillness of a church, where all anger is drugged to sleep and only the sorrow that one learns of can hold against the spell and keeps its eyes awake.

Now, in the desolation of his mind, John was learning, of the things that have true value and of those which have none. It is not an easy lesson to acquire, for the sacrifice of pre-conceived ideas can only be accomplished on the altar of bitterness and only the burning of despair can reduce them to the ashes in which lies the truth concealed.

Having deposited his belongings in his rooms in the *Rio della Sacchere*, where he always stayed, he set off on foot by the narrow little pathways to the *Palazzo Capello*.

That was always a moment in John's life when, upon his arrival every year, he first opened the big gate that closed on to the *fondamenta*. It was always a moment to be remembered when first he beheld, from beneath the archway, the glow of the flaming sunset in that old Italian garden, framed in the lace-worked trellises of iron.

Life had these moments. They are worth all the treasure of the Indies. The mind of a man is never so possessed of wealth as when he comes upon them; for in such moments as these, his emotions are wings which no sun of vaunted ambition can melt; in such moments as these, he touches the very feet of God.

Closing the big door behind him, John stood for a moment in contemplation. The great disc of the sun had just sunk down behind the cypress trees. Their deep black forms were edged with a bright thread of gold. Everything in that old garden was silhouetted against the glowing embers of the sunset, and every bush and every shrub was rimmed with a halo of light.

This was the last moment of his warfare. Had his ideal not lifted again before the sight of such magnificence as this, it would inevitably have been the moment of defeat. Through the blackness of the tunnel, it is inviolably decreed that a man must pass before he shall reach the ultimate light; but if, when that journey is accomplished, the sight of beauty, which is only the symbol of the good, if that does not touch him and, with a beckoning hand, raise his mind into the mystery of the infinite, then that immersion in the darkness has not cleansed his soul. He has been tainted with it. It clings like a mist about his eyes, blurring all vision. He has been weighed in the balance that depends from the nerveless hand of Fate, and has been found--wanting.

But as a bird soars, freed from the cage that held it to earth, John's mind rose triumphantly. Acknowledging all the credit that was Amber's due--and but for her, he could not have seen the true beauty, the beauty of symbolism, in that sunset there--he yet had passed unscathed from the depth of the shadow into the heart of the light.

Here was a moment such as they would have known had the story of the City of Beautiful Nonsense come true. Here was a moment when they would have stood, hands touching, hearts beating, seeing God. And yet, though she was hundreds of miles from him then, John's mind had so lifted above the bitterness of despair, had so outstripped the haunting cries of his body, that he could conjure Jill's presence to his side and, in an ecstasy of faith, believe her with him, seeing the beauty that he saw; there.

In the text-books of science, they have no other name for this than hysteria; but in those unwritten volumes--pages unhampered by the deceptive sight of words--a name is given to such moments as these which we have not the eyes to read, nor the simplicity of heart to understand.

Forcing back the rush of tears to his eyes, John passed under the little archway in the wall, mounted the dark stone steps, dragged down the chain, and with the clanging of the heavy bell was brought back, tumbling to reality.

With a rattling of the rings, the heavy curtain was pulled, the little door was thrown open. The next moment, he was gripping Claudina's hand--shaking it till her earrings swung violently to and fro.

Then came his father, the old white-haired gentleman, looking so old to have so young a son.

They just held hands, gazing straight, deep down into each other's eyes.

"God bless you, my boy," said the old man jauntily. He stood with his back to the light. He would not for the world have shown that his eyes were filled with tears. Old men, like little boys, think it babyish to cry--perhaps it is partly because the tears rise so easily.

And last of all, walking slowly, because her paralysis had affected her whole body, as well as rendering powerless her hands, came the little old white-haired lady. There was no attempt from her to hide the tears. They were mixed up in a confusion of happiness with smiles and with laughter in the most charming way in the world.

She just held open her thin, frail arms, and there John buried himself, whispering over and over again in her ear--

"My dearest--my dearest--my dearest----"

And who could blame him if Jill were there still in his mind. There comes a time when a man loves his mother because she is a woman, just as the woman he loves. There comes a time when a mother loves her son, because he is a man just as the man she has loved.

CHAPTER XXVII
THE TRUE MOTHER

It was not that evening that she plied her questions, this gentle, white-haired old lady. That first evening of his arrival, there was John's work to talk of, the success of his last book to discuss, the opinions upon his criticisms to lay down. The old gentleman had decided views upon such matters as these. He talked affirmatively with wise nods of the head, and the bright brown eyes of his wife followed all his gesticulations with silent approval. She nodded her head too. All these things he was saying then, he had said before over and over again to her. Yet they every one of them seemed new when he once more repeated them to John.

This critic had not understood what he had been writing about; that critic had hit the matter straight on the head. This one perhaps was a little too profuse in his praise; that one had struck a note of personal animosity which was a disgrace to the paper for which he wrote.

"Do you know the man who wrote that, John?" he asked in a burst of righteous anger.

John smiled at his father's enthusiasm. One is so much wiser when one is young--one is so much younger when one is old.

"I know him by sight," he said--"we've never met. But he always reviews me like that. I suppose I irritate him."

His mother felt gently for his hand. Without looking down, he found the withered fingers in his.

"How could you irritate him, my darling?" she asked. It seemed an impossibility to her.

"Well--there are always some people whom we irritate by being alive, my dearest. I'm not the only one who annoys him. I expect he annoys himself."

"Ah, yes!" The old gentleman brought down his fist emphatically upon the arm of his chair--"But he should keep these personal feelings out of his work. And yet--I suppose this kind of thing will always exist. Oh--if it only pleased the Lord that His people should be gentlemen!"

So his father talked, giving forth all the enthusiasm of his opinions which for so long had been stored up in the secret of his heart.

It was no longer his own work that interested him; for whatever contempt the artist may have for his wage, he knows his day is past when the public will no longer pay him for his labour. All the heart of him now, was centred in John. It was John who would express those things his own fingers had failed to touch. He had seen it exultantly in many a line, in many a phrase which this last book had contained; for though the mind which had conceived it was a new mind, the mind of another generation than his own, yet it was the upward growth from the thoughts he had cherished, a higher understanding of the very ideas that he had held. He, Thomas Grey, the artist, was living again in John Grey, the writer, the journalist, the driver of the pen. In the mind of his son, was the resurrection of his own intellect, the rejuvenescence of his own powers, the vital link between him, passing into the dust, and those things which are eternal.

It was not until John had been there two or three days, that his mother found her opportunity.

The old gentleman had gone to the *Merceria* to look after the Treasure Shop. Foscari, it seemed, had been selling some more of his beloved curios. A packet of money had been sent to him the evening before for a set of three Empire fans, treasures he had bought in Paris twenty years before. With a smothered sigh, the little old lady had consented to their going to the *Merceria*. Only to make a show, he had promised her that. They should never be purchased by anyone, and he put such a price upon them as would frighten the passing tourist out of his wits. It was like Foscari to find a man who was rich enough and fool enough to buy them. With his heart thumping and, for the first time in his life, not quite being able to look John in the eyes, he had made some excuse--a picture to be framed--and gone out, leaving them alone.

This was the very moment John had dreaded. He knew that those bright brown eyes had been reading the deepest corners of his heart, had only been biding their time until such moment as this. He had felt them following him wherever he went; had realised that into everything he did, they were reading the hidden despair of his mind with an intuition so sure, so unerring, that it would be quite useless for him to endeavour to hide anything from her.

And now, at last they were alone. The sun was burning in through the windows into the little room. The old garden below was pale in the heat of it.

For a little while, he stood there at the window in nervous suspense, straining to think of things to say which might distract her mind from that subject which he knew to be uppermost in her thoughts. And all the time his face was turned away as he gazed down on to the old garden, he could still feel her eyes watching him, until at last the growing anticipation that she would break the silence with a question to which he could not reply, drove him blindly to speak.

He talked about his father's pictures; tried in vain to discover whether he had sold enough for their wants, whether the orders he had received were as numerous, whether his strength permitted him to carry them all out. He talked about the thousand things that must have happened, the thousand things they must have done since last he was with them. And everything he said, she answered gently, disregarding all opportunity to force the conversation to the subject upon which her heart was set. But in her eyes, there was a mute, a patient look of appeal.

The true mother is the last woman in the world to beg for confidence. She must win it; then it comes from the heart. In John's silence on that one subject that was so near as to be one with the very centre of her being, it was as though she had lost the power of prayer in that moment of her life when she must need it most.

At last she could bear it no longer. It could not be want of confidence in her, she told herself. He was hurt. Some circumstance, some unhappiness had stung him to silence. Instinctively, she could feel the pain of it. Her heart ached. She knew his must be aching too.

"John," she said at length and she laid both those poor withered hands in his--"John--you're unhappy."

He tried to meet her eyes; but they were too bright; they saw too keenly, and his own fell. The next moment, with straining powerless efforts, she had drawn him on to his knees beside her chair, his head was buried in her lap and her hands were gently stroking his hair in a swift, soothing motion.

"You can tell me everything," she whispered; and oh, the terrible things that fond heart of hers imagined! Terrible things they seemed to her, but they would have brought a smile into John's face despite himself, had he heard them. "You can tell me everything," she whispered again.

"There's nothing to tell, dearest," he replied.

For there was nothing to tell; nothing that she would understand. The pain of his losing Jill, would only become her pain as well, and could she ever judge rightly of Jill's marriage with another man, if she knew? She would only take his side. That dear, good, gentle heart of hers was only capable of judging of things in his favour. She would form an utterly false opinion and, he could not bear that. Much as he needed sympathy, the want of it was better than misunderstanding.

"There's nothing to tell," he repeated.

Still she stroked his head. There was not even one thought of impatience in the touch of her fingers. It may be said without fear or hesitation that a mother at least knows her own child; and this is the way with children when they are in trouble. They will assure you there is nothing to tell. She did not despair at that. For as with John asking his question of Jill in Kensington Gardens, so she asked, because she knew.

"Isn't it about the Lady of St. Joseph?" she said presently. "Isn't that why you're unhappy?"

He rose slowly to his feet. She watched him as he moved aimlessly to the window. It was a moment of suspense. Then he would tell her, then at that moment, or he would close the book and she would not see one figure that was traced so indelibly upon its pages. She held her breath as she watched him. Her hands assumed unconsciously a pathetic gesture of appeal. If she spoke then, it might alter his decision; so she said nothing. Only her eyes begged mutely for his confidence.

Oh--it is impossible of estimate, the worlds, the weight of things infinite, that swung, a torturing balance, in the mind of the little old white-haired lady then. However much emotion may bring dreams of it to the mind of a man, his passion is not the great expression by which he is to be judged; is the woman who loves. It is the man who is loved. He may believe a thousand times that he knows well of the matter; but the great heart, the patience, the forbearance, these are all the woman's and, from such are those little children who are of the kingdom of heaven.

If these qualities belonged to the man, if John had possessed them, he could not have resisted her tender desire for confidence. But when the heart of a man is hurt, he binds his wounds with pride and it is of pride, when one loves, that love knows nothing.

Turning round from the window, John met his mother's eyes.

"There's nothing to tell, dear," he said bitterly. "Don't ask me--there's nothing to tell."

Her hands dropped their pathetic gesture. She laid them quietly in her lap. If the suffering of pain can be reproach, and perhaps that is the only reproach God knows of in us humans, then, there it was in her eyes. John saw it and he did not need for understanding to answer to the silence of its cry. In a moment he was by her side again, his arms thrown impulsively about her neck, his lips kissing the soft, wrinkled cheek. What did it matter how he disarranged the little lace cap set so daintily on her head, or how disordered he made her appearance in his sudden emotion? Nothing mattered so long as he told her everything.

"Don't think I'm unkind, little mother. I can't talk about it--that's all. Besides--there's nothing--absolutely nothing to say. I don't suppose I shall ever see her again. We were just friends, that's all--only friends."

Even this was more than he could bear to say. He stood up again quickly to force back the tears that were swelling in his throat. Tears do not become a man. It is the most reasonable, the most natural thing in the world that he should abominate them, and so he seldom, if ever, knows the wonderful moment it is in the life of a woman when he cries like a baby on her shoulder. It is only right that it should be so. Women know their power well enough as it is. And in such a moment as this, they realise their absolute omnipotence.

And this is just why nature decrees that it is weak, that it is foolish for a man to shed tears in the presence of a woman. Undoubtedly nature is right.

Before they had well risen to his eyes, John had left the room. In the shadows of the archway beneath the house, he was brushing them roughly from his cheek while upstairs the gentle old lady sat just where he had left her, thinking of the thousands of reasons why he would never see the lady of St. Joseph again.

She was going away. She did not love him. They had quarrelled. After an hour's contemplation, she decided upon the last. They had quarrelled.

Then she set straight her cap.

CHAPTER XXVIII
THE TREASURE SHOP

At a quiet corner in the *Merceria*, stood the Treasure Shop. In every respect it had all the features which these little warehouses of the world's curiosities usually present. Long chains of old copper vessels hung down, on each side of the doorway, reaching almost to the ground. Old brass braziers and incense burners stood on the pavement outside and, in the window, lay the oddest, the wildest assortment of those objects of antiquity--brass candlesticks, old fans, hour-glasses, gondola lamps, every conceivable thing which the dust of Time has enhanced in value in the eyes of a sentimental public.

At the back of the window were hung silk stuffs and satin, rich old brocades and pieces of tapestry--just that dull, burnished background which gives a flavour of age as though with the faint scent of must and decay that can be detected in its withering threads.

All these materials, hanging there, shut out the light from the shop inside. Across the doorstep, the sun shone brilliantly, but, as though there were some hand forbidding it, it advanced no further. Within the shop, was all the deepest of shadow--shadow like heavy velvet from which permeated this dry and dusty odour of a vanished multitude of years.

The Treasure Shop was a most apt name for it. In that uncertain light within, you could just imagine that your fingers, idly fumbling amongst the numberless objects, might chance upon a jewelled casket holding the sacred dust of the heart of some Roman Emperor or the lock of some dead queen's hair.

Atmosphere has all the wizardry of a necromancer. In this dim, faded light, in this faint, musty smell of age, the newest clay out of a living potter's hands would take upon itself the halo of romance. The touch of dead fingers would cling to it, the scent of forgotten rose leaves out of gardens now long deserted would hover about the scarce cold clay. And out of the sunshine, stepping into this subtle atmospheric spell, the eyes of all but those who know its magic are wrapt in a web of illusion; the Present slips from them as a cloak from the willing shoulders; they are touching the Past.

Just such a place was the Treasure Shop. Its atmosphere was all this and more. Sitting there on a stool behind his heaped-up counter, in the midst of this chaos of years, the old gentleman was no longer a simple painter of landscape, but an old eccentric, whose every look and every gesture were begotten of his strange and mysterious acquaintance with the Past.

It came to be known of him that he was loth to part with his wares. It came to be told of him in the hotels that he was a strange old man who had lived so long in his musty environment of dead people's belongings that he could not bring himself to sell them; as though the spirits of those departed owners abode with him as well, and laid their cold hands upon his heart whenever he would try to sell the treasures they once had cherished.

And all this was the necromancy of the atmosphere in that little curio shop in the *Merceria*. But to us, who know all about it, whose eyes are not blinded with the glamour of illusion, there is little or nothing of the eccentric about Thomas Grey.

It is not eccentric to have a heart--it is the most common possession of humanity. It is not eccentric to treasure those things which are our own, which have shared life with us, which have become a part of ourselves; it is not eccentric to treasure them more than the simpler necessities of existence. We all of us do that, though fear of the accusation of sentimentality will not often allow us to admit it. It is not eccentric to put away one's pride, to take a lower seat at the guest's table in order that those we love shall have a higher place in the eyes of the company. We all would do that also, if we obeyed the gentle voice that speaks within everyone of us.

But if by chance this judgment is all at fault; if by chance it is eccentric to do these things, then this was the eccentricity of that white-haired old gentleman--Thomas Grey.

Whenever a customer--and ninety per cent. of them were tourists--came into the shop, he treated them with undisguised suspicion. They had a way of hitting upon those very things which he valued most--those very things which he only meant to be on show in his little window.

Of course, when they selected something which he had only recently acquired, his manner was courtesy itself. He could not say very much in its favour, but then, the price was proportionately small. Under circumstances such as these, they found him charming. But if they happened to cast their eyes upon that Dresden-china figure which stood so boldly in the fore-front of the window; if by hazard they coveted the set of old ivory chess men, oh, you should have seen the frown that crossed his forehead then! It was quite ominous.

"Well--that is very expensive," he always said and made no offer to remove it from its place.

And sometimes they replied----

"Oh, yes--I expect so. I didn't think it would be cheap. It's so beautiful, isn't it? Of course--really--really old."

And it was so hard to withstand the flattery of that. A smile of pleasure would lurk for a moment about his eyes. He would lean forward through the dark curtains of brocades and tapestries and reach it down for inspection.

"It is," he would say in the gratified tone of the true collector--"It is the most perfect specimen I have ever seen. You see the work here--this glaze, that colour----" and in a moment, before he was aware of what he was doing, he would be pointing out its merits with a quivering finger of pride.

"Oh, yes--I think I must have it," the customer would suddenly say--"I can't miss the opportunity. It would go so well with the things in my collection."

Then the old gentleman realised his folly. Then the frown returned, redoubled in its forbidding scowl. He began putting the Dresden figure back again in the window from whence it had come.

"But I said I'd take it," the customer would exclaim more eager than ever for its possession.

"Yes--yes--I know--but the price is--well it's prohibitive. I want seventy-five pounds for that figure."

"Seventy-five!"

"Yes--I can't take anything less."

"Oh----" and a look of disappointment and dismay.

"You don't want it?" he would ask eagerly.

"No--I can't pay as much as that."

Then the smile would creep back again into his eyes.

"Of course--it's a beautiful thing," he would say clumsily--"a beautiful thing."

And when he went home, he would tell the little old white-haired lady how much it had been admired, and they would call back to memory the day when they had bought it--so long ago that it seemed as though they were quite young people then.

So it fell out that this old gentleman of the curio shop in the *Merceria* came to be known for his seeming eccentricities. People talked of him. They told amusing stories of his strange methods of doing business.

"Do you know the Treasure Shop in the *Merceria*," they said over the dinner tables in London when they wanted to show how intimately they knew their Europe. "The old man who owns that--there's a character for you!" They even grew to making up anecdotes about him, to show how keenly observant they were when abroad. Everyone, even Smelfungus and Mundungus, would be thought sentimental travellers if they could.

It was the most natural coincidence in the world then, that John, strolling aimlessly in the arcades of the Square of St. Mark's that morning after he had left his mother, should overhear a conversation in which the eccentric old gentleman in the *Merceria* was introduced.

Outside Lavena's two women were taking coffee, as all well-cultured travellers do.

"--my shopping in Kensington----" he heard one of them say, concluding some reference to a topic which they were discussing.

John took a table near by. It is inevitable with some people to talk of Kensington and Herne Hill when abroad. John blessed them for it, nevertheless. There was that sound in the word to him then, which was worth a vision of all the cities of Europe.

He ordered his cup of coffee and listened eagerly for more. But that was the last they said of Kensington. The lady flitted off to other topics. She spoke to her friend of the curio shop in the *Merceria*.

Did she know the place? Well, of course not, if she had not been to Venice before. It was called the Treasure Shop. She had found it out for herself. But, then, it always was her object, when abroad, to become intimate with the life of the city in which she happened to be staying. It was the only way to know places. Sightseeing was absolutely waste of time. And this old gentleman was really a character--so unbusiness-like--so typically Italian! Of course, he spoke English perfectly--but, then, foreigners always do. No--she could not speak Italian fluently--make herself understood at table, and all that sort of thing--anyhow, enough to get along. But, to go back to the old gentleman in the Treasure Shop, she ought to go and see him before she left Venice. She was going early the next week? Oh--then, she ought to go that morning. He was such a delightful personality. So fond of the curios in his shop that he could scarcely be persuaded to part with them. There was one thing in particular, a Dresden figure, which he had in the front of the window. He would not part with that to anyone. Well--asked such a price for it that, of course, no one bought it.

But would it not be rather amusing if someone did actually agree to pay the price--not really, of course, only in fun, restoring it the next day, but just to see how he would take it? Was she really going next week? Then why not go and see the Treasure Shop at once? She would? Oh--that was quite splendid!

And off they went, John following quietly at their heels. This old Italian who could not bear to part with his wares because he loved them so much, there was something pathetic in that; something that appealed to John's sense of the colour in life. This was a little incident of faded brown, that dull, warm tint of a late October day when life is beginning to shed its withering leaves, when the trees, with that network of bare, stripped branches, are just putting on their faded lace. However unsympathetic had been the telling, he had seen the colour of it all with his own eyes. He followed them eagerly, anxious to behold this old Italian gentleman for himself, to confirm his own judgment of the pathos of it all.

Letting them enter first, for he had no desire to listen to their dealings, he took his position outside the window, intending to wait till they came out.

There was the Dresden figure the lady had mentioned. Ah! No wonder that he asked a large price for it! They had one just like that at the *Palazzo Capello*. His father had often said that if he could get a pair of them, they would be almost priceless. Supposing he bought it for his father? Would it be cruel to the old gentleman inside? Perhaps, if he knew that it was to make a pair, he would be more reconciled to its loss.

John waited patiently, gazing about him until the ladies should come out and leave the field free for him to make his study--his study in a colour of brown.

Presently the draperies in the back of the window were pulled aside. An old man leaned forward, hands trembling in the strain of his position, reaching for the Dresden figure. John bit on the exclamation that rose to his lips.

It was his father! Had he seen him? No! He slipped back again into the darkness of the shop and the brocades and the tapestries fell together once more into their place as though nothing had happened.

What did it mean? Was it true? With an effort, he held back from his inclination to rush into the shop, making sure of the reality of what he had seen. If it were true, then he knew that his father had not meant him to know. If it were true, he knew what the pain of such a meeting would be.

Crossing to the opposite side of the street, he tried to peer in through the shop door; but there was that clear-cut ray of sunshine on the step, barring the entrance. Only vaguely, like dim, black shadows on a deep web of gloom, could he see the moving figures of the two ladies who had entered. On an impulse, he turned into the magazzino by which he was standing.

Who was the owner of the curio shop on the other side? They did not know. What was his name? They could not say? Had he been there long? Not so very long. About a year. He was an Englishman, but he spoke Italian. He lived in Venice. They had heard some say in the *Rio Marin*. He was not used to the trade. It was quite true that he did not like to sell his things. They had been told he was a painter--but that was only what people said.

That was sufficient. They needed to say no more. This answered the questions that John had put that morning to his mother. His father could no longer sell his pictures. In a rush of light, he saw the whole story, far more pathetic to him than he had imagined with his study in brown.

One by one, they were selling the treasures they had collected. Now, he understood the meaning of those empty night-caps which Claudina carried away with her every evening. They said the things were broken; they had said it with nervous little glances at each other and then at Claudina. At the time, he had read those glances to mean that it was Claudina who had broken them. But no--it was not Claudina. This was the work of the heavy, the ruthless hand of cruel circumstance in which the frailest china and the sternest metal can be crushed into the dust of destruction.

In a moment, as it was all made clear, John found the tears smarting in his eyes. As he stood there in the little shop opposite, he painted the whole picture with rapid strokes of the imagination.

The day had come when his father could no longer sell his pictures. Then the two white heads had nodded together of an evening before Claudina came in with the night-caps. More emphatically than ever, they had exclaimed--"You don't mean to say it's ten o'clock, Claudina?" And Claudina, laying the box on the table, beginning to take out the night-caps and place forth the treasures before she tucked them up, would vouchsafe the answering nod of her head. At last, one evening, watching the Dresden figure being put to bed, his father had thought of the way out of the difficulty.

They had not decided upon it at once. Such determinations as these come from the head alone and have to pass before a stern tribunal of the heart before license is given them. He could just imagine how bitter a tribunal that had been; how inflexibly those two brave hearts had sat in judgment upon so hard a matter; how reluctantly in the end they had given their consent.

Then, with the moment once passed, the license once granted, John could see them so vividly, questioning whether they should tell him, their decision that it would not be wise, his father fearing that it would lessen his esteem, his mother dreading that he would feel called upon to help them. Finally, that first day, when the Treasure Shop had been opened and his father, the artist, the man of temperament, with all the finest perceptions and sensibilities that human nature possesses, had gone to business.

So truly he could see the moment of his departure. Nothing had been said. He had just taken the little old white-haired lady in his arms and kissed her. That was all. It might have been that he was merely going out, as he had quietly said that morning, to see about the framing of a picture. No one would ever have thought that he was about to pass through the ordeal of becoming a shop-keeper, because, in his old age he had failed as an artist.

All this, incident by incident, he painted, a sequence of pictures in his mind.

Presently the curtains in the shop-window stirred again. John's eyes steadied, his lips parted as he held his breath. The Dresden figure appeared, like a marionet making its bow to the public. Then followed the head and shoulders of his father. There was a smile on his face, a glow of genial satisfaction. They had not bought it. The price had been too much. That little Dresden figure, playing upon its lute, decoyed many a customer into the Treasure Shop, with its living tunes; but like a will-o'-the-wisp, it always evaded them. Back it danced again into the fore-front of the window where the old ivory chess-men stood stolidly listening to its music of enchantment. You might almost have seen them nodding their heads in approval.

John felt a lump rise quickly in his throat. He knew just what his father was feeling; he knew just what was in his mind. He realised all his sense of relief when the Dresden figure made its reappearance. If it had not come back into the window, he could not have restrained his desire to march into the shop and repeat every word of the conversation to which he had listened.

But it was safe once more and, with a breath of satisfaction, he moved away towards the *Rialto*, his head hanging as he walked.

That afternoon at tea, with the little cups that had no handles, he made no comment on his father's absence. The little old white-haired lady was trembling that he would ask, but he said not a word.

Only that evening, after Claudina had come in for her ceremony and he was saying good-night, he put both hands on his father's shoulders and, impulsively drawing him forward, kissed his forehead. Then he left the room.

The two old people sat staring at each other after he had gone. What did it mean? Why had he done it?

"Why, he hasn't kissed you since he was eight years old," said his mother.

The old gentleman shook his head thoughtfully--"No--I can't understand it. Don't you remember that first evening he refused, when I bent down to kiss him and he blushed, drew back a little and held out his hand?"

She smiled.

"You were hurt about it at first," she reminded him.

"Yes--but then when you said--'John's thinking about becoming a man'--of course, it seemed natural enough then. And he's never done it since--till now. I wonder why."

The old gentleman went to bed very, very silent that night, and long after Claudina had taken away the lamp, he could feel John's lips burning on his forehead and the blood burning in his cheeks. Something had happened. He could not quite understand what it was. Some change had taken place. He felt quite embarrassed; but he fell asleep before he could realise that he was feeling just what John had felt that night when he was eight years old. That was what had happened--that was the change. The child was now father to the man--and the man was feeling the first embarrassment of the child--so the last link had been forged between the irrevocable past and the eternal present.

CHAPTER XXIX
THE CANDLE FOR ST. ANTHONY

If you know aught of the history of Venice; if the strenuous efforts of all those little lives that have done their work and lived their day in that vast multitude of human ephemera should have any meaning for you; if, in the flames of colour that have glowed and vanished in the brazier of Time, you can see faces and dream dreams of all that romantic story, then it is no wasting of a sunny morning to sit alone upon the *Piazetta*, your face turned towards *San Giorgio Maggiore* and, with the sun glinting upwards from the glittering water, weave your visions of great adventure in the diaphanous mist of light.

It was in such a way as this that John was spending one day when he could not work, when the little old white-haired lady was busy with Claudina over the duties of the house, when his father had departed upon that engrossing errand of seeing to the framing of a picture.

The sun was a burning disc, white hot in a smelter's furnace. A few white sails of cloud lay becalmed, inert, asleep in a sky of turquoise. John sat there blinking his eyes and the windows in the houses on *San Giorgio* blinked back in sleepy recognition as though the heat was more than they could bear. Away down the *Giudecca*, the thin bare masts of the clustering vessels tapered into the still air--giant sea-grass, which the sickle of a storm can mow down like rushes that grow by the river's edge. Their reflections wriggled like a nest of snakes in the dancing water, the only moving thing in that sleepy day. Everything else was noiseless; everything else was still.

John gazed at it all through half-closed eyes, till the point of the Campanile across the water seemed to melt in the quivering haze, and the dome of the chiesa was lost in the light where the sun fell on it. What had changed? What was different to his eyes that had been for the eyes of those thousands of workers who had toiled and fought, lived and died, like myriads of insects to build this timeless city of light, this City of Beautiful Nonsense? What had altered? A few coping stones, perhaps, a few mosaics renewed; but that was all. It was just the same as it had been in the days of the Council of Ten; just the same as when Petrarch, from his window on the *Riva degli Schiavona*, sat watching the monster galleys ride out in all their pomp and blazonry across the pearl and opal waters of the lagoons.

In another moment the present would have slipped from him; he would have been one of the crowd upon the Piazetta, watching the glorious argosy of Domenico Michieli returning from the Holy Land, with its sacred burdens of the bodies of St. Isidore from Chios and S. Donato from Cephalonia; in another moment he would have been seeing them unload their wondrous spoils of the East, their scents and their spices, their silks and their sandalwood, had not a most modern of modern hawkers, his little tray slung by straps from his shoulder, chosen him out for prey.

"Rare coins, signor," he said--"coins from every country in the world."

And for the price of one lira, he offered John an English penny.

John looked him up and down.

"Is this your idea of humour?" he asked in Italian.

The man emphatically shook his head.

"Oh, no, signor! It is a rare coin."

John turned away in disgust.

"You'd better go and learn your business," he said. "That's an English penny. It's only worth ten centesimi."

The hawker shrugged his shoulders and walked away. He had got the coin from a Greek whose ship lay in the *Giudecca* there. It was no good saying what the Greek had said. The signor would never believe him. He cast a wandering eye at the ships and shrugged his shoulders once more.

John watched his retreating figure with a sense of irritation-- irritation because the man had gone away thinking him an English fool--irritation because, unasked, the hawker had betrayed to him his loss of a sense of humour.

To be offered an English penny for one lira! To be told quite seriously that it was a rare coin! And to take it in all seriousness; to go to the trouble of saying in an injured voice that it was only worth ten centesimi! Was this what he had fallen to? Was his sense of humour so far gone as this? Of course it was a rare coin! Had there not been times when an English penny would have saved him from the dire awkwardness of an impossible position. How about the chair in Kensington Gardens? How about the friend who mounted the 'bus with him in the cheerful expectation that he was going to pay? Of course it was a rare coin! Why, there were times when it was worth a hundred lire!

He called the hawker back.

"Give me that coin," he said.

The man took it out with a grin of surprise.

"It cost me half a lira, signor," he said, which was a lie. But he told it so excellently that John paid him his price.

"Do you think they'll find it worth a candle at the shrine of St. Anthony?" asked John.

"You have lost something, signor?"

He said it so sympathetically.

"My sense of humour," said John, and off he strode to St. Mark's, the hawker gazing after him.

Without laughter in it, the voice is a broken reed; without laughter in it, the heart is a stone, dullened by a flaw; without laughter in it, even a prayer has not the lightness or the buoyancy of breath to rise heavenwards.

Can there be one woman in the world who has never prayed to St. Anthony in all seriousness for some impossible request which, by rights, she should have enquired for at the nearest lost property office--for a lost lock of hair that was not her own--one of those locks of hair that she ties to the wardrobe in the morning and combs out with all the seriousness in the world? Surely there must have been one out of the thousands? Then why not for a lost sense of humour? There is no office in the world that will return you such valuable property as that, once it has slipped your fingers. He has the sense himself, has St. Anthony. Think of the things he has found for you in your own hands, the jewels that he has discovered for you clasped about your own neck! Why, to be sure, he must have a sense of humour. And if it is impossible to pay an English penny for his candle in an Italian church--an English penny, mind you, which has profited some poor beggar by the sum of one lira; if it is a sacrilege, a levity, to ask him for the return of so invaluable a quality as a lost gift of laughter, then why pray at all, for without laughter in it, even a prayer has not the lightness or the buoyancy of breath to rise heavenwards.

If, when one drops upon one's knees at night and, beginning to deceive oneself in one's voluntary confessions, making oneself seem a fine fellow by tardy admissions of virtue and tactful omissions of wrong, if when one shows such delightful humanity in one's prayers as this, and cannot laugh at oneself at the same time, cannot see that it is but a cheating at a game of Patience, then it might be as well not to pray at all. For the humour in which a prayer is prayed, is the humour in which a prayer will be judged, and if, seriously, one deceives oneself into believing that one is a fine fellow, just so seriously will that deceit be weighed; for there are mighty few of us who are fine fellows, which is a great pity, for so mighty few of us to know it.

By the time John had reached the shrine of St. Anthony in the Duomo, by the time his English penny had rattled in the box along with all the other Italian coins, by the time the first words of his prayer were framed upon his lips, a laugh began to twinkle in his eyes; he had found his sense of humour, he had found his gift of laughter once more. It was in his own prayer. Before he could utter it, he was smiling to think how St. Anthony must be amused by the whole incident. Then, all it needed was for him to be grateful and, dropping his head in his hands, he expressed his gratitude by asking for other things.

St. Mark's is one of the few churches in the world where you can pray--one of the few churches in the world where they have not driven God out of the Temple, like a common money-changer, driven Him out by gaudy finery, by motley and tinsel. Mass at the High Altar there, is the great Passion Play it was meant to be, performed upon a stage unhung with violent colours, undecked with tawdry gems. They had no pandering fear of the God they worshipped, when they built that theatre of Christianity in the great Square of St. Mark's. The drama of all that wonderful story has a fit setting there. No stage is lit quite like it; no tragedy is so tragic in all its awful solemnity as when they perform the Mass in the duomo of St. Mark's. As the Host is elevated, as that sonorous bell rings out its thrilling chime and as the thousand heads sink down within two thousand hands, a spirit indeed is rushing upwards in a lightning passage to its God.

Once his head was bowed, once his eyes were closed, John was lost in the contemplation of his prayer. He did not observe the party of people who came by. He raised his head, but his eyes were fixed before him towards the little shrine. He did not see one separate herself from the party, did not notice her slip away unobserved and, coming back when they had gone on, seat herself on the chair close by his side.

Only when his thoughts were ended, when St. Anthony had listened to all that he had lost, to all the aching story of his heart, did he turn to find what St. Anthony had brought him.

His lips trembled. He rubbed and rubbed his eyes.

There on the seat beside him, her hands half pleading, her eyes set ready to meet his own, sat Jill.

CHAPTER XXX

THE QUALITIES OF IGNATIA

In amazement, John put out his hand. He touched her to see if she was real. Her hand answered. She caught his finger. Then she let it fall.

"Are you sorry?" she whispered.

He looked up at the image of St. Anthony, then back at her; around the church, then back once more at her.

"Where have you come from?" he asked.

"From home--from London."

"When?"

"I arrived last night."

"Alone?"

"No! No! With the Crossthwaites."

"Then what has happened?"

"Why--nothing has happened--and----" her voice dropped below the whisper--that strange pitch in which you hear not a syllable, yet know the worst--"and everything has happened."

"You're going to be married?"

It sounded no less terrible in his voice because he knew it.

"Yes."

"Then why have you come here?"

"The Crossthwaites were going. They asked me to come too. It was the only chance I knew I should ever have--our City of Beautiful Nonsense--I had to come."

Still John gazed at her, as though she were unreal. One does not always believe one's own eyes, for there are some things, which the readiness to see will constitute the power of vision. He put out his hand again.

"I can hardly believe it," he said slowly. "Here, just a minute ago, I was telling St. Anthony all I had lost. You--the best thing in my life--my ideal as well--even my sense of humour."

She looked up at his face wondering. There had been strange lost things for which she had prayed to St. Anthony--things to which only a woman can act as valuer. But to pray for a lost sense of humour. She touched the hand that he put out.

"You're very funny," she said gently--"You're very quaint. Do you think you'll find the sense of humour again?"

"I've found it," said John.

"Already?"

"Yes--already." One eye lifted to St. Anthony.

Then he told her about the hawker and that rare, that valuable coin--the English penny--and in two minutes, they were laughing with their heads in their hands.

This is not a reverent thing to do in a church. The least that you can offer, is to hide your face, or, turning quickly to the burial service in the prayer-book--granted that you understand Latin--

read that. Failing that of burial, the service of matrimony will do just as well.

But before the image of St. Anthony, to whom you have been praying for a lost gift of laughter--well, you may be sure that St. Anthony will excuse it. After all, it is only a compliment to his powers; and the quality of saintliness, being nothing without its relation to humanity, must surely argue some little weakness somewhere. What better then than the pride that is pardonable?

At length, when she had answered all his questions, when he had answered all hers, they rose reluctantly to their feet.

"I must go back to them," she said regretfully.

"But I shall see you again?"

"Oh, yes."

"Does Mrs. Crossthwaite know that you have seen me?"

"Yes. Her husband doesn't. He wouldn't understand."

John smiled.

"Men never do," said he. "They have too keen a sense of what is wrong for other people. When shall I see you?"

"This afternoon."

"Where?"

"Anywhere----" she paused.

"You were going to say something," said John quickly. "What is it?"

She looked away. In the scheme of this world's anomalies, there is such a thing as a duty to oneself. They have not thought it wise to write it in the catechism, for truly it is but capable of so indefinite a rendering into language, that it would be only dangerous to set it forth. For language, after all, is merely a sound box, full of words, in the noisy rattling of which, the finer expression of all thought is lost.

But a thousand times, Jill had thought of it--that duty. Its phrases form quite readily in the mind; they construct themselves with ease; the words flow merrily.

Why, she had asked herself, should she sacrifice her happiness to the welfare of those who had brought her into the world? What claim had they upon her, who had never questioned her as to a desire for existence?

All this is so simply said. Its justice is so palpably apparent. And if she had gained nothing herself by the transaction, it would have been so easy of following. But the mere knowledge that she stood to win the very heart of her desire at the cost of some others' welfare, filled her with the apprehension that she was only inventing this duty of self for her own gratification, as a narcotic to the sleeplessness of her own conscience.

The education of the sex has so persistently driven out egotism from their natures, that the woman who finds paramount the importance of herself, has but a small place in this modern community.

Fast in her very blood, was bred in Jill that complete annihilation of selfishness, that absolute abandonment to Destiny. Strive as she might, she could not place her own desires before the needs of her father and mother; she could not see the first essential of happiness in that gain to herself which would crush the prospects of her brother Ronald.

To such women as these--and notwithstanding the advent of the tradeswoman into the sex, there are many--to be able to give all, is their embarrassment of riches, to withhold nothing is their conception of wealth.

In the ideal which she had formed of John, Jill knew that he was possessed of more in himself, than ever would be the bounty bequeathed to those three people dependent upon her generosity. And so, she had given her consent of marriage to one, whom she might have valued as a friend, whom, as a man, she respected in every way, but who well, since brevity is invaluable--like poor St. Joseph, had a brown beard.

All this, in the pause that had followed John's question, had passed for the thousandth time through Jill's mind, bringing her inevitably once more to the realisation of her duty to others. And when he pressed her again, offering, not perhaps the penny for her thoughts, but an equivalent, just as valuable as that most valuable of coins, the promise of his eyes, she shook her head.

"Ah, but you were going to say something!" he pleaded.

"I was going to ask you," said she, "if you would take me to see your people." She hesitated. "I--I want to have tea with them out of the little blue and white cups with no handles. I want to go and buy lace with the little old white-haired lady in the arcades."

He seized her hand so that she winced.

"You've not forgotten! You shall come this afternoon." And there, with a smile, she left him, still standing by the silent image of St. Anthony; and, gratitude being that part of prayer which belongs to the heart and has nothing in common with delay, John knelt down again. When Jill looked back over her shoulder, his head was buried in his hands.

The little old white-haired lady was waiting over the mid-day meal for him when he returned. His father had taken his food and gone out again, leaving her alone to keep John company. She was sitting patiently there at the head of the table and, by the side of her empty plate, stood a small bottle containing white pills, over which she hurriedly laid her hand as he entered.

But clever as they are, in their cunning, childish ways, old people lose all the superior craft of deceit. They go back to childhood when they imagine that once a thing is hidden, it is out of sight. That is not at all the case. There comes a moment when it is too late to conceal; when curiosity will bring the hidden thing twice vividly before the eyes. Under the very nose of John, was the best place for that secret bottle of pills, had she needed it not to be seen.

As it was, his eyes travelled more quickly than her hand. She made a gentle little effort to hide her concern as well. She smiled up at him, asking where he had been. But it would not do. The child is parent to the man, he is parent to the woman too--a stern parent, moreover, who will brook no simple trifling with his authority, who overlooks nothing and whose judgments are the blind record of an implacable justice. John could not let that little deception pass. Instead of answering her question, instead of taking his place at the table, he came to her side and put one arm gently round her neck.

"What are you hiding, dearest?" he asked.

Like a child, who is discovered in the act of nefarious negotiations with the good things of this world, she quietly took her hand away. There stood the innocent little bottle in all its nakedness. John stared at it questioningly--then at his mother.

"Is it something that you have to take, dearest?" he asked. "Aren't you well?"

"Yes, I'm quite well," she said, and she played nervously with the cork in the little bottle. It was a delicate subject. She began to wish that she had never embarked upon it at all. But faith brings with it a rare quality of courage, and so firmly did she believe, with the quaint simplicity of her heart, in the course she had determined to adopt, that the wish broke like a bubble on the moment.

"Well, what is in the bottle?" persisted John.

"Ignatia."

There was just the faintness of a whisper in her voice. She had not found full courage as yet. Even in their firmest beliefs, old people are pursued by the fear of being thought foolish. The new generation always frightens them; it knows so much more than they.

"Ignatia?" John repeated.

"Yes--I--I want you to take it."

She began uncorking the bottle.

"Me? What for? I'm all right. I'm not ill."

"No--but----" she paused.

"But what?"

"It'll do you good. Try it, to please me."

She hid her white head against his coat.

"But what for, dearest?"

"Have you never heard of Ignatia?" she asked.

John shook his head.

"It's a plant. It's a homeopathic medicine. It's a cure for all sorts of things. People take it when their nerves are bad, for worry, for insomnia. It's a cure for trouble when--when you're in love."

She said it so simply, in such fear that he would laugh; but when he looked down and found the hopefulness in her eyes, laughter was impossible. He caught it back, but his nostrils quivered.

"And do you want to cure me of being in love?" he asked with a straightened face.

"I thought you'd be happier, my dear, if you could get over it."

"So you recommend Ignatia?"

"I've known it do wonders," she asserted. "Poor Claudina was very much in love with a worthless fellow--Tina--one of the gondolier!--surely you remember him. He lived on the *Giudecca*."

John nodded smiling.

"Well, she came to me one day, crying her heart out. She declared she was in love with the most worthless man in the whole of Venice. 'Get over it then, Claudina,' I said. But she assured me that it was impossible. He had only to put up his little finger, she said and she had to go to his beckoning, if only to tell him how worthless she thought he was. Well--I prescribed Ignatia, and she was cured of it in a week. She laughs when she talks about him now."

John was forced to smile, but as quickly it died away.

"And is that what you want me to do?" he asked. "Do you want me to be able to laugh when I talk about the lady of St. Joseph? You'd be as sorry as I should, if I did. It would hurt you as much as it would me."

"Then you won't take it, John?" She looked up imploringly into his face.

"No--no charms or potions for me. Besides--" he bent down close to her ear--"the lady of St. Joseph is in Venice. She's coming to see you this afternoon."

With a little cry of delight, she threw the bottle of Ignatia down upon the table and caught his face in her trembling hands.

CHAPTER XXXI
THE SACRIFICE

A belief in Ignatia argues a ready disposition for Romance.

The mind of the little old white-haired lady belonged to that period when love was a visitation only to be cured by the use of simples, herbs, and magic. She called the treatment--homeopathic. It was her gentle way of assuring herself that she marched bravely with the times; that the superstition of the Middle-Ages had nothing whatever to do with it.

This is all very well; but there is no such scientific name for the portents told by the flight of a magpie; you cannot take shelter behind fine-sounding words when you admit to the good fortune brought by a black cat; there is no marching with the times for you, if you are impelled to throw salt over your left shoulder. You are not stepping it with the new generation then. And all these things were essentials in the life of the little old white-haired lady. Certainly there were no flights of magpies over the tiny Italian garden at the back of the *Palazzo Capello* to disturb the peace of her mind with joyous or terrible prognostications. But the resources of an old lady's suspicions are not exhausted in a flight of magpies. Oh, no! She has many more expedients than that.

The very day before John's announcement of the advent of the lady of St. Joseph to Venice, she had seen the new moon, a slim silver sickle, over her right shoulder. There is good omen in that. She had gone to bed the happier because of it. What it betokened, it was not in the range of her knowledge at the time to conceive. Destiny, in these matters, as in many others, is not so outspoken as it might be. But immediately John told her, she remembered that little slip of a moon. Then this was what it had heralded--the coming of the lady of St. Joseph.

As soon as their meal was finished, John went out to the Piazza, the meeting place which he had arranged with Jill, leaving his mother and Claudina to make all preparations for his return. How fast the heart of the little old white-haired lady beat then, it would be difficult to say. She was as excited as when Claudina put the treasures away to bed in their night-caps. Her little brown eyes sparkled, for a party to old people is much the same as is a party to a child. The preparations for it are the whirlwind that carries the imagination into the vortex of the event. And this, for which she was getting ready, was all illuminated with the halo of Romance.

Sometimes, perhaps, a wave of jealousy would bring the blood warmly to her cheeks. Supposing the lady of St. Joseph was not equal to her expectations? Supposing she did not fulfil her hopes and demands of the woman whom she had destined in her mind to be the wife of her son? How could she tell him? How could she warn him that he was unwise? How could she show him that the woman he loved was unworthy of him? It would be a difficult task to accomplish; but her lips set tight at the thought of it. She would shirk no duty so grave or serious as that.

Yet all these fears, with an effort, she put away from her. A generous sense of justice told her that she might judge when she had seen, so she sent out Claudina when everything was ready, to buy some cakes at Lavena's and, stealing into her bedroom, knelt down before the little altar at her bedside.

There, some ten minutes later, her husband found her. It was not her custom to pray at that time of the afternoon, unless for some special request and, for a moment, he stood in silence,

140

watching the white head buried in the pathetically twisted hands, the faint rays of the little coloured lamp before the image shining through the silken silver of her hair.

When at last, she raised her head and found him standing there, a smile crept into her eyes. She beckoned to him silently to come to her, and when he reached her side, she pulled him gently to his knees.

"What is it?" he whispered.

"I'm praying for John," she whispered back, for when you kneel before an altar, even if it is only rough-made out of an old box, as was this, you are in a chapel; you are in a cathedral; you are at the very feet of God Himself and you must speak low.

"What about him?" he whispered again.

She put her dear lips close to his ear with its tuft of white hair growing stiffly on the lobe, and she whispered:

"The lady of St. Joseph is in Venice. She's coming to tea this afternoon."

And then, looking round over his shoulder, to see that he had closed the door--because old gentlemen are sensitive about these things--his arm slipped round her neck and both their heads bent together. It was, after all, their own lives they were praying for. Every prayer that is offered, every prayer that is granted, is really for the benefit of the whole world.

What they prayed for--how they prayed; what quaint little sentences shaped themselves in her mind, what fine phrases rolled in his, it is beyond power to say. Certain it is that a woman comes before her God in all the simplest garments of her faith, while a man still carries his dignity well hung upon the shoulder.

Presently, they rose together and went into the other room. Everything was in readiness. The blue and white cups were smiling in their saucers; the brass kettle was beginning its tempting song upon the spirit stove.

"Do you like my cap?" asked the little old white-haired lady and, looking down to see if his waistcoat was not too creased, the old gentleman said that it was the daintiest cap that he had ever seen.

"Poor John will be very shy," she continued, as she sat down and tried to fold her hands in her lap as though she were at ease.

"John! shy!"

The old gentleman laughed at the idea of it and kissed her wrinkled cheek to hide his excitement. John, shy! He remembered the days of his own love-making. He had never been shy. It was like an accusation against himself. Besides, what woman worth her salt would have anything to do with the love-making of a man who was shy? John, shy! He straightened his waistcoat for the second time, because it was getting near the moment of their arrival, the kettle was nearly boiling, and he was beginning to feel just a little bit embarrassed.

"Did John say when they were going to be married?" he asked presently.

"Oh, but you mustn't say that to him!" she cried out quickly. "Why, he told me that he would never see her again. He said that they were friends--just friends. But d'you think I can't guess! Why has she come to Venice? She must have known he was here. Oh, he'll tell nothing about it. We must just treat her as if she were a friend. But----" She shook her head knowingly, not caring to finish her sentence.

Of course, she guessed it all--their meeting in the chapel-- their meeting in Kensington Gardens! A young man and a young woman do not meet like that, unless it be that there is some good reason for it. Besides--that last candle! What woman could fail to fall in love with a man, who had thought of such a gentle consideration as that, even letting alone the fact that that man was her son? There are some things in this world which a woman knows and it is not the faintest use trying to contradict her. To begin with, she is bound to be right, and secondly, if it were possible to prove her wrong, it would only convince her the more firmly of her opinion.

The old lady knew quite well what she was talking about. These two were as fondly in love with each other as it was possible for them to be. Their meeting here in Venice, after John had assured her that they were never going to see each other again, was all the proof that she needed of it. And with this knowledge held firmly in the heart of her, she was already pre-disposed to see those signs by which, in spite of all their cleverness, two people are bound in this predicament to show their hands.

At last the bell clanged loudly. Its jangling hammered like echoes beating to and fro against the walls of their hearts. The old lady set straight her cap for the twentieth time; for the twentieth time, the old gentleman pulled down his waistcoat, then he crept to the door and looked out into the big room.

"Claudina's going!" he whispered back over his shoulder. "She's opened the door. Yes--it's John!"

He came back quickly to his seat and there, when the two visitors entered, they were sitting opposite to each other, quite placidly, quite calmly, as though there were nothing left to happen in the world. Yet I doubt if four hearts ever beat so quickly beneath such quiet exteriors as these.

"This is Miss Dealtry," said John--in much the same tone of voice as when he had told the cabman to drive to the opera.

The old gentleman had risen from his chair and, coming forward, with that air--it is the air of courtesy--which makes a woman feel a queen, if she is only a washerwoman, he took her hand, bowed low as he gently shook it and then, drawing her further into the room, he bowed solemnly again.

"My wife," said he, just catching the last note from the tone of John's voice.

The little old white-haired lady held out her hands and, as Jill saw the tortured, twisted fingers, her heart shuddered in pity. But before that shudder could be seen, she had bent down and kissed the wrinkled face that was lifted up to hers and from that moment, these two loved each other.

With women, these things are spontaneous. A woman will go through the play of pretending to kiss another; she will put forward her cheek, mutter an affectionate word and kiss the air with her lips. No one is deceived by it. The lookers-on know quite well that these two must hate each other. The actors know it perfectly well themselves. But once the lips of two women meet, their hearts go with the touching.

From the instant that the lips of the little old lady touched Jill's, there was sealed a bond. They both loved John, and in that kiss they both admitted it. The mother wanted no further proof than this. Then all jealousy vanished. With that kiss, she made the mother's sacrifice, the sacrifice which is the last that the incessant demands of nature makes upon her sex. She gave up the love of her son into the keeping of another woman. And when Jill stood up again, the old lady's heart had died down to a quiet, faint measure, fainter perhaps a little than it had been before. Her life was finished. There was only left the waiting and her eyes, still bright, sought John's, but found them fixed on Jill.

CHAPTER XXXII
THE DEPARTURE--VENICE

Before that little tea party was over, these two old people had won the heart of Jill. For all the world, they were like two children, making believe with the most serious things in life. Like children, they looked at each other in surprise when anything happened, or when anything was said. Like children, they laughed or were intensely earnest over their game. Like children, it seemed as if they were playing at being old, he, with his nodding of the head, she, with her crumpled figure and withered hands.

Sometimes at a thing that John would say, they would look at each other and smile. It had reminded them of something far back in the years of which neither John nor Jill knew anything. And in this again, they were like children, upon whose faces one may sometimes trace a distant look of memory--a look that is very marvellous and very wise--as though they were gazing back into the heart of Time from which the hand of destiny has brought them.

Yet it was not only this--this charm of wonderful simplicity--but that whenever Jill looked up, she found their eyes resting tenderly on her. It seemed--she did not understand why just then--as though they were trying mutely to tell her how fond of her they were.

Then, when the old gentleman handed her her cup of tea, she recognised from the description, the china of blue and white and turned with a smile to John.

"Aren't these the cups?" she asked gently.

He nodded his head and tried to smile, too. The old lady watched those smiles. Her eyes never left them for a moment.

"I've been told about these cups," Jill explained to the others. "Your son told me one day when--when he was giving me a description of where you lived."

"That's the real Chinese cobalt," said the old gentleman. "John told you that of course."

"Well--no--they were not described in detail--at least----" suddenly she found the blood mounting to her cheeks. "I--I knew that they had no handles."

Why did she blush? The little old lady had not failed to see that sudden flame of colour. Why did she blush? Something she had remembered? Something that John had said? She looked quickly at her son. His eyes were bent on Jill.

Oh, yes, they loved. There was no fear of her mistaking that. There was a secret between them; a secret that had set free a flood of colour to Jill's cheeks, that had brought a look of fixed intent into John's eyes. What other could such secret be between a boy and girl, than love? No one can keep it; but it is the greatest secret in the world.

Before the tea was over, they had betrayed it in a thousand different ways to the sharp, bright eyes of the little old white-haired lady. When vying with John to do honour to their guest, the old gentleman persuaded Jill to take from the plate he proffered, then she bent her head and smiled to see her husband's pride and poor John's discomfiture.

"She loves him! She loves him!" she whispered in her heart. "She is the very woman for my John!"

"A charming little girl," whispered the old man's vanity, as he proudly bore the plate back to the table. "Exactly the woman I would have chosen for John myself."

And John was disconsolately wondering why, if she loved him, Jill had so patently refused his offering.

Why had she refused? The little old white-haired lady knew that. She wanted to please his father, because she loved John. That was their secret. How it affected the blue and white china, she could not guess; but that was their secret--they loved.

Only by exercising the greatest control over herself, could she refrain from drawing her aside and telling Jill all she had seen, all she had guessed, and all she hoped.

Presently, without seeking for it, the opportunity presented itself. They had been eating little jam sandwiches--jam sandwiches, which Claudina knew how to cut so thin, that the bread was almost threadbare, and looked as if it wanted darning. They melted in your mouth, but then, they made your fingers sticky. Jill looked ruefully at hers when the tea was over. Holding them away from her at arm's length, she made a little grimace. When one was young, one's mouth was the best, the quickest, the most approved-of remedy for these matters. She might have wished she were a child then, but wishing was all. She asked to be allowed to wash them.

"You will come into my room, dear," said the little old lady eagerly, and away she led her, where John could not hope to follow.

Ah, then she was cunning, when once she had her alone! What subtle little compliments she paid! You would scarcely believe how cunning she could be.

"That is your little altar?" said Jill, when she had dried her hands. As she walked across to it, the old lady took her arm. It needed but little manipulation from there to slip her hand into Jill's. It needed but little management to show her in a hundred tender ways as she clung to her for support, that she found her very dear, very loveable.

The hearts of women are responsive things. When there is sympathy between them, they touch and answer, as though some current united them, as well indeed it may.

So gentle, so expressive were those simple signs that passed between Jill and the little old white-haired lady, that Jill was stricken in conscience, realising all that they meant and wondering, almost guiltily, what they would think of her if they knew. They must never know. She could not bear the thought that these two old people, far away in Venice as they might be, should hold in their hearts anything but the affection which they were showing to her then.

"I was praying here just before you came," said the little old lady in a whisper.

Jill pressed the withered hand.

"Do you know what I was praying for?"

A sudden fear seized Jill. She felt her forehead cold.

"No----" she tried to smile--"How could I know?"

"I was praying for John." She looked up simply into Jill's face. "He's such a dear boy, you don't know. Look at the way he comes every year to see us--all the way from London. I wonder would any other son do as much. Do you think they would?"

She asked the question as naïvely as if, were there any doubt about it, she really would like to know. You might have known there was no doubt in her mind.

Before that little altar then, was a dangerous place to discuss such subjects. Jill drew her gently away towards the door.

"Do you think there are any other sons have such a mother?" she said. "Why don't you ask yourself that question?"

The little old lady looked up with a twinkle in her eyes. "I thought perhaps you'd understand it better that way," she answered. "Besides--it's easy to be a mother. You have only to have a son. It's not so easy to be a son, because you need more than a mother for that."

Jill looked at her tenderly, then bent and kissed her cheek.

"I think John's very like you," she whispered. She could not keep it back. And that was as much as the little old white-haired lady wanted; that was all she had been playing for. With her head high in triumph, she walked back with Jill to join the others.

Soon afterwards Jill declared she must go; that her friends would be waiting for her.

"But when----" the old people began in a breath, then stopped together.

"You say, my dear," said the old gentleman--"I can wait."

Oh, no--she would not hear of it. He began first. Let him say what he wanted to. He shook his head and bowed. John caught Jill's eye and they held their laughter.

"Then when----" they both began again together and this time, they finished out their sentence--"are we going to see you again?"

We share the same thoughts when we know each other well. But life runs along in its separate channels with most people. They may be many years beneath the shadow of one roof, yet for all they know of each other, they might live at opposite ends of the earth, so little is it given to human beings to understand humanity; so little do people study it except in the desires which are in themselves.

In these two old people, it was quite charming to see one standing out of the way to let the other pass on, as if they both were going in vastly different directions, and then, to find that one was but speaking the other's thoughts.

They all laughed, but their laughter died away again when Jill announced that in two days she was leaving Venice for Milan, passing through the Italian lakes on her way back to England.

"You only stay three days!" exclaimed the little old lady, and she looked quickly at John. But John had known of it. There was

146

no surprise in his face. He breathed deeply; looked away out of the window over the old Italian garden--that was all.

They made her promise to come the next day to lunch--to tea again if she would--to stay with them the whole day. John looked to her appealingly for her answer.

"But I can't leave my friends all that time," she said reluctantly. "I'll come to lunch--I'll try and stay to tea. I can't do more than that."

Then John took her down to her gondola. In the archway, before they stepped on to the *fondamenta*, he took her arm and held her near him.

"You're sure it's too late?" he said hoarsely, below his breath. "You're sure that there is nothing I could do to make things different--to make them possible?"

She clung to him quietly. In the darkness, her eyes searched impenetrable depths; stared to the furthest horizons of chance, yet saw nothing beyond the track of many another woman's life before her.

"It is too late," she whispered--"Oh, I should never have come! I should never have seen these two wonderful old people of yours. Now I know all that the City of Beautiful Nonsense meant. You very nearly made them real to me that day in Fetter Lane; but now I know them. Oh, I don't wonder that you love them! I don't wonder that you would come every year--year after year to see them! If only my mother and father were like that, how different all of it would be then."

"You haven't the courage to break away from it all?" asked John quietly--"to make these old people of mine--to make them yours. If I couldn't support you over in London, you could live with them here, and I would do as much of my work here as possible."

Jill looked steadily into his eyes.

"Do you think I should be happy?" she asked. "Would you be happy if, to marry me, you had to give up them? Wouldn't their faces haunt you in the most perfect moments of your happiness? Wouldn't his eyes follow you in everything you did? Wouldn't those poor withered hands of hers be always pulling feebly at your heart? And if you thought that they were poor----?"

"They are," said John. He thought of the Treasure Shop; of that pathetic figure, hiding in the shadows of it, who would not sell his goods, because he loved them too well.

"Could you leave them to poverty then?" said Jill.

"So it's too late?" he repeated.

"I've given my word," she replied.

He lifted her hand generously to his lips and kissed it.

"Then you mustn't come to-morrow," he said quietly.

"Not see them again?" she echoed.

"No. You must send some excuse. Write to my mother. Say your friends have decided to stop at Bologna on their way to Milan and that they are going to start at once. She loves you too well--she counts on you too much already. It'll be a long time before I can drive out of her head the thought that you are going to be my wife. And I don't want to do it by telling her that you are going to be married to someone else. She wouldn't understand that. She belongs to an old-fashioned school, where ringlets and bonnets and prim little black shoes over dainty white stockings, make a wonderful difference to one's behaviour. She probably couldn't understand your wanting to see them under such a circumstance as that. She could scarcely believe that you cared for me and, if she did, would think that we shouldn't see each other, as perhaps, after this, we shan't. No, I shall have quite enough difficulty in driving you out of her mind as it is. You mustn't come and see them to-morrow. She'll nearly break her heart when she hears it, but nearly is not quite."

"Shan't I ever see them again then?" she asked below her breath.

He shook his head.

"This is the last time you'll see any of us."

She put her hands on his shoulders. For a moment, she clung to him, her face closely looking into his as though she must store him in her memory for the rest of time. He shut his eyes. He dared not kiss her. When the lips touch, they break a barrier through which floods a torrent there is no quenching. John shut his eyes and held back his head, lest the touching of her hair or the warmth of her breath should weaken his resolve.

"How am I to do it?" she whispered. "I feel as though I must stay now; as though I never wanted to go back home again."

He said nothing. The very tone of his voice would have been persuasion to her then. Slowly, she unclasped her fingers; as slowly she drew herself away. That was the last moment when he could have won her. Then she was his as the blood was rushing through him, as her pulses were throbbing wildly in time to his. But in love--it may be different in war--these things may not be taken so. Some vague, some mystical notion of the good does not permit of it.

"You must be going," said John gently. "We can't stay here."

She let him lead her to the door. As it came open to his hand and the greater light flooded in, he knew that it was all finished.

She stepped down into her gondola that was waiting, and the gondolier pushed off from the steps. Until it swayed out of sight, John stood motionless on the fondamenta, watching its passing.

Sometimes Jill looked back over her shoulder and waved a little handkerchief. John bent his head acknowledging it.

But neither of them saw the two white heads that, close together in a window up above, were whispering to each other in happy ignorance of all the misery which that little white handkerchief conveyed.

"You see how long they took to get down the steps," whispered the old lady.

"Oh, I don't know that you can judge anything by that," replied her husband. "Those steps are very dark to anyone not accustomed to them."

She took his arm. She looked up into his face. Her brown eyes twinkled.

"They are," she whispered back--"very dark--nearly as dark as that little avenue up to the house where I lived when you first met me."

CHAPTER XXXIII
THE SIXTEENTH OF FEBRUARY--LONDON

The abhorrence of Nature for a vacuum, is nothing to her abomination of unfinished work. In the great Tapestry which Time sits eternally weaving with the coloured threads of circumstance, there are no loose ends allowed. Every little picture which finds its way into the mighty subject of that vast material, must be complete in its symbol of accomplished Destiny. No ragged edges must there be; no lines unfinished, no shadow left out. And even, in so inconsequent a matter as a story of Beautiful Nonsense, some definite completion must be shown to round the whole, to leave no hanging thread by which the picture might be unravelled.

When John said good-bye to Jill on the steps of the *fondamenta*, when the last wave of her little white handkerchief had fluttered into a curling light upon the water, he had turned back into the house, believing that the story was irretrievably ended. The last word had been written. So far as Jill was concerned, he might well close the book and thank the pen of Chance that it had shown him an ideal as high above the common conception of life as it is good for the eyes of a man to lift.

But he had not, in this calculation, counted the presence of those two white heads in the window up above. For him, so far as his eye could see, Destiny had had its fill, had drained the cup of possibility to its utmost dregs. But this was not so for them. They had yet to be appeased. For them, the matter had only just begun. To them, it was the last shuttle, whose speeding to and fro, would weave in the past with the present and so fulfil their final justification.

From that day, the little old white-haired lady looked forward to John's marriage with Jill as to the consummation of her whole life's desire. She lived--she thought--she ordered her existence for nothing else. Her disappointment was pathetic to witness when she received Jill's little note telling her departure the next day. But her beliefs were not shaken; her hopes were not thwarted. She still saw the last burning of her romance before the flame should flicker and become a light no more.

She spoke to John about it of course. Sitting in the window one day, the window that looked down on to the old gentleman's garden, she told him what she knew; what was not the slightest use his contradicting. They loved each other. Oh, not a doubt of it! She spoke authoritatively, as women will on these subjects. Who better able to than they?

"You really think she loves me, mother?" he asked in a quick moment of hopefulness.

She took his hand. She lifted one tired arm about his neck.

"Why do you think she came like that to Venice?" she asked. "There's not a thing she wouldn't do for you--not a place she wouldn't go to in order to see you. Don't you realise that?"

It was unfortunate she should have chosen that phrase. There were things, Jill would not do for him. It had needed every effort from him to find the full value of unselfishness in what she was about to do; but he could not think that she loved him as his mother would have him believe. It was unfortunate, her choosing of that phrase. From that moment, John shrank into himself. He could not bring himself to tell her the whole truth of it; therefore, it was no good talking any more.

"Her people are too well off," he said, rising with a gesture of despair from the seat in the window. "They're in a different position altogether. I've no right to tell her. I've no right to try and win her affection. It would only be a hopeless business all through."

From that moment, he avoided the subject; from that moment, he became impregnable whenever the little old white-haired lady tried to assail him with the weapons of her worldly knowledge.

"I can get John to say nothing," she said one night to her husband. "He won't speak about it at all."

He put his arms round her in the darkness.

"You're worrying yourself, little woman," he said, sleepily. "I woke up once last night and you were wide awake. Did you sleep at all?"

"Very little," she admitted.

"Well--you mustn't worry. Leave it to Nature. John will tell her everything about it one of these days. Young men are always getting on the high horse and trying to tilt against Nature, and women are forever offering to assist Nature, thinking she must come off the worst. It's waste of time either way, my dearest.

Nature's a windmill. It'll grind the flour out of everyone of us when the wind blows. It's no good tilting at it on a windy day; and it's no good trying to turn the sails round when it's calm. The wind'll blow,"--he yawned and turned over on his side--"soon enough." And he was asleep.

She believed so much in what her husband said, did the little old white-haired lady. It is not often, that after twenty odd years of married life, a man keeps still alive that ideal of unquestionable reliability which his wife first found in everything he said. Usually there comes a time--sad enough in its way, since ideals are almost everything--when those which once were words of wisdom, fall tainted with the odour of self-interest. It becomes a difficult thing to believe in then, that aphorism of your philosopher, which brings him the warmest seat in the chimney corner, or the softest place in the bed. And that is the wisdom of a lot of people--a philosophy of self, translated into a language for others.

By some kink of chance perhaps--though rather it would be kinder to think, by some quality of mutual affection--the old gentleman had avoided this tragedy. It is a tragedy; for no man likes a mean motive to be attributed to his philosophy--especially when it is true. And so, the old lady still believed in the infallibility of her husband's wisdom which in its way was quite good. That night at least then, she worried no more. She turned over her white head in his direction and she fell asleep. And whenever he turned through the night, she turned as well. After twenty years or so, these things become mechanical. Life is easier after twenty years, if you can bear with it till then.

But before John had left, her worries began again and, not daring to speak to him any more, she was driven to bear her trouble in silence.

She hoped up to the last that he would mention it once more, and a thousand different times in a thousand different ways, decoyed their conversations into topics which would suggest it to his mind. Yet always with the caution of some wary animal pursued, John avoided it--sheered off and chose another path.

Even on the day of his departure, she yet thought that he would speak and, clinging gently to him, with her arms about his neck, she whispered:

"Have you nothing to say to me, John?"

"Nothing--nothing, dearest," he replied, adding the term of endearment as he saw the bitter look of disappointment in her eyes.

Then he was gone. For another year that vast chamber with its high windows, and that tiny room which peeped out into it, would be silent of the sound of his voice. For another year, night after night, these two old people would continue to look up in surprise when Claudina entered for the ceremony; they would continue to exclaim: "You don't mean to say it's ten o'clock, Claudina!" And perhaps, as the days wore on and the year drew itself out to the thin grey thread, the surprise would get fainter, the note of exclamation not so emphatic as it used to be. She took her breath in fear as she thought of it. Supposing the year were to pass and John had not married Jill? She went into the little altar in her bedroom and commenced a novena--one of the many that she began and dutifully finished, before that year had gone.

So, it may be seen, in these two old people, who have woven themselves so inextricably into this whole story of Nonsense, how Time has by no means finished with the picture it set itself the weaving on that mysterious 18th of March, whereof the calendar still keeps its secret.

John went back to his labours in London, but he left behind him, forces at work of which he knew nothing. The old gentleman was quite right. Nature has no need of the meddling hand. The seed had been transplanted into the mind of the little old white-haired lady and, in her, will the completion of Destiny be found.

For the first few weeks, she wrote her usual letters to John, avoiding the subject with a rigid perseverance which, she might have known, which certainly her husband knew, she could never hope to maintain. This perseverance did not break down all at once. She began with inconsequent allusions to Jill; then at last, when they called forth no word of a reply from John, she gave way to the passionate desire that was consuming her, commencing a long series of letters of counsel and advice such as an old lady will give, who believes that the world is the same place that it was when she was a girl.

"*Have you ever spoken to her, John?*" she asked in one of her letters. "*With your eyes you have. I saw you do it that afternoon at tea. But the language of the eyes is not enough for a woman, who has never heard the sound of the spoken word in her ears.*"

"*Tell her you love her--ask her to marry you, and if she says no--don't believe her. She doesn't mean it. It's more or less impossible for a woman to say yes the first time. It's over so soon.*"

"*You say her people are wealthy; that they are in a very different position to you. Of course, I know blood is thicker than water, but love is stronger than them both. And, after all, their position is one of luxury--that is of the body. Your's is a position of the mind. There is no comparison.*"

"*I lie awake sometimes at night, thinking of all the trials and troubles your father and I had to go through before we found our corner in the world, and then I know how much more worth than youth or luxury, pleasure or ease, is love.*"

"*I believe in that short time she was here, she became very fond of me, and in one of those moments when one woman shows her heart to another--they are very seldom--it was when she came to wash her hands after eating the jam sandwiches--she said she thought you were very like me. Now comparisons, with women, are not always odious; it is generally the only way they have of describing anything."*

"I am sending you a bracelet of jade to give to her. It is very old. I will send you the history of it another time. I have it all written out somewhere. Anyhow, it belonged to one of the great Venetian ladies when Leonardo Loredano was Doge. Give it to her as coming from you. It does come from you. I give it you. A gift, however small, however poor, means a great deal to a woman. She reads a meaning into it--the very meaning I send with this."

"Oh, my dear boy, will you tell me nothing. Don't you know how my heart must be aching to hear some news of your happiness. It is the last happiness I shall know myself. Don't delay it too long."

These extracts from the letters written by the little old white-haired lady to her son, John, over that period of the first three months after her meeting with Jill, could occupy the space of many a page in this history. But these few which, with John's permission, I have quoted here, are sufficient to show how close her heart was wrapt up in the fortunes of his love-making.

Hoping, that, in his reticence on the subject, she might in time grow to lose interest, finally even forgetting Jill's existence altogether, John procrastinated, putting off, putting off the day when he must tell her all the truth. There was, too, he has admitted it, some fanciful sense of satisfaction intricately woven in with the pain he felt when he read those letters of hers every week. It was nonsense again, perhaps, but it kept the idea a living reality in his mind. He came to look forward to them as to the expression of a life that was too wonderful, except to dream of. And so, as an Eastern takes his opium and, retiring into the gloomy shadows of his den, is transported into the glorious heavens of a phantom creation, John read these letters of his mother's in his room in Fetter Lane. There, the passings to and fro of Mrs. Rowse, the hawker's cries and the screams of the parrot on the other side of the road, had no power to waken him from his sleep, so long as it lasted.

For nearly three months--week after week--he received these letters, dreamed his dreams and, in writing back to the little old white-haired lady, tried to allay the expectancy of her mind.

At last it could be done no longer. You may put back the hands of a clock to your heart's content, but there is no warding off of the inevitable. There came a letter saying she would write of it no more. It was not impatient, it was not in anger, but in the spirit, as when an old lady lays down her sewing in her lap as the sun sets and, gently tells you, she can see the stitches no longer.

It was then, that John, knowing what he had lost, conceived another felonious means of transport--this time the transport of the mind.

Jill was only known to his people as Miss Dealtry. They did not know where she lived. They knew nothing of her relations. They could not communicate with her in any way.

For a long while he sat looking at that last letter of his mother's, where she had said she would write no more of Jill.

"She wants a love story--bless her heart," he said musingly--and Mrs. Morrell's sandy cat coming at that moment into the room, he repeated it for the cat's benefit--"She wants a love story," he said. The cat blinked its eyes, curled a rough red tongue lovingly about its whiskers, and sat down as though, having half an hour to spare and the tortoiseshell not being in the way, it was quite ready to listen to it then.

"And, by Jove!" exclaimed John--"She shall have it!"

Miss Morrell curled her tail comfortably round her in the most perfect attitude of attention.

"I'll write her a story," said John to Miss Morrell--"a story of beautiful nonsense--some of it true and some of it made up as I go along."

And, therewith, he sat himself down to answer her letter.

It was necessary, if he were to re-create the interest of the little old white-haired lady, for him to meet Jill again. Accordingly, with some ingenious preamble, in which he explained his silence of the preceding months, he began with the description of his second meeting with Jill in Kensington Gardens--that time when she came and spent the entire morning in telling him that she could not come and meet him that day.

"*Undoubtedly God could have made a place more fitted for Romance than Kensington Gardens,*" he began--"*but unquestionably He never did.*"

And this was how the last tissue of nonsense came to be woven.

Of course, he told her, that it was all a secret. Jill had to keep it a secret from her people. He had to do that. Well--surely it was true? He put the question boldly for his conscience to answer, and a look of the real thing came into his eyes. It was as well, however, that he thought of doing it, for the old lady was nearly landing him in an awkward predicament. She enclosed a letter to Jill and asked him to forward it, as, of course, she did not know the address.

He made a grimace at Miss Morrell when he received it, as though asking her what she would do under the circumstances. Miss Morrell yawned. It was so simple. So far, she had taken an interest in the case, had come in every day since the writing of the first letter to get her saucer of milk and hear the latest. But if he was going to put questions to her like this, there was all probability that she would be bored. Of course there was only one thing to be done. Miss Morrell could see that. And John did it. He answered the letter himself--wrote in a woman's hand; which is to say, he wrote every letter slanting backwards--said all that was important when the letter was finished, and scribbled it in and out between the date and the address, then, with a last effort at realism, spelt two words wrong on every page.

By this means, he was getting two letters every week, answering them both himself with as much industry and regularity as he ever put into his work.

This was all very well--all very simple so long as it lasted. But even Miss Morrell, whose eye to the main chance was unerring when it concerned a saucer of milk, warned him of what would follow. One morning, he received a letter from the little old white-haired lady, asking him when they were going to be married.

Quite placidly, he sat down and wrote----

"*We're to be married on the 16th of February. I've taken a small cottage down in the country. It costs forty pounds a year. I thought it wise to begin on economical lines. There's a little rustic porch to the front door, with William Allan Richardson roses climbing all over it. In the front, there are ten feet of garden, protected from the road by a wooden railing about two foot and a brick high with a tiny gate that's always locked to prevent burglars getting in. Three pink chestnuts combine to give it the appearance of an ambrosial park. At the back, there's a little lawn, just large enough for pitch and toss--I've measured it myself, it takes thirty-nine and a half of the longest steps I can take. And in the middle there's an apple tree,--that's likely to have a crop of three this year.*"

Miss Morrell closed her eyes in silent acquiescence when he read it out to her. It is possible that she may have considered him extravagant and, having that eye to the main chance, wondered whether he would be able to afford her her basin of milk with all this expenditure on two establishments. She did not say it, however, and listened patiently when he told her of other arrangements he had made.

"I forgot to tell you," he said, taking Miss Morrell on his knee--"that Lizzie Rowse is going to give up sticking labels on the jam-jars at Crosse and Blackwell's and is coming to do housemaid, cook, and general help for seven and sixpence a week--including beer money as she doesn't drink. I wanted to pay her more, but she wouldn't take it. I asked her why and she said, because she mightn't get it; that it was better to be certain of things in this world, rather than spending your life in hoping for what was too good to be true. It was no good my telling her that the whole business was only going to be transacted on paper, and that black and white would be the colour of everything she'd ever make out of it. But no! Seven and six was what she stuck at. As it was, it was a rise of sixpence to what she was getting at the jam-jars, and she wouldn't take a penny more. She said I'd been too kind to her as it was."

Miss Morrell listened to all this with contempt. Mrs. Rowse was not in good repute just then. They thought very nasty things about her on the third and second floors--what is more, they said them, and in tones quite loud enough for Miss Morrell and her tortoiseshell companion to hear.

Mrs. Rowse, it appeared, had spilt some water on the landing mid-way between the first and second floor where was the water cock common to the entire uses of the whole establishment. Five drops would convey an idea of about the amount she had spilled. At a first glance, this may seem very slight, but when it is explained that the stairs from the first to the second floor were covered with linoleum specially purchased by Mrs. Brown to make the approach to her residence the more ornate, it will be easily understood what a heinous offence this was.

Mrs. Brown had spoken about it and the untidy habits of the people on the first floor generally, in tones so opprobrious and so loud that not only the first floor, but indeed the whole house had heard her. Following this, there had appeared, stuck upon the wall so that all who approached the fountain must read, the accompanying notice--"If persons spill the water, will they have the kindness to slop it up."

It may be imagined how, in the effort to compose so reserved a notice as this, the feelings of Mrs. Brown, aided and abetted by Mrs. Morrell, must have overflowed in speech, all of which, of course, Miss Morrell would undoubtedly have heard. Hence her contempt.

When John had finished his dissertation upon the generosity and good qualities of Lizzie Rowse, Miss Morrell climbed down quietly from his knee. She was too dignified to say what she thought about it and so, with tail erect, stiffened a little perhaps for fear he might not perceive the full value of her dignity, she walked from the room.

The time passed by. It grew perilously near to that 16th of February. But John took it all very placidly; probably that is the way, when one does these things on paper. He invented all day long, and took as much pride in the ingenuity and construction of those letters as ever he took over his work.

"We went last night to the pit of a theatre," he said one morning to Miss Morrell. "Took Mrs. Rowse and Lizzie and Maud.

The two girls persisted in eating oranges till Maud put a piece of a bad one in her mouth; then they both stopped. I was rather glad, Maud got hold of a bad one, because I was just racking my brains to know how I could stop them without giving offence."

Miss Morrell looked quietly up into his face.

"You shouldn't take those sort of people to a theatre," said she.

John took no notice of her grammar. "It was Jill's idea," he replied.

On the 16th of February, right enough, they were married. Miss Morrell came that morning to drink her saucer of milk in honour of the event.

She walked in without knocking. It was her privilege. John was seated at his table, with his head buried in his hands, his shoulders shaking like a woman's with sobs that had no tears in them. And there, before him, with their paper wrappings all scattered about the place, were a pair of Dresden china shepherds, playing gaily on their lutes. Hanging about the neck of one of them was a card, on which was written: "*To John on his wedding day-- from his loving father.*"

CHAPTER XXXIV
THE DISSOLUBLE BONDAGE

If only it were that these things could continue--but alas! they cannot! We make our bubbles with all the colours of heaven in them, but cannot abide to see them only floating in the air. The greens and purples, the golds and scarlets, they seem so real upon the face of that diaphanous, crystal disc, that to touch them, to find their glorious stain upon the fingers, becomes the desire of every one of us. Out stretches the hand, the fingers tighten! The bubble is gone!

That was much the way with John's beautiful bubble of Nonsense. So long as Jill knew nothing of it; so long as he played with the fairy thing by himself, it was enough; but the every-day business of life, in which death is one of the unavoidable duties, intervened. One cannot play at these wonderful games for long. You cannot be married on paper--more perhaps is the pity. There would be fewer separations, fewer misunderstandings if you could. Life unfortunately does not permit of it. The law of Gravity is universal. You come down to earth.

When John had been living a married life of unbroken happiness for two months, there came two letters on the same day to Fetter Lane. He looked at one with no greater bewilderment than he did at the other. The first was from Venice in a strange handwriting; the second, from Jill. He opened it apprehensively. It could not be an invitation to her wedding? She could not have done that? Then what?

"Is there any reason why we should not see each other again? I shall be in Kensington Gardens to-morrow at 11.30."

He laid it down upon the table. For the moment, he forgot the existence of the other letter. In the midst of all his make-believe, this message from Jill was hard to realise; no easy matter to reconcile with all the phantoms in whose company he had been living.

What strange and unexpected things were women! Did ever they know what they wanted? or, knowing, and having found it, did any of them believe it to be what they had thought it at first?

Was she married? Since he had come back from Venice, the world might have been dead of her. He had heard nothing--seen nothing--and now this letter. Like the falling of some bolt of destruction from a heaven of blue, it had dropped into his garden, crushing the tenderest flowers he had planted there, in its swift rush of reality.

She wanted to see him again. The mere wish was a command; the mere statement that she would be in Kensington Gardens, a summons. All his sacrifice, his putting her away from him that day of her departure in Venice, was in one moment gone for nought. All this dream in which he had been living, became the bubble broken in the hand of such circumstance as this. While it had lasted, while he had continued to hear nothing of her, it had been real enough. Up till that moment, he had been happily married, quietly living down at Harefield in the county of Middlesex, in his cottage with its William Allan Richardson roses and its insurmountable wooden railing, two foot and a brick high. Every day, he had been coming up to London to work in Fetter Lane and to get his letters. Some very good reason, he had given to the old people why they should write to him there. And now, because he must obey this summons to go to Kensington Gardens and talk of things, perhaps, that little mattered, for fear they might embark upon the sea of those things that did, all his dream had vanished. The only reality left him, was that he was alone.

With a deep breath of resignation, he turned to the other letter and opened it.

"Dear Mr. Grey--I am writing this for your mother, to tell you the unfortunate news that your father is very ill. He has had a heart seizure, and, I fear, cannot live more than a few days. I am told by Mrs. Grey to ask you and your wife to come here as soon as possible. He knows the worst, and is asking to see you before he dies."

The paper hung limply in John's fingers. He stared blindly at the wall in front of him. One hand of ice seemed laid upon his forehead; the cold fingers of another gripped his heart.

Death--the end of everything--the irrevocable passing into an impenetrable darkness. It was well enough to believe in things hereafter; but to put it into practice wanted a power greater than belief. The old gentleman was going to die. The little old white-haired lady was to be left alone. How could he believe it? Would she believe it? Old people must die. He had said that often enough to himself while they had been well, while there had been no fear of it. He had said it, as the philosopher says that everything that is, is for the best. Now, as the philosopher so frequently has to do, he had to put it to the test.

His father was going to die. In a few days, he would see the last of him. Then pictures--scenes in his father's life--rode processionally through his mind. Last of all, he saw him, hands trembling, eyes alight and expression eager, placing back the Dresden Shepherd in the window of the Treasure Shop--that same gay figure in china which, with its fellow, he had sent to John on his imaginary wedding day.

With that picture, came the tears tumbling from his eyes. The wall opposite became a blurred vision in shadow as he stared at it. And all the time, the two Dresden Shepherds, perched upon his mantel-piece, played gaily on their lutes.

In the light-heartedness of his imagination, he had not conceived of this aspect of his deception. His father had asked to see his wife before he died. Now, he would give the world that the description had never been. Already, he could see the look of pain in the old gentleman's eyes, when he should say--as say he must--that he had had to leave her behind. Already, he could feel the sting of his own conscience when, by that bedside in the little room, he invented the last messages which Jill had sent to make his passing the easier.

It had been simple matter enough to conceive a thousand of these messages and write them upon paper; it had been simple matter enough to write those letters, which they were to suppose had come from Jill's own hand. But to act--to become the mummer in mask and tinsel, beside his father's death-bed, hurt every sensibility he possessed. It was beyond him. He knew he could not do it. Jill must know. Jill must be told everything, the whole story of this flight of his imagination. He trusted the gentle heart of her, at least, to give him some message of her own; something he could repeat for his father to hear, without the deriding knowledge in his heart that it was all a lie, all a fabrication, which, if the old gentleman did but know, he would reproach him with in his last moments.

There, then, with the tears still falling down his cheeks, he wrote to Jill, telling her everything; enclosing the last letter which he had just received.

"Give me something to say," he begged--*"something which comes from the kindness of your heart and not from the fiendishness of my imagination. In those few moments you saw him, he must have shown you some of the gentleness of his nature; must have shown you something which, putting aside the blame which I deserve at your hands for all I have said, expects this generosity from you. I have become a beggar, an importunate beggar, scarcely to be denied; but I become so with all humility. Just write me a line. You can see now, that I dare not meet you to-morrow, now that you know. But send me a line as soon as you receive this, which I may learn by heart and repeat to him with a conscience made clear, in so much as I shall know that such words have actually been said by you."*

When he had posted this, John began the packing of those things which he would require for the journey. Into the chapel of unredemption he marched and made an indiscriminate offering of everything he possessed on his list of sacrificial objects. The high priest swept them all into his keeping and winked at his acolytes.

The next morning came Jill's reply. John tore it open, and read and re-read and re-read again.

"Meet me on Friday morning on the Piazetta at 12 o'clock."

CHAPTER XXXV
THE WONDER OF BELIEF

To believe, is the greater part of reality.

Despite all argument that flung itself at his credulity, John believed that Jill would be true to her word. Reasons in multitude there were, why it should be impossible for her to take such a journey and at such short notice. He admitted them all, as his mind presented them before him; yet still he believed. Though his faith trembled a thousand times in the balance; though common sense warned him insistently that hope was fruitless; nevertheless, he believed. Even when the little men on the Plaza began the striking of their twelve strokes on that Friday morning and, searching the gondolas as they rode in sight, searching them with eyes burning and pupils dilated in nervous expectancy, yet finding no sight of Jill, he still had faith that triumphed above all reason and overcame all doubt.

The vibrations of the last stroke from the great clock in the Square had died down to the faint trembling in his ear; the single bell in all the churches was tolling for the Angelus; hope was just beginning to flicker in John's heart as a candle trembles that feels its approaching end and then, round the corner of the *Rio San Luca*, shooting quickly into the Grand Canal, came the twentieth gondola John had espied, in which one solitary lady was seated. Something about the haste with which this gondolier plied his oar, something in the attitude of the lady as she half leant forward, half reclined upon the cushion at her back, something even in the crisp, swift hiss of the water as it shot away from the bows, brought him the conviction at last that it was Jill. When instinct is once awake, it finds a thousand little proofs to give it assurance.

As the gondola came nearer, the lady moved her position. She had observed John waiting. He strained his eyes to see through the glare of light that sparkled up from the dancing water. Then a little white handkerchief darted out, and fluttering, shook the beating of his heart with realisation. It was Jill.

In another moment, he was holding her hands and saying the most common-place words of greeting, but in a voice that held in it all the joy of his heart. The gondolier stood by smiling, waiting to be paid. The signora had wanted to be taken quickly to the *Piazetta*, and he had travelled as fast as if they were going to a funeral. It was almost payment enough to see her meeting with the signor. Not quite enough, however, for when they walked away, forgetting, in the embarrassement of their happiness, what he was owed, he stepped forward and, very politely, touched John's arm.

"*Doue lire, signor,*" he said and showed some wonderful teeth in a brilliant smile. John thought of a London cabby under similar circumstances, giving him three and a smile as well.

Then he turned back to Jill.

"Well--are you going to explain it all?" he asked.

"There's nothing to explain," she said, half laughing. "I'm here--isn't that enough?"

"But your husband?"

"We're not married yet. I pleaded for a long engagement."

"Then your people?"

"Aren't you satisfied that I'm here?" she said gently. "Does it matter how I got here? You might just as well be curious to know whether I came by the St. Gothard or the Simplon. But you don't ask that. I'm here--you don't worry about that. Then why worry about the other?" and her eyes twinkled with mystery.

"Is it Mrs. Crossthwaite again?"

She nodded her head with a laugh.

"She's with you?"

"No--she's at her cottage in Devonshire."

"But you'll be found out."

"Not if I go back to-morrow."

"And you are going back?"

"Yes."

"And you came all this way----?"

"Yes--here I am--in the City of Beautiful Nonsense again."

"The little old white-haired lady was right then!" he exclaimed.

"How right?"

"She said that you would come anywhere, that you would do anything for me."

Jill tried to meet his eyes.

"When did she say that?" she asked.

"Last year--after you had gone."

He watched her as he waited for her to reply, but she kept silent. It was not a moment in which she dared to speak; moreover, other matters were waiting.

In St. Mark's, beneath the image of St. Anthony, where they had met the year before, they chose to go and make their arrangements. There is everything that is conservative about Romance. Places become dear for themselves, for the spirit of the Romance which, like a lingering perfume, still hangs about their corners. The times alter perhaps, sometimes even the woman herself is different; but the spirit, the Romance and with them often the place, remain the same.

"You understand all it means, your coming to see them?" he asked when they were seated. "You understood my letter? You realise what I've been saying?"

"Yes, every word."

"Then why did you come?"

"I couldn't bear to think of his dying without----" she hesitated, or did she hang upon the words--"without seeing your--your wife as he wanted to. Oh, John! Why did you say it? It wasn't right of you! You ought not to have done it!"

She was angry! His beautiful nonsense had offended her! Might he not have known that? What woman in the world was there who could have understood so well as to sympathise with the trick which he had played.

"If it has annoyed you," said he, "why did you come? Of course, I know it was unpardonable; but then, I thought you'd never know. I didn't understand how much a fabrication, an invention it was, until I heard that he was dying and wanted to see you before the end. It had been so easy to make up till then. I'd become infatuated with my own success. Then, when I got the letter from the doctor, I realised that I was done. I couldn't go to his death-bed, making up lies, giving him messages that had never passed your lips, never entered into your thoughts. I was done. And I hoped you'd understand. I hoped--like a fool, I suppose--that you wouldn't be offended."

"But I'm not offended."

He stared at her. Even St. Anthony stared, because St. Anthony does not know so much about women as you would expect. He knows full well their extraordinary valuation of trifles, but on serious matters such as these, he is as ignorant of them as the rest of us.

"You're not offended!" echoed John.

"No."

"Then why did you say I was wrong? Why did you say I ought not to have done it?"

"Because it was not fair to them. They might have found out. The little old white-haired lady may find out even now."

"Then you don't think it was unfair to you?"

"You thought I should?"

He nodded emphatically two or three times.

"That, I believe, is the way you judge women. That is why their actions are so incomprehensible to you. You form an opinion of them and then, naturally, everything they do seems a mystery, because you won't change your opinion. They're not the mystery. I assure you women are very simple. The mystery is that their actions don't conform with your pre-conceived opinion." She stumbled over those last big words. She was not quite sure of them. They sounded very large, moreover, they sounded as if they expressed what she felt. What they really meant was another matter. She could have told you nothing about that. That is not the way women choose their words.

"Well now," he said--"we must be going. Of course I haven't been, though I arrived last night. I counted on your coming."

"Yes," she whispered, "that's the wonderful part about you-- you believe."

She thought of her father--she thought of the man with the brown beard like St. Joseph. They believed nothing until it was before their eyes. But a woman likes to be trusted, because at least, she means to do what she says; sometimes--God knows--she does it.

CHAPTER XXXVI
THE PASSING

It was a greater ordeal than they knew of, for Death, though he is for ever in our midst, always covers his face, and you may never recognise the features until that last moment when, with the sweeping gesture of the arm, he throws aside the folds that enshroud him, and in his quiet voice, so low, yet so distinct, announces "It is finished."

At the opening of the little door, they beheld the dear old white-haired lady. Her arms fell about them both and, in her feeble way, she clasped them to her. It was not hysterical, not that cry of the witless woman who is faced with the stern matters of life and will lean upon any shoulder to support her weight. She was losing that which was hers alone, and these two, though she thought they belonged irrevocably to each other, belonged also in their way to her. They were all now that was left her.

"How is he?" asked John, as she led them down that vast chamber to the deep-set door which opened to the tiny bedroom.

"You're only just in time," she replied. "The priest is with him. It's just the end."

There was a true, a steady note of reconciliation in her voice. She knew and had accepted the inevitable with that silent courage which brave women have. You knew that there would be no sudden passionate outburst of cries and tears when at last it actually was all over. His time of departure had come. She recognised it; had faced it bravely for the last few days. On Claudina's ample bosom, the first wild torrent of weeping had been made; for your servant, your meanest slave is a woman when she understands in such moments as these. When her agony had passed, she had raised her head, brushed away the tears. With warm water, Claudina had bathed her eyes and then, bravely setting a smile upon her trembling lips, she had gone to watch by his bedside.

Gently, now, she opened the door and admitted them, then silently closed it behind her. The jalousies were closed. In faint bars of light, the sunshine stole into the room and lit it faintly as though stained through the amber-coloured glass of church windows. In a deep shadow, burnt the tiny flame of red upon their bedroom altar. Bowed humbly down before it, knelt the priest, whose even, muttered tones just stirred in a gentle vibration of sound as of some hive of bees muffled with a heavy cloth and, only with the sibilant lisping of the breath between his lips as he pronounced certain letters, did it seem that a man was speaking at all. It was all so quiet, so even, so monotonous, a gentle noise to waft a spirit to its last sleep.

In a dark corner of the room, away from the rest, almost lost in the shadow, knelt Claudina, her head bent low upon her breast, her shoulders gently lifting and falling in sobs that were tuned low to the silence. She did not look up as they entered. The priest did not move his head. It all continued, just as if nothing had happened and, lying still, inert upon the pillow, almost lost in the big bed, was that silent figure of the old white-haired gentleman, who never stirred, nor uttered any sound, as though the chanting of the priest had already lulled him to his infinite sleep.

They all knelt down by the bedside, buried their faces in their hands, and the chanting continued.

What thoughts passed through the minds of those two who knelt there, playing their part, acting the life which both of them knew could never be real, it would be impossible to say. In the face of death, the mind has such simple thoughts, that words can scarcely touch their expression. Remorse may have scourged them; it may have been that, in seeing the peaceful passing of his spirit, they were satisfied that what they did was for the best; or, in the deepest secrets of their hearts they may have been longing that it all were true. Yet, there they both knelt, with the little old white-haired lady by their side. For all the world you might have thought, as did all the others in the room, that they were husband and wife on the very threshold of that journey through the years of which this death-bed meeting was the gate where all must pass out into the land that is in the blue haze beyond.

Presently, the voice of the priest became silent. The heads of all sank lower in their hands as the Extreme Unction was given. God visits the earth in great silences. It was a wonderful silence then. The wine gurgling softly into the cup, the unfolding of the little napkin, the patten lying on the tongue, the last brave effort as the old gentleman swallowed the sacred bread, were all noises that thrilled and quivered in that silence.

Then it was all passed, all finished, the spirit cleansed, the last gentle confession made of such sins of thought and deed as a brave and generous gentleman is capable of. The priest rose to his feet and, taking his little vessels with him in their case, stole quietly from the room. A moment or so passed in still deeper silence. At last Claudina rose. She crossed herself as she passed the little altar, crept also to the door and went away.

Now the silence was still deeper than before, as though, in the mere functions of their living, these two had taken with them their disturbing elements of full-blooded life from this place where life was so fainting and so weak. When they had gone, the very vibrations of air seemed more still and a greater quietness fell with their absence.

And the three who remained, continued there motionless on their knees--motionless, until, in the midst of the silence, came the whispering of a tired voice--a voice, pronouncing with infinite difficulty, one, single word,

"John--John."

John knelt quickly upright. He stretched out his hand and found a hand to meet it, a hand that could not hold, that only lay in tender submission upon his own.

"Father," he said; and that, after all, is the only word that a son can say--father or mother--they are the last words left in the deepest heart of a man. He utters them, incoherently almost, when emotion is choking speech.

"Where is Jill?" the voice whispered again.

Jill crept round on her knees to his side. With one hand below in the darkness, John held hers. They clasped them and unclasped them as the sobs rose and broke silently in their throats.

The old gentleman's eyes took a light into them, as he saw their heads together by his bedside. With a great effort, he strained himself to rise upon one elbow in the bed and, laying the other hand upon their heads, he whispered that blessing which it has been in the power of the father to give from time immemorial.

"God bless you," he whispered. "Make your lives out of love, as I have made mine. Make your children out of love, as I have made mine. Make your work out of love--as I have made mine."

His voice burnt low, but yet it burnt. The flame of it was there. It seared into the very hearts of them. Jill's fingers lay in John's as a bird that is starved and cold, lies limply in the hand that succours it. Her cheeks were ashen white. Her eyes stared wildly before her at the pattern on the counter-pane and tears rolled from them without heed or stay.

The moments passed then, as the old gentleman leant back upon his pillows. Without moving, they stayed there with heads bowed down before him. At last, he moved again. His hand stretched out once more and felt for John's.

"God bless you my boy," he said, as his son bent over him. "You've made us very happy. You've set your life just as we could wish. Now do your work. I expect I shall hear how you get on. They won't keep that from me. They'll let me see your first happy ending. It's the only way to end--like this. Now kiss me--you don't mind--this time--do you?"

John kissed him, as pilgrims kiss the feet of God.

"And tell me----" the old gentleman whispered. He paused to breathe as the thought came swiftly on him. "Tell me--why did you kiss me--on the forehead--that night--a year ago?"

"I'd seen you in the Treasure Shop, sir--and I----" the words wrestled in his throat--"I thought you were the finest man I'd ever known."

The old gentleman lay back again upon his pillows. The light of a great pride was flashing in his eyes. His son had called him--sir. That was all. Yet in that moment, he felt like a Viking being borne out upon his burning ship into the sea of noble burial. His son had called him, sir. He lay still, listening to the great sound of it, as it trumpeted triumphantly in his ears. His son, who was going to be far greater than he had ever been, whose work was above and beyond all work that he had ever done--his son had called him--sir.

Then, for some time, everything was still once more. They bent their heads again within their hands. At last, the little old white-haired lady, like

CHAPTER XXXVII
THE CIRCULAR TOUR

The evening, with her quiet feet, had stolen across the sky; night was fast riding in the wake of her, when at last they left the little old white-haired lady alone.

Repeatedly John had offered to stay and keep her company.

"You may not sleep, dearest," he said gently. "Someone had better be with you."

"I shall have Claudina," she replied with a smile of gratitude. "And I think I shall sleep. I've scarcely been to bed since he was ill. I think I shall sleep." And her eyes closed involuntarily.

Jill offered to stay, to help her to bed, to sit by her side until she slept. But, patiently and persistently, she shook her tired, white head and smiled.

"Claudina understands my little fidgety ways," she said--"and perhaps I shall be better with her."

Down the vast chamber, she walked with them again to the little door. Her head was high and brave, but the heart within her beat so faintly and so still, that sometimes, unseen by them, she put her hand upon her bodice to assure herself that it beat at all.

Before they pulled the heavy curtain, she stopped and took both their hands in hers.

"My dear--dear children," she whispered, and for the first time her voice quivered. A sob answered it in Jill's throat. She tried to face the old lady's eyes, bright with a strange and almost unnatural brilliance, but a thousand reproaches cried at her courage and beat it back.

"My dear--dear children," said the old lady once more, and this time her voice took a new power into itself. Her figure seemed to straighten, her eyes to steady with resolve.

"I have something I want to say; something your father would have said as well, had there been time. I thought of waiting till to-morrow, perhaps till he was buried. But I'm going to say it now; before you can tell me what I know you mean to. I discussed it all with your father before you came, and he quite agreed with me." She paused. A great, deep breath she drew, as does a painter when he nerves his hand. And in the gathering darkness in that great room, they waited with all attention expectant.

"When your father is buried," she began slowly, drawing with reserve from that long deep breath, "I am going to live on here." Quickly she raised her hand before John could answer. She thought she knew what he was going to say. "No!" she said, "you must let me finish. I'm going to live on here. For the next ten years, these rooms belong to us--and ten years----" she smiled--"are more than I shall need. I could not leave here. I know it so well. You want me to come and live with you--but no----" the white head shook, and a curl fell out of place upon her cheek. She did not notice it. "No--I know what is best," she went on. "Your father and I decided what was right. Old people have their place. They should never get in the way of the ones who are just beginning. I shall be contented waiting here for the year to come round to bring you both to see me. Don't think I shall be discontented. Claudina will take care of me, and I shall not be in your way. You'll like me all the better in the summer. I get tiresome in the winter. I know I do. He used not to say so, but Claudina has to admit it. I get colds. I have to be looked after. Sometimes I'm in bed for days together and have to be nursed. All of which things," she added, turning with a bright smile to Jill, "Claudina can do so much more easily than you. She's more accustomed to them."

And look at my poor hands, she might have said, how much would you not have to do for me? You would have to dress me, to undress me, to get me up, to put me to bed. But she hid her hands. Those withered hands had their pathos even for her. She would not press them upon their notice.

"Think over what I've said, dear," she concluded, looking up to John. "Tell me what you've thought about it to-morrow, or the next day. I know all this evening, it has been in your mind to tell me of the arrangements you have thought of making for me in your little cottage; but think over it again, from my point of view. Understand it as I do, and I'm sure you'll find I'm right."

And they could say nothing. In silence, they had listened to all this indomitable courage, to this little old white-haired lady preparing to face the great loneliness after death. In silence, Jill had bent down and kissed her. The last lash had fallen upon her then. She could not speak. By the bedside of the old gentleman, the utmost tears had tumbled from her eyes. And now this, from the little old lady, had been more than she could bear. That sensation which they call the breaking of the heart, was almost stifling the breath within her. The whole army of her emotions had been thundering all this time at the gates of her heart. When she had heard his blessing, she had flung the gates open wide. Now, they were trampling her beneath their feet. She could not rise above them. She could not even cry out loud the remorse and pain she felt.

With John, this silence that was forced upon him was more cruel still. On a scaffold, set before the crowd, he stood, listening to the loathing and reproach that groaned in every throat. The little old lady was making this sacrifice, and yet, he knew a thousand times that he should not let it be. To stand there then and, in that derisive silence, to quietly give consent, was the utmost penalty that he could pay. Then, in the teeth of all reproach, as though to shut out from his ears the moaning of that cruel, relentless crowd, he caught her slender figure in his arms and strained her to him.

"My little mother," he said wildly in his breath, "it can't be like that--it can't be! Something must be done. I'll think it out, but something must be done."

Then, kissing her again and again, he put her down from him, as you put back a little doll into its cradle--a little doll which some thoughtless hand has treated ill.

They said no word to each other as they passed through the archway this time. In silence, they stepped into the gondola which had been waiting for them at the steps for an hour and more.

John told him the hotel at which Jill was staying, and the gondolier pushed out into the black water. Another moment, and they were swaying into the soft velvet darkness, rent here and there with little points of orange light, where a lamp burnt warmly in some tiny window.

"And to-morrow," said John presently, "you must go back? Perhaps that's the hardest part of it."

"I shall not go for a few days," Jill replied quietly.

He looked quickly at her white face. Impulsively his hand stretched out to hers. She stared before her as he took it. She was like a figure of ivory, set strangely in black marble, as black as the water itself. There was no movement from her, no stir, scarcely a sign of life.

"That's good of you," he said in honest thankfulness. "You're being wonderfully good to me." He repeated it, ruminating, with his eyes looking out into the distance where hers were set. "But, I might have known you'd be that."

She shuddered. Praise from him, then, hurt more than all. She shuddered as if a wind had chilled her.

After a long pause, he moved and spoke again.

"How are you going to manage?" he asked. "What are you going to do?"

"I shall write."

"Home?"

"No--to Mrs. Crossthwaite."

"Is it safe?"

"I think so."

"But you mustn't be discovered," he said quickly. Conscience pulled him first one way, then another. Every instinct prompted him to accept her generosity without question. "You must not take too great a risk. Why, indeed, should you take any?"

The words came slowly. He felt both glad and sorry when once they were spoken. The tragedy of life is indecision. They bury suicides at the crossroads, for that is where lurks all tragedy-- the indecision of which way to choose.

At last, she turned her head and looked at him. The hand he held quickened with feeling. It became alive. He felt the fingers tighten on his own.

"You are thinking of me?" she said.

"I must," he replied.

"You feel it your duty because I'm here alone?"

He shook his head.

"I don't feel duty," he answered. "There is no such thing. People do what they do. When it is a disagreeable thing to do, they make it worth the doing by calling it duty. That is the satisfaction they get out of it. But everything that is done, is done for love--love of self or love of other people. Duty is the name that enhances the value of disagreeable things. But it's only a name. There's nothing behind it--nothing human, nothing real. I don't feel duty as some do, and so I never attempt anything that's disagreeable. A thing that is weighed is repugnant to me. Just now things are very hard--just now I scarcely know which way to turn. The little old white-haired lady puts her arms round me and I feel I can't let her go. You hold my hand and I feel that I would move heaven and earth to save you from a moment's unhappiness." Reluctantly, he let go her hand and sat upright. "Here we are; I say good-night here. You must think before you write that letter."

She put out a detaining hand.

"Tell him to go back to your rooms," she said--"I'll take you back there before I go in. I've got a lot to say."

John smiled incredulously. He could have asked heaven for no greater gift. His heart was sick. There was nothing but disillusionment to which he could look forward. His own disillusionment had come already; but that of the little old white-haired lady was harder to bear than his own. Stretching before him, an ugly shadow, he saw the unswerving promise of that day when he must tell her all the truth; that day, a year perhaps to come, when, arriving in Venice without Jill, he must explain her absence, either by another fabrication or the naked fact.

To hide his face from it all a little longer; to have Jill's presence closing his eyes to it, even though it were only for a speck of time in the eternity that was to follow, was a reprieve for which he had not dared to hope.

"You mean that?" he said eagerly.

"Yes."

John gave the order. The gondolier did not smile. Perhaps the motion of his oar as he swung them round was a gentle comment. Every man has his different medium of expression. There was once a ballet dancer who, whenever she became excited and was driven to gesticulation, always caught her skirt just below the knee and lifted it to show her instep. It meant more than any words she could ever have uttered.

John sat back again by Jill's side.

"Oh! it's good," he said, half aloud, half to himself.

"What is good?" she whispered.

"To be just a little while longer with you. I dread to-night, I dread the next few nights to come. I shall see his eyes. I shall hear that sound in his voice when he called to her. I shall see that brave look in her face, and hear that whole speech of her sacrifice as we stood by the door. My God! What wonderful things women can be when they love."

"She's so gentle and yet so brave," said Jill.

"Brave!" he echoed it, but it had not the force of all he felt. "Great Heavens! Think of her there now, alone. Everything but us gone out of her life; a sudden rent in the clouds--just a flash, and but for us, in that moment she's made destitute. And then, with a smile in her eyes, to give up what little she has. And I, to have to accept it. Lord! what a fool I've been. I remember that day when Mrs. Morrell's sandy cat came slouching into the room and I'd just received the letter saying she would write no more of you. I took that confounded cat into my confidence--'The little old lady wants a love story,' I said. And the cat seemed to wink as though it had no objection to hearing one, too. Then I began. Lord! what a child I am. Not the faintest idea of the future! No conception of consequence! Just a blind idea of doing things as they come, without the smallest consideration of results! I never foresaw that it was going to lead to this. What a child! My heavens! What a child! He was a child! She's a child! I'm a child, too! We're a family of children, not fit for one of the responsibilities of life."

"Do you think you're any the worse for that?" she asked softly.

"I don't know," he shrugged his shoulders. "Upon my soul, it seems now the greatest crime a man can commit. In a world of grown-up men and women who can pay their rents and taxes, meet their bills and save their money, to be a child is a monstrous, a heinous crime."

"Only to those who don't understand," she answered.

"Well--and who does?"

"I do."

"You do? Yes, I know that--but how can you help? You've done more than a thousand women would have done. You helped me to make his passing a happy one; you can't do more than that. You're even going to stay on a few days longer to help this fool of a child still more. That proves you understand. I know you understand--God bless you."

He shrank into himself despairingly. His whole body seemed to contract in the pain of self-condemnation, and he pressed his hands violently over his eyes. Suddenly, he felt her move. He took his hands away and found her kneeling at his feet, that white face of ivory turned up to his, her eyes dimmed with tears.

"Do you call it understanding if I leave you now--little child?" she whispered, and her voice was like the sound in a long-dreamt dream which, on the morning, he had forgotten and striven to remember ever since.

Slowly, he took away his hands. Now he recalled the voice. The whole dream came back. It was summer--summer in England. They were in a field where cattle grazed under the warm shadows of high elm trees. Cowslips grew there, standing up through the grass with their thin, white, velvet stems; here and there an orchid with spotted leaves, a group of scabii bending their feathered heads in the heat of the day. Jill sat sewing little garments, and he lay idle, stretched upon his back, gazing up into the endless blue where the white clouds sailed like little ships, making for distant harbours. And as she sewed, she talked of things more wonderful than God had made the day; of things that women, in the most sacred moments of their life, sometimes reveal to men.

This was the dream he had forgotten. In his sleep, he had known that it was a dream; had known that he must remember it all his life; yet in the morning, but faintly recollected he had dreamt at all. Now, those two words of hers--little child--and the summer day, the browsing cattle, the white flutter of the tiny garments, the scent of the fields and the sound of her voice had all returned in one swift rush of memory.

"What do you mean?" he asked slowly--"if you leave me now, what do you mean? What do you mean by--little child?"

Both hands, she put out; both hands to clasp on his. The tears ceased gathering in her eyes. Before God and in great moments, the eyes forget their tears; there is no trembling of the lips; the voice is clear and true.

"Don't you remember what he said?" she asked. "'Make your lives out of love, as I have made mine. Make your children out of love as I have made mine.' Did you think I could hear that from him without knowing what you yourself have said just now, that there is no such thing as Duty?"

John stared at her. He dared not interpose. He dared not even answer the question she had asked, for fear his voice should break the linking of her thoughts.

"Can you hear him saying--'Make your lives out of duty, as I have made mine. Make your children out of duty as I have made mine?' Can you imagine him saying that? Can you feel how it would have grated on your ears? Yet that's just what I'm going to do; but I didn't realise it till then."

"What is it you're going to say?" he asked below his breath. "What is it you're leading to? All this is leading to something. What is it?"

"That I'm not going to leave you, little child. That if, after all, there is such a thing as Duty, he has shown me what it is."

The gondola bumped against the steps. The voice of the gondolier called out that their destination was reached. John rose quickly to his feet.

"Go back," he said. "Go back to the hotel."

Away they started again and as he plied his oar, the gondolier gazed up at the stars, and hummed a muffled tune.

For a few moments, John remained standing. She was not going to leave him. She was never going to leave him. That was the big thought, triumphant in his mind. But a thousand little thoughts, like grains of dust in a great sunbeam, danced and whirled about it. He thought of those rooms of his in Fetter Lane; of his own improvidence, of the disreputable appearance of Mrs. Morrell on Saturday mornings when she cleaned the stairs of the house, and conversed, in language none too refined, with Miss Morrell. He thought of the impudence of Mrs. Brown, when she appeared in curling papers and made remarks about her neighbours with a choice of words that can only be said to go with that particular adornment of the hair.

But these were only cavilling considerations, which made the big thought real. He could change his address. Now, indeed, he could go down to Harefield. He could work twice as hard; he could make twice as much money. All these things, ambition will easily overcome in the face of so big a thought as this. She was never going to leave him.

He took her hands as he sat down.

"Do you think you realise everything?" he said; for the first instinct of the grateful recipient is to return the gift. He does not mean to give it back; but neither does he quite know how to take it.

She nodded her head.

"All my circumstances? How poor I am?"

"Everything."

"And still----?"

"And still," she replied. "Nothing but your asking could change me."

He sat gazing at her, just holding her hands. Only in real stories do people at such a moment fall into each other's arms. When the matter is really nonsense, then people act differently-- perhaps they are more reserved--possibly the wonder of it all is greater then.

John sat silently beside her and tried to understand. It was so unexpected. He had scarcely even wished that it might be so.

"When did you think this?" he asked presently.

"Just--before he died."

"When he blessed us?"

"Yes."

"Why haven't you said so before?"

"I couldn't. I haven't been able to speak. I've suddenly seen things real----"

"In the midst of all this nonsense----"

"Yes--and it's taken my breath away. All in a few hours, I've seen death and love, and I don't know what the change is in me, but I'm different. I've grown up. I understand. You say I have understood before; but I've understood nothing. I should never have come here last year, if I had understood. I should never have continued meeting you in Kensington Gardens, if I had understood. Women don't understand as a rule; no girl understands. She would never play with love, if she did. I know, suddenly, that I belong to you; that I have no right to marry anyone else. In these last few hours, I've felt that a force outside me determines the giving of my life, and it has frightened me. I couldn't say anything. When you said you were a child, then I suddenly found my tongue. I wasn't afraid any more. I knew you were a child, my child--my little child--not my master. There's no mastery in it; you're just my child."

Suddenly she closed her arms round him; she buried her head on his shoulder.

"I can't explain any more!" she whispered--"It's something I can't explain--I haven't any words for it."

And, as he held her to him, John thought of the dream he had dreamt, of the field and the cattle, and the white fluttering of the tiny garments, and the clouds sailing in the sky, and again came to him the note in her voice as she told him the most wonderful thing in the whole world. Then, leaning out from the hood, he called out to the gondolier:

"Just take us out on the Lagoon before we go back."

And they swung round again to his oar.

CHAPTER XXXVIII
A PROCESS OF HONESTY

The very best of us have a strain of selfishness. The most understanding of us are unable to a nicety to grasp the other person's point of view; and there will always be some little thing, some subtle matter, which it is not in the nature of us to perceive in the nature of someone else. Perhaps this is the surest proof of the existence of the soul.

When, on the steps of the hotel, John bid good-night to Jill, there was but one regret in the minds of both of them, that that blessing which they had received at the hands of the old gentleman had come too soon; that in the receipt of it, they had been impostors, unworthy of so close a touch with the Infinite.

174

There is nothing quite so distressing to the honest mind as this and, to avoid it, to mitigate the offence, it is quite a simple process for the honest mind to project itself into some further evil of selfishness, so long as it may gain peace and a free conscience.

"There is only one thing that we can do," said John, and, if good intentions weigh, however lightly, in the sensitive scales of justice, let one be here placed in the balance for him.

"I know what you are going to say," replied Jill.

Of course she knew. They had begun to think alike already.

"We must tell her."

She nodded her head.

"We can't deceive her," he went on--"It's bad enough to have deceived him. And now--well, it's such a different matter now. She must understand. Don't you think she will?"

With a gentle pressure of his hand, she agreed.

They both pictured her glad of the knowledge, because in the hearts of them both, they were so glad to be able to tell. For this is how the honest deceive themselves, by super-imposing upon another, that state of mind which is their own. With all belief, they thought the little old white-haired lady must be glad when she heard; with all innocence and ignorance of human nature, they conceived of her gratitude that such an ending had been brought about.

"When shall we tell her?" asked Jill.

"Oh--not at once. In a day or so. The day you go, perhaps."

"And you think she'll forgive me?"

He smiled at her tenderly for her question.

"Do you think you know anything about the little old white-haired lady when you ask that? I'll just give you an example. She abominates drunkenness--loathes it--in theory has no pity for it, finds no excuse. Well, they had a gardener once, when they were better off. There's not a school for the trade in Venice, as you can imagine. Tito knew absolutely nothing. He was worthless. He was as likely as not to pull up the best plant in the garden and think it was a weed. But there he was. Well, one day Claudina reported he was drunk. Drunk! Tito drunk! In their garden! Oh, but it was horrible--it was disgusting! She could scarcely believe that it was true. But Claudina's word had to be taken and Tito must go. She could not even bear to think he was still about the place.

"Tito--I have heard so and so--is it true?" she said.

Well--Tito talked about not feeling well and things disagreeing with him. At last he admitted it.

"Then you must go," said she--"I give you a week's wages."

But a piteous look came into Tito's face and he bent his head and he begged--'Oh, don't send me away, *egregia signora*!' and that cry of his went so much to her heart, that she almost took his head on her shoulder in her pity for him. And you say--will she forgive you? Why, her capacity for forgiveness is infinite! I often think, when they talk of the sins that God cannot pardon, I often think of her."

She looked up and smiled.

"Do you always tell a little story when you want to explain something?" she asked.

"Always," said he--"to little children."

She shut her eyes to feel the caress in the words.

"Well, then," she said, opening them again--"we tell her the day after to-morrow."

"That is the day you go?"

"Yes--I must go then. And may I say one thing?"

"May you? You may say everything but one."

"What is that?"

"That I have been dreaming all this to-night."

"No, you haven't been dreaming. It was all real."

"Then--what do you want to say?"

"That the little old white-haired lady is not to live alone. I'm going to live with her as much of the year as you'll let me--all of it if you will."

For one moment, he was silent--a moment of realisation, not of doubt.

"God seems to have given me so much in this last hour," he said, "that nothing I could offer would appear generous after such a gift. It shall be all the year, if you wish it. I owe her that and more. But for her, perhaps, this would never have been."

He took her hand and pressed his lips to it.

"Good-night, sweetheart. And the day after to-morrow then, we tell her everything."

CHAPTER XXXIX
THE END OF THE LOOM

When the little door had closed behind them, the old lady stood with head inclined, listening to the sound of their footsteps. Then, creeping to the high window that looked over the *Rio Marin*,--that same window at which, nearly a year before, she had stood with her husband watching Jill's departure--she pressed her face against the glass, straining her eyes to see them to the end.

It was very dark. For a moment, as John helped Jill into the gondola, she could distinguish their separate figures; but then, the deep shadow beneath the hood enveloped them and hid them from her gaze. Yet still she stayed there; still she peered out over the water as, with that graceful sweeping of the oar, they swung round and swayed forward into the mystery of the shadow beyond.

To the last moment when, melting into the darkness, they became the darkness itself, she remained, leaning against the sill, watching, as they watch, who long have ceased to see. And for some time after they had disappeared, her white face and still whiter hair were pressed against the high window in that vast chamber, as if she had forgotten why it was she was there and stood in waiting for her memory to return.

Such an impression she might have given, had you come upon her, looking so lost and fragile in that great room. But in her mind, there was no want of memory. She remembered everything.

It is not always the philosopher who makes the best out of the saddest moments in life. Women can be philosophic; the little old white-haired lady was philosophic then, as she stood gazing out into the empty darkness. And yet, no woman is really a philosopher. To begin with, there is no heart in such matter at all; it is the dried wisdom of bitterness, from which the burning sun of reason has sucked all blood, all nourishment. And that which has no heart in it, is no fit food for a woman. For a woman is all heart, or she is nothing. If she can add two and two together, and make a calculation of it, then let her do it, but not upon one page in your life, if you value the paper upon which that life be written. For once she sees that she can add aright, she brings her pen to all else. The desire of power, to a woman who has touched it, is a disease.

But it was other than the calculation of philosophy which sustained the mind of the little old lady at this, the saddest and the most lonely moment of her life.

As she leant, gazing out of the window down the black line of water that lost itself in the silent gathering of the houses, there almost was triumph in her mind. She had lost everything, but she had done everything. She was utterly alone; but only because she had outlived her world. And last of all, there was triumph in her heart, because her world was complete. She could have asked nothing more of it. Her Romance was rekindled. If there was anything to live for, it was to see the flames leaping up in some other brazier--those flames which she had given the spark of her life to ignite. And had she not seen them rising already? Had she not seen the fire blessed by the only hand to whom the power of blessing is given? For all she knew, for all she dared to guess, the old gentleman's blessing had fallen upon a future, further distant than, perhaps, he dreamed of. What more had desire to ask for than that?

She remembered how, in those days of doubt and troubling, she had counted in fear the time which was left in which John should take his wife. She remembered doubting that they might even live to see the realisation of such happiness as that.

They were old people. There had no longer been certainty for them in the counting of the years. And, as this very day had proved, John's marriage had come none too soon. Had it been later, had they not received that blessing to which, with all such things as the flights of magpies and the turnings of the moon, this simple soul of hers gave magic virtue, then, indeed, she might have looked sorrowfully out of the high window in the great room.

But no--there had been no such mischance as that. The vivid sense of completeness filled her heart and raised the beating of it for a few moments, as the hope of a dying priest is raised by the presentation of his beloved cross.

And this is the philosophy, the stoicism of women, who will face the fearsome emptiness of a whole desert of life, so be it, that their heart is full and satisfied.

Who, passing below on the black strip of water and, seeing her pale, white face looking out from that high window into the night, could have conceived of such wonderful reconciliation as this? Who could have imagined the whole moment as it was? An old gentleman lying in a tiny room, the lamp still burning on the altar at his side, his hands crossed upon his breast in an unbreaking sleep; away out upon the water of the Lagoon, two lovers, young, alight with life, exalted in a sudden realisation of happiness, and this little old white-haired lady, alone in that great, high-ceilinged room, with its heavy, deep-coloured curtains and its massive pictures hanging on the wall and in the heart of her, a great uplifting thankfulness in the midst of such absolute desolation as this, a thankfulness that her life was a great, an all-comprehending fulfilment, that her greatest work was done, her highest desire reached--who, in the first inspiration of their imagination, seeing that frail white face pressed close against the window pane, could have conjured to their mind such a moment as this?

And yet, these simple things are life. A face peering from a window, a hand trembling at a touch, a sudden laugh, a sudden silence, they all may hide the greatest history, if one had but the eyes to read.

For more than half-an-hour she remained there without movement almost, except when she pressed her hand inquiringly to her breast to feel for the beating of her heart. At last, with a little shudder, as though, in that moment, she realised the vast space of emptiness in the great room behind her, she moved away.

Still her steps were steady, still her head was high, as she walked back to the little room where, evening after evening, year after year, the old gentleman had sat with her and talked, until the time came when they must go to bed. For with old people, as you know, it comes to be a state of--must--they must go to bed. It is not kind to tell them so, but there it is.

The room was disordered; for a time of sickness is as a time of siege--the time when Death lays siege upon a house and there are no moments left to put things as they were.

On any other occasion, she would have fretted at the sight. The world is sometimes all compassed in an old lady's work-basket, and to upset that, is to turn the world upside down. But now, as she saw all the untidiness, the little old white-haired lady only sighed. She took her accustomed chair and, seating herself, stared quietly at the chair that was empty, the chair that was still placed, just as he had left it that morning when, going down to see to his garden and to speak to Tito, he had fallen in the great room outside, and they had carried him straight to his bed.

Now it was empty. The whole room was empty. She heard sounds, sounds in Venice, sounds that she had never realised before. She heard the clock ticking and wondered why she had never heard that. She heard Claudina moving in the kitchen. She heard the voice of a gondolier singing on the canal.

Presently, she rose to her feet and walked slowly to a drawer that had long been closed. Opening it, she took out some part of an old lace shawl, unfinished, where it had been laid from that moment when God had withered her hands and she was powerless to do her work.

Bringing it with her, she came back to her chair; sat down and laid it on her lap. This was the only thing incomplete in her life. Memory became suddenly vivid as she looked at it. She almost remembered--perhaps pretended that she did recall--the last stitch where she had left off.

And there, when she came in for her unfailing ceremony, Claudina found her, gazing towards the door with the unfinished lace shawl in her hands.

The little white head moved quickly, the eyes lighted for one sudden moment of relief----

"Surely it's after ten o'clock, Claudina," she said.

And Claudina shook her head gravely.

"No, signora. It wants some minutes yet. But I thought if Giovanino was gone, you ought to go to bed."

They had prepared another little room for her to sleep in; but she insisted first upon going to see him once more.

By the light of the altar lamp, she found her way to the bed. Without the sound of a cry, or the hesitation of those who are suddenly brought into the presence of Death, she lifted the sheet from his face. It was almost as though she had expected to find that he was asleep.

For a little while, she stood there, looking quietly at the peacefulness of it all, then she bent over the bed. Claudina saw her whisper something in his ear. At the last, she crossed him with trembling finger, laid back the sheet upon his face and, without a sound, slowly turned away.

In Claudina's hands she was like a little child. Like a little child, she was undressed, like a little child put into her bed, the clothes pulled warmly round her, her beads given into her hand to hold.

With candle lighted and held above her head, Claudina stood at the door before she went out. The tears rushed warmly to her eyes as she saw the white head alone upon the pillow, and thought of the silent figure they had just left in the other room.

"*Buona notte, signora,*" she said as bravely as she could.

"*Buona notte,*" replied the little old white-haired lady.

At her accustomed hour of the morning, came Claudina into the little room. Feeling her way to the window, she threw open wide the jalousies. A flood of sunshine beat into the room and made all dazzling white. Claudina felt thankful for it. It was a new day. It was a wonderful day.

She turned to the bed. There was the still white head, alone upon the pillow, the powerless hand just showing from beneath the coverlet, still holding its string of beads.

"*Buona Giorno, signora,*" she said, trying to make the note of some cheerfulness in her voice.

But there was no reply.

Far away out in the wonderful city, she heard the cry of a gondolier,--"Ohé"--and in through the window, there floated a butterfly of white, that had been beating its wings against the jalousies outside. Into the room it flew, dipping and dancing, swaying and lifting in the free air of the day just born.

THE END

Made in United States
North Haven, CT
23 December 2021

13573832R00102